The Colour of Grass

Dorset Libraries
Withdrawn Stock

The Colour of Grass

NIA WILLIAMS

Seren is the book imprint of
Poetry Wales Press Ltd
57 Nolton Street, Bridgend,
Wales, CF31 3AE
www.serenbooks.com

ISBN 978-1-85411-539-3

A CIP record for this title is available from the British Library.

Cover image: 'Under the Elder'. Photograph by Andrew Gilmore.

Inner design and typesetting by Sarah Theodosiou

Printed by The Berforts Group Ltd, Stevenage

The publisher works with the financial assistance of
the Welsh Books Council.

Part One

1

'That's it then.'

She says it aloud. It's a habit: speaking to him without expecting an answer. She can barely remember what it's like, that counterpoint of statement and response. Hum, ha, some sign that he knows she's there, or cares. All that stopped a long time ago.

'How long ago?' she asks him.

He lies there, not answering. He looks thinner, lighter, without all the wires and tubes and other moorings. He might float away. It took them ages – unplugging, unhooking, pulling a fast slither of lines from beneath the skin, switching off the noises and lights that had taken his place and become her company in this white-walled room. And then, she reckons, they must have tidied him up. After draining the excess fluids, fixing the jaw to prevent it lagging open, spiriting away the bags and stinking pads – they must have finished off with some ordinary dressing-table brush-up. Combed the hair, straightened the shirt, layered the hands neatly. Helen assesses her husband and delicately draws her fingers along his cheek. They've given him a shave.

She wonders when she's meant to leave. Maybe they'll come and get her. Is there an allotted period for saying goodbye? She doesn't want to seem too brisk about it. She wanders to the window. They've shut the blinds. She prises a gap between the slats. The tree outside is a liquid yellow now. Lovely. They were so lucky – as she told him many times – to get this room, with its view of the tree, their guide to the passing seasons. She sits on the plastic chair next to his bed and plumps her handbag on her lap. Five minutes more. Then she'll poke her head through the door, see if there's a nurse nearby. Or are they all hanging about outside, waiting for her to finish?

'We'll leave you for a while,' they said, 'to say goodbye.' And then they left her, shutting the door with exaggerated care, as if there were anyone to disturb.

Helen raises a hand to Nick and says, 'Goodbye'.

She starts to giggle. He lies there, straight-faced. She says, 'Sorry, Nick' – and that makes her giggle even more.

It's release of tension, she tells herself. You couldn't call it shock. He's been dying for two years.

'It hardly took me by surprise,' she tells him, and now she's really laughing, her eyes watering, her throat pulsating with a glandular ache.

On the bus home she asks herself again how long it is since he stopped answering her. This helps – concentrating on a question, a problem: it gives her mind somewhere to go.

Well, let's see. There was a time, many years back, when Nick would talk to her in whole sentences. He even initiated conversations, once upon a time. Come to think of it, though, he was never that chatty in private. That was a revelation, early in their relationship – that Nick, the storyteller, the raconteur, life and soul of the pub, was quiet and introspective when alone with her. She was touched, at the time. It made her feel special.

''Scuse me, love.'

A large woman, breathless under her own weight, is forcing herself into the seat next to Helen.

'Don't know why they put these seats so close together!' she says.

Helen's chest starts to whinny. Don't start. Don't start. She has to turn to the window, where her mirth escapes in sharp gusts and thaws telltale splashes in the glass. The woman's still manoeuvring herself into place and Helen knows, from a quality of silence, that she's offended. Helen feels terrible. With an almighty effort she heaves in a steadying breath and turns back to the woman, who's looking away, containing her embarrassment.

'Sorry,' says Helen. 'My husband died this morning.'

The woman glances towards her – not at her – and blinks. *She thinks I'm mad*, Helen tells herself. *She's thinking, trust me to sit by the weird one.*

'I've just come from the hospital,' she goes on. Too late. The giggling's started again. 'I keep doing this…' she chortles.

The woman makes eye contact. Something in Helen's expression – desperation, perhaps – must be convincing.

'I'm so sorry, love,' says the woman, so kindly that tears billow over Helen's cheeks. She gives a moist sniff and the woman rifles in her bag and passes her a tissue. 'So sorry for your trouble,' she says. Helen guesses it's a phrase inherited from an older generation, a generation more skilled at handling crises with simple, compassionate formulas. She opens the tissue around her face and laughs and laughs and laughs.

2

Lisa sounds relieved.

'Oh,' she says. 'Oh.' Then, 'I'll come over. Are you still in his room?'

'No,' says Helen, 'I'm at home.'

'At home?'

Helen's gut contracts, as usual, at the spike of disapproval in her daughter's voice. Obviously, going home was the wrong move.

'I didn't know what else to do,' she says.

'You didn't think I might want to see him?'

Oh, dear, thinks Helen. No, I didn't.

'Well…' she says, 'why don't you call in at the hospital first, and…'

'It's a bit late for that,' snaps Lisa. 'They've probably put him in the freezer by now.'

A kernel of silence. Then the wheezing begins.

Lisa's voice returns, diminished: 'Mum, I'm sorry…'

Helen says: 'It's all right,' but can't bring herself to confess that she's not crying.

Maybe it was after Lisa's birth that the talking stopped. Not abruptly – not as a matter of policy; only because there was no time, no space, between nappies and feeds and worries and work and mess and guilt and wailing zombie nights. No – that's not right. Helen remembers ringing the surgery to tell Nick about Lisa's first steps. He wasn't annoyed at all. She remembers him repeating her words to the receptionist – 'Lisa's started walking!' – and then broadcasting to the pet-owners in the waiting room – 'My daughter's taken her first steps!' Someone in the background spoke and Nick relayed the words to Helen: 'Gentleman here says, next thing it'll be "Dad, can I borrow the car",' and Helen heard distant laughter and the echo of yaps and grunts from the animals, and her own laughter, close and loud.

She's being melodramatic. Of course Nick spoke to her. All the time. Right up until the last few years. They were an ordinary married couple. He loved to hear about Lisa's little achievements and comic turns. On Fridays he used to buy a bottle of wine on the way home, and after Lisa was asleep they'd settle on the sofa and Helen would tell him how Lisa had tried to sing 'Baa Baa Black Sheep', and speculate about her faddy appetite, and worry about the red flush on her forehead, and Nick would say, 'It'll be fine, it's just normal,' as if he knew, and Helen would tuck her bare feet under her and offer her glass to be topped up.

It would be easier, though, if she could pinpoint a year, a day, when it changed: when the words shrank into noises. They seemed to be noises learned from his animals – warding-off noises, noises to keep her sweet and buy him time. There's no one moment of transition of course, but still Helen can't help searching for it. She finds it even harder to track the time when the mumbles and growls disappeared into nothing.

The hospital staff used to praise her for keeping up her commentary and gossip. They'd say, 'That's the way, Helen. Deep down, he's probably taking it all in.'

But it was no effort. She'd been doing it for years, in the hope he might overhear.

'Right. I don't suppose you've eaten.'

Two straining carrier bags yank Lisa up the hall at high speed and attach themselves to the kitchen table with a clunk.

Helen, still holding the front door, is surprised to see that it's getting dark. She stares at the throbbing light of the lamppost outside her front garden. The fresh sheen of rain highlights gold nuggets among the chippings in her drive and picks out the leaf frills on the elm across the road.

'Shut the door, Mum, you're letting in the cold.'

Helen obeys. Lisa is easing her hands free of the bag handles and examining the palms.

'God, look at this.' She holds up the rutted flesh and Helen takes one of her hands, just for the sake of touching her.

'Serves me right for using plastic bags, I guess,' says Lisa, snatching her hand back and starting to unload. 'But I was in a rush. I knew you wouldn't have any food in the house. Why are you in the dark?'

She breaks off from her task to switch on the kitchen light, and both women blink in the sudden burst of halogen.

'I hadn't realised,' says Helen. Lisa stands next to her, hesitates, then gives her a quick, awkward hug.

'I'll make us a spag bol,' she says, and returns to her unpacking. A craggy mountain of ingredients accumulates on the table. Pasta rattling in cellophane. See-through bags of carrots, mushrooms, tomatoes. Shrink-wrapped nests of meat. Shiny baubles of fruit: grapes, apples, peaches... Helen picks a grape from its bunch and eats it.

'I'll never manage all this,' she complains.

'You need to get some proper meals down you,' insists Lisa. 'All that canteen gunk you've been living on – it's poison, that stuff. Look at you. How much weight have you lost?'

Something moves in the darkened garden and Helen peers. A fox, probably. There's one who visits regularly. She's seen it in the early hours.

Lisa's ripping packets open now, clanging around for pans, boiling the kettle, and she hasn't even taken off her coat.

'Shall we put all this away?' suggests Helen, tentatively extracting a tin of tomatoes from the pile and bracing herself for a landslide. Suddenly there's a sound like rain on a tin roof, and dry spaghetti is cascading onto the floor.

'Bollocks! Bollocks and buggery!' shouts Lisa. Spaghetti rolls and skids and crackles under their feet. Helen says, 'It doesn't matter. I've got some in the cupboard I think.'

Lisa buckles into a chair. She hangs her head and lets her hands dangle between her knees. Helen considers the possibility of embracing her, but knows how uncomfortable they'd both be. As a family they've never been very touchy-feely. She crouches to start picking up the pasta, and says, 'I'll be all right, sweetheart. I'll be fine. Go home and have dinner with Mark. Go on.'

'Come with me.' Lisa's voice is dragging. But Helen doesn't reckon she'll cry just yet.

'No,' she says, with finality. 'I'll be fine.'

Mark and Lisa are bad enough at the best of times. Mark and Lisa trying to be sensitive is more than she can face at the moment. She had to ask them not to visit Nick together. The nurse thought their constant bickering might provoke his mind back to life, but Helen said, 'It'll drive me to distraction first' – and suffered a glare of reproval for her levity.

'I wanted to cook you spag bol,' says Lisa, despondently. 'You're not eating enough.'

Helen looks at her daughter's fair hair descending in a curtain over her misery, just as it always did during the teenage calamities and heartbreaks. A great lava-tide of love washes through her and she says, 'Spag bol *does* sound rather tempting…'

The curtain parts and Lisa straightens in her chair.

'I *knew* it. You haven't had a square meal in months. Where did you say your pasta is?'

3

There it goes. Slipping behind the birch at the end of the lawn. There's a fox-sized gap between the trunk and the back fence. Lisa used to hide there when she was playing Mob with her friends. Helen remembers making a plate-load of bread and butter, going to the window to summon them and seeing a small hand and a long plait sticking out from behind the tree. She remembers the hidden pockets of repressed energy escaping in splutters here and there from the garden's nooks and crannies. She remembers how happy it made her, and how she postponed calling them in, just so that she could watch their game a little longer.

Another shifting in the shadows and a brief, breathless glimpse of the creature's muzzle and jewel eyes before it vanishes. Next-door's security lamp clicks on, casting an imitation of moonlight across the garden, sketching the curve of plant pots and the dip and shiver of shrubs. Helen goes on watching; she feels rested. She and Lisa had a good meal and some wine, and talked logistics. Funeral arrangements. Dates. Hymns. Speakers. Lisa suggested Nick's Aunt Fay and they had a laugh about that. Nick and Fay never did get on. Helen asked about pension payments and closing accounts, and Lisa said she'd ask Mark. Actually, a lot of that was sorted out when Nick went into hospital, but Helen enjoyed discussing it, having an issue to grapple with. Something to talk about, other than death. Because after all, what can you say about death?

'Nothing,' says Helen to the garden. 'That's why we gibber on about life.'

Lisa left late and reluctantly; Helen had to convince her to go. She told her she wanted some space, knowing this to be a phrase Lisa would accept. Only afterwards did it occur to her that Lisa had been drinking and shouldn't drive. Still. Helen really had wanted to be alone. And she'd slept, soundly, deeply, for several hours, with no half-presence in the way to stir up her dreams.

At 8.30 next morning Nancy calls round. Helen knows who it is as soon as the doorbell goes. It takes on a shriller tone. Through the bubbled glass panel, Nancy's abstracted head and shoulders bow in condolence. Helen stiffens her spine and prepares her brightest smile. As soon as she opens the door Nancy's earnest eyebrows are assailing her: 'Oh, Helen! I just heard – how are you…' and she's clamping herself around Helen's midriff and burying her face in her chest. Helen staggers back and pushes Nancy firmly away. She sees the rapid sequence of expressions as Nancy overcomes her indignation and makes allowances. *It's the grief. Poor Helen.*

'I saw Lisa leaving last night,' says Nancy. 'In fact it was Finn who noticed – the sound of the engine woke him up, but don't worry, don't worry – and he said "Mummy, who's driving away?" And I looked out and I thought, oh dear, has something happened… I did try to ring earlier on, but maybe you didn't…'

'I was probably in the shower,' says Helen. She has a dim recollection of the phone ringing, and a burble of words on the answering machine.

'Of *course*,' coos Nancy. 'You don't want me pestering you at a time like this, I understand…'

'It's not that. I was in the shower.' Helen tries to maintain a glassiness tough enough to withstand Nancy's torrent of sympathy.

'Well, I was worried about you,' says Nancy, and jostles Helen into the kitchen. 'So I rang Lisa.'

Helen boggles at her. She imagines Lisa's rage at the intrusion and her nostrils flare as she represses another bout of giggling.

'She told me the news,' Nancy goes on, dropping her voice to a meaningful pitch. 'Helen. I don't know what to say, I really don't. I said to Carl – I said, you can get the kids off today, Carl, I don't care, I'm going over to see Helen. That's what friends are for. So…' she clutches Helen's elbow and starts steering her towards the chair – 'you sit down and I'll make a pot of tea, and, you know, if you want a good cry…'

'Actually,' sings Helen, reclaiming her arm, 'I'm just off out to the hospital.'

'The hospital?' Nancy's whole body halts at this departure from the script.

'Yes, they said there were forms to fill in. That sort of thing.'

And thank god, thinks Helen, *for forms to fill in*. Thank god for the professionals who give you appointments to make and papers to sign, and who dole out commiserations in small, efficient portions before moving on to their next case.

'Oh, how awful!' wails Nancy. 'Red tape! At a time like this! Surely they can…'

'No. It's got to be next of kin.'

Nancy begs to give her a lift. 'You can't *possibly* go on your own.'

'Sorry. Family only,' says Helen. She hopes it sounds like a feasible regulation. But she knows she's being clipped and – frankly – rude. Well, she's allowed to be rude today. She's grieving.

Nancy leaves. As always, Helen is tripped up by guilt at the front door and thanks her with last-minute effusiveness. That'll guarantee another visit. But if Nancy didn't visit, who would? Apart from Lisa, she realises with a start, Nancy is the only other human being who ever sets foot in the house. Everyone else Helen knows is a voice on the phone or a scrawl on a card. Maybe she should treat Nancy with greater care. The tyranny of that word makes her shudder. Time to go and sign some forms.

4

When Helen leaves the hospital it's stopped raining and the whole day has changed. On the way in, the streets coughed and limped with rush-hour traffic. White and yellow globules of reflected light trembled in the pavements under wet footsteps. Pedestrians shut their faces under flowering umbrellas. And now, within a couple of hours, the sky and streets have cleared and almost dried; stray leaves and takeaway boxes clatter in the wind; the day is high with possibility. *I'm free*, thinks Helen. *I can go where I like.*

When Nick was in hospital her days were composed of infinities, broken by quick, bustling intervals of life. She thought of them as a piece of music: the soft, sustained drone of her sessions at his bedside; the short passages of percussion as she visited the hospital shop or the refreshment kiosk. She used to arrive every day with a plan of survival. A newspaper to read to him before her coffee break. Between coffee and lunch, any post that had come before she left the house – including bills, leaflets and brochures. She read through them all.

'Three-quarter length winter coat,' she'd recite, 'wool and polyester mix, sizes eight to twenty, three colours: russet, chocolate and berry.' She'd hold up the catalogue to show him.

'Bit young for me, d'you think?'

His breathing pipe would click and suck, click and suck. *Yes, a bit young for you.*

In the first weeks, she had lunch in his room, on a trolley, like a patient. Then one of the nurses said it was an administrative mistake, and would she mind buying herself a sarnie from the kiosk? Helen wouldn't mind. Every day at 1.30 she was at the hatch, exchanging cheery words with the WI volunteers. Those encounters were as vital a lifeline as the oxygen driven into Nick's inert lungs.

'That'll be three pounds twenty please, dear.'

'I've only got a twenty-pound note, I'm sorry…'

'Not to worry, but I'll have to give you pound coins. That'll weigh you down a bit!'

'Never mind, I need something to keep my feet on the ground.'

Ha, ha, ha.

Then she'd sit at a round table with her mug of tea and a ham and cheese sandwich, and listen to the beat of the hospital. Clack, clack, clack, as staff hurried to the scanner or the X-ray room. Squelch, squelch as slippered patients trudged from ward to loo.

Afternoons were worse than mornings. Sometimes Helen found herself at the window, watching the movement of the tree, and couldn't tell how long she'd been there. Then she'd feel bad for neglecting him, and she'd jabber at him frantically. And why would Nick want to come round to that?

The kiosk shut at four. Helen would try to get there just before the shutter rumbled down, for a final cup of strong tea. But everything was decelerating at that time of day, gathering energy for the evening rush. Only Nick's click and suck, click and suck remained constant.

Lisa usually took over in the early evening. Sometimes Helen would take the opportunity to stretch her legs. She'd walk the mile into town to look at the shop windows and watch the security grids being flung down. There was a café with tables outside, always thrumming with chat, always laced with a delicious roasting scent. It was busy whenever she went by. It had long windows at the front that were opened in summer; in winter there were pearls of white light strung around the frames. Helen never went in. It was always time to return to Nick. But she enjoyed seeing the place, as she might enjoy a painting, or a memory.

Today, she can go where she likes. Helen sets off towards town. Her excitement rises to the edge of a scream. She feels as though she could fly, if she put her mind to it. Anything is possible.

When she gets there the café is full. For a moment she stands outside, deflated. So it's not a place for her, after all. But before she can move on, there's a minor scuffling at one of the pavement tables and a woman stands up and says to her companion, 'Leave it alone, will you?' She says it quietly, but with a fierce intensity that makes a few other customers look round and then swiftly away. Her companion stays in his seat and says something in an undertone, but the woman is slamming money down and making her exit, kicking the chair aside and hugging her shoulder bag to her ribs. Helen sidles towards the empty chair and hovers. The man is glowering at the tideline of froth in his cup, but lifts his eyes briefly and mutters, 'Feel free.'

And Helen sits, and breathes in the sophistication of caffeine and conversation, and feels the cold air on her face. Someone at a nearby table starts talking into his mobile. He's not speaking English. Helen doesn't recognise the language. She listens, trying to figure it out. The vowels are taut and nervous, the consonants soft. Lots of 'sh' and 'th'. Spanish? No, she's sure she'd recognise Spanish…

'What can I get you?'

Helen opens her eyes and smiles at the waitress.

'Just a coffee please. A white coffee.'

'Americano?'

'Yes please.'

Americano. It sounds like a dance. Just right for this new, romantic setting. She thinks of the sludgy instant served at the hospital kiosk; the rattle of grains in a cracked mug, the bite of its chemical fumes as the volunteer pours on the water. A spasm of guilt knots her stomach. She should be getting back. *Oh, no* – she reminds herself, before the thought has fully formed – *there's no need any more.*

The waitress returns with the americano. A remarkably pretty girl, with haughty cheekbones and blonde hair pulled back into a ponytail.

Her little square apron emphasises the slim swoop of her hips.

'Enjoy,' she commands, and Helen thanks her with maternal affection. The man sitting opposite makes a subtle gesture, tilting his hand at his empty cup.

'Another one?' asks the waitress.

'Yes.'

Yes *please*, thinks Helen. She's noticed that other people don't say please or thank you as much as she does, but the waitress doesn't seem to mind. Maybe it's Helen who's at fault. Maybe she gushes. She sips her coffee. Sublime. Smooth and strong, neither sweet nor sour – a taste like autumn, like the hint of bonfire in the air… *I should have been a copywriter*, thinks Helen. She bandages her hands around the mug, soaking in its heat and anticipating the next sip. A girl hurries along the other side of the road steering a pushchair and tugging an older child in her wake. Passing cars divide the air into a soporific beat. The man at the table has turned to a black bag and is searching for something. When his coffee is brought he looks up, distracted, with a curt thanks. Good, thinks Helen, and grins at the pretty waitress.

The man brings out papers and cardboard rectangles and busies himself dealing through them. He takes perfunctory slurps at his coffee, his eyes still fixed on his task. The waitress has gone back in, leaving the café door open. Over the mesh of customer chatter, odd phrases ring out.

– 'I'm sorry, but honestly, he's better off without her…'

– 'Basically, the whole programme is a bloody disaster…'

– 'Needles in the butt are not my idea of therapy.'

Helen's in danger of giggling again. To deflect her mind she focuses on her companion and his documents. She can see, now, that the cardboard rectangles are photographs. Old photographs, sepia portraits. And some of his papers, by the looks of it, are photocopies of photographs, grey and ghostly. Others are facsimiles of handwritten documents. He must be a researcher, she decides. An archivist. She considers asking him. Rehearses her opening question: *That looks interesting. Do you work for a museum?*

No, of course she won't ask. He'd think she was mad. Or trying to chat him up, which – given her age and his – would be tantamount to madness. So she contents herself with eyeing his work and savouring her coffee and watching the traffic and the passers-by. There's a sudden interruption in the parade of cars. One mounts the kerb a couple of feet away. Almost immediately Helen hears the mew of an ambulance. It races through the chasm, siren rising to a painful peak and subsiding again. The cars struggle back into their places and the stream resumes its flow. Helen remembers about Nick and squeezes her mug to catch its receding heat. She won't think about it yet. She'll just carry on until the next appointment. Funeral director. Ten thirty tomorrow morning. It's in her diary.

The man is scribbling notes in a notebook. Urgent, minimal coils and tails. His hair, which is quite long, sways and shudders over the page in time to his hand. This would have been useful material for those languid hospital afternoons. *Guess what, Nick. I sat by an archivist today. And I drank an americano.*

5

Nick's Aunt Fay is wearing the most extraordinary hat. A great flat dish with black fronds hanging from the brim. As if someone put a huge plate of noodles on her head.

Oh, stop it. The effort to quell the bubbling in her chest makes Helen twitch. Lisa touches her arm, and Helen winks reassurance at her. The minister approaches.

'Shall we go in now, Mrs Pascoe?'

A clump of hair detaches itself from his swept-back fringe and he smoothes it quickly back. She can tell he's stressed. He's got end-to-end funerals today and any delays will result in a coffin pile-up. Helen's already thrown a spanner in the works by standing outside the chapel in the fresh air, instead of allowing herself to be escorted solemnly indoors and filed into the front pew to wait for the pall-bearers.

'Mum, come on,' says Lisa, hardly opening her mouth. Her skin has a greenish, sickly tinge. She keeps glancing towards the street. Mark loiters beside her looking bored. If we don't go in soon, thinks Helen, Nick's going to go straight to the crematorium, and cut out the middle man. She locks her fingers together hard, till the joints are burning. Trouble is, funerals have so many comic possibilities.

'Oh, my dear, it was vile!' – Aunt Fay's fag-end growl. She's relating a funeral anecdote to some mourners who are trying not to smile.

'Look at her. What a sight,' mumbles Lisa. But Helen quite likes the way Fay's decked herself out, with that gash of lippie and the panda eyes, defiant brushstrokes of colour on crumpled and powdered flesh. That's how I want to look, thinks Helen, when I'm in my eighties. She spots Nancy's car turning into the car park and says, 'Right. Let's get on with it.'

'Follow me, Mrs Pascoe,' croons the minister, only just failing to disguise his relief.

The clearing of throats. The mutter of responses and prayers. The groan of a hymn. I wish, thinks Helen, I'd learned to sing. She wants to bellow out the tune, but that wouldn't be fitting. For the English, singing is like nose-picking: shameful, but occasionally necessary. When the last note straggles away Helen can hear Aunt Fay holding her husky semibreve to its full value. Lisa tuts softly. Helen remonstrates silently with her daughter: *But she's singing, Lisa. That's what we're meant to do.*

Caddie, the surgery receptionist, says a few words. They couldn't think of anyone else. Helen had suggested one of the nurses who tended to Nick in hospital, but Lisa had sneered: 'What would they say? "He never gave us any trouble"?'

So Caddie gets up with her trembling piece of paper and gamely stutters through a short speech about what a good and supportive boss Nick was, and how he loved the animals in his care… 'and of course,' she adds shakily, 'his family'.

Don't laugh. Don't laugh. Helen feels Lisa's hand pressing on her thigh and she reins herself in. Caddie steps down from the lectern, wiping her nose with a tissue. Helen is deeply, genuinely grateful. She knows how much Caddie must have dreaded that, and how much it means that she did it all the same. Her eyes flick helplessly towards the coffin resting on its temporary plinth. *Hear that, Nick? Can you hear what you put her through?*

Afterwards Helen and Lisa and Mark stand at the exit to thank the mourners as they leave. Helen feels like the queen, touching hands and inclining her head as each departing guest intones a few awkward words. Nancy tries to fling her arms around Helen but is frogmarched past by her husband, like a drunk being chucked out of the pub.

'Thank God,' whispers Lisa, 'it's family only at the crem.'

Aunt Fay is the last to leave, clopping like a thoroughbred on her high black heels.

'Bizarre, isn't it,' she drawls to Helen. 'It feels as though we should have done all this months ago!' and out she canters, while Lisa's eyes and mouth expand in outrage. But she's right, thinks Helen. That is how it feels, this funeral. Like an afterthought.

Helen, Lisa and Mark in the front row. Aunt Fay three rows behind them. A man with a close-cut white beard, who says he's Nick's second cousin, sitting at the back. The crematorium is modern and corporate, with pale green chairs and magnolia walls. There must have been hours of discussion about that by some committee or other. Nothing brash, nothing depressing; clean and clinical but warm and welcoming... from the minister's inflexion Helen guesses he's rounding up his address. His head is slightly bowed; Helen sneaks a look to her right and sees Lisa and Mark attempting respectful but not excessive attitudes of prayer. *In case someone catches them at it*, thinks Helen.

'And thank you, Lord,' sighs the minister, 'for the mercy you show in the midst of your great power.' He moves his hand behind his console and there's a click and a low hum.

'As God our Eternal Father,' he goes on, seamlessly, 'has received our brother Nicholas...'

Helen feels Lisa tensing up beside her, and realises that the coffin is moving. The buzz of machinery reminds her of something – what is it? A lift. That's what it sounds like. A lift, in a posh hotel. The minister has raised his voice slightly to cover the sound. '...we now commit his body to the elements...' The coffin noses its way between short mustard-coloured curtains. A bit tacky, thinks Helen. Should have gone for a different shade.

There he goes.

The curtains drag along the lid as he glides towards...

A door shuts in Helen's mind.

Lisa is making strange gulping noises.

Helen thinks about Aunt Fay's implausible hat and impassive old face. She can smell her perfume. Aunt Fay has seen it all before. Good old Aunt Fay.

The curtains swallow him whole.

Guess what, Nick. Aunt Fay turned up. She's not such a bad old stick. You knew that really, didn't you? She came up trumps in the end.

They've decided not to do the whole ham-and-sherry thing. It didn't seem appropriate, somehow. What would people say to each other? Helen pictured them trooping to the front door, averting their eyes from the garage, where Nick did the deed. She couldn't face it. So now the mourners have drifted off. The second cousin strides away, taking his name out of Helen's memory. Aunt Fay folds her thin legs into her Mini Clubman and roars off down the road in a cloud as black as her hat. And now Helen thinks it was a mistake, sending everyone away. She understands, watching the first car arrive for the next shift, why people gather after funerals, and why they eat. She wants to be in a room full of the living, the talking, seeing the crustless sandwiches disappear from heaped plates, seeing the mouths munch them into gloopy pulp and pass them into the system, fuelling the body, continuing the whole mechanical process that differentiates the survivors from the dead. A Sainsbury's bag balloons over the car park in a gust of wind and then drops and settles at the foot of the low wall. Lisa is next to her again.

'Mum? Are you all right?'

Mark is jangling his car keys.

'Come on. Let's get going, before we're blocked in.'

More cars are drawing up. The minister has disappeared, presumably to swot up on names.

'Oh, thanks, Mark,' Lisa is yapping, 'very sensitive, thank you...'

'Well, do you want to be stuck in a crematorium car park for another hour?'

'I've just lost my father, Mark, thanks...'

'So let's get home, that's what I'm saying…'

'Actually,' says Lisa, 'could you possibly think about someone else for a change, instead of what football you might be missing on the telly?'

'What the hell are you talking about, *football*? We need to get the car – unless you want to catch the bus home?'

'Right from the off you've been acting like a…'

'Actually,' says Helen, then 'STOP!' She holds both hands up. 'I want to be on my own for a while. You two go home. I'll be fine.'

'Mum, don't be – you can't…'

'DON'T.' Helen startles herself, and switches to a gentler tone. 'Please, sweetheart, don't tell me what I can and can't do. I'm not a child.'

Lisa's eyes are brimming. Mark scrutinises his shoes. Helen smiles. 'I'm just going for a walk. That's all. On my own. I'll ring you later.'

She gives Lisa's arm a squeeze, turns and walks away, staying ahead of the wave of recrimination that immediately floods the forecourt.

'See what you've done?'

'What *I've* done! Can you *hear* yourself?'

Helen accelerates until their argument merges with the city's Saturday hubbub.

She'd assumed the café would be full today, but there are quite a few free places inside. It must be the dip between lunch and tea. Just like the hospital. Helen takes a seat near the window. The waitress comes to clear the dishes and scrunched-up napkins and wipes the table in rapid circles, one, two, three.

'What can I get you?'

'A large americano, please.'

The waitress gives Helen's funeral clothes a swift but comprehensive glance.

Helen's glad she didn't wear a hat. She contracts the muscles in her feet to ease the pressure of her shoes. Then, on a sudden impulse, she levers the shoes right off and breathes out luxuriously as her feet regain their natural shape. *Guess what, Nick. I went to a café while you were being cremated. And I took off my shoes.*

The café door is propped open. Someone pauses there, blocking the light, then moves forward. Helen recognises the woman who stormed off, that day. The woman whose seat she took, the day after Nick died. She's got heavy swirls of hair and an angled face – like a fox, thinks Helen. Quite attractive, but serious-looking. Grumpy, even. The woman sits two tables away, with her back to Helen, in a corner. She seems on edge, turning constantly, looking towards the door, towards the window, towards the door again. As Helen's coffee arrives there's an outburst of tinny hysteria from her own handbag.

'Good ring tone!' comments the waitress. Fumbling in her bag, Helen says, 'I thought I'd switched it off.'

Why on earth did she take it in the first place? What if it had gone off during the funeral, accompanying Nick's exit with the theme from The Simpsons? She hasn't figured out how to change it since Lisa bought her the wretched thing a year ago. Helen snorts, and pretends to be laughing at something in the text message.

'HOPE U R OK GOD BLESS U LOVE NANCY.'

Helen switches the phone off and buries it at the bottom of her bag.

Outside, the daylight dims. Passers-by start buttoning their coats and picking up their pace. The waitress shuts the door and switches on the lights.

'We're in for it now,' she says, to no one in particular, and right on cue there's a rip of rain across the windows and a muted teenage scream from the street. Two, three, four new customers stagger in dripping, and disperse to the free tables, gasping with laughter and shock. A fifth appears and scans the room. It's the archivist. He goes straight up to the woman with the foxy face and sits opposite her, unpeeling his coat and letting it sag over the back of his chair. Helen strains to hear their conversation over the increased background noise. She hears annoyance in the woman's voice, sees her spread her hands and shrug, then swivel away from his reply.

'It matters,' Helen hears him say. 'It's important.'

Then a couple enters the café, with a baby yelling from the downpour, and everything else is lost under that livid howl.

In the early hours, decades ago, Nick brought her tea while she comforted Lisa back to sleep. They stood facing each other in their dressing gowns. Nick held the two cups of tea, waiting until he could hand hers over. Helen rocked Lisa with that half-swinging, half-bouncing, hypnotic rhythm that she hadn't realised she knew. The bellow had subsided into occasional whimpers; Lisa's head was growing heavy on Helen's breast.

'You're a witch,' growled Nick, who always had more trouble getting Lisa down.

'Flattery,' whispered Helen, 'won't get you out of your turn.' But she did feel like a conjurer, every time Lisa's eyelids slid shut.

When all resistance had evaporated and Helen had deposited the limp little body into the cot, they drank tea and spoke in hoarse dawn voices as light opened the sky. Helen told Nick about her recurring nightmare of hearing Lisa cry and being unable to reach the cot.

'Even while I'm thinking, "oh shut up",' she confessed, 'something's pulling me. I *need* to comfort her. I knew that would happen. But I didn't realise how strong it would be. Or how much I'd resent it.'

'Resent?' Nick cocked an eyebrow. The blue skin under his eyes had folded itself into layers.

'The *feeling*,' she explained. 'Not Lisa. Just the feeling.'

He nodded. He rubbed his hand over his stubble. He said, 'I used to feel a bit like that about the animals.'

They both snuffled like naughty kids. He tried to justify himself.

'I mean, it's not the same. But when they're hurt, and scared, and don't understand … and they're at your mercy. It used to…'

He gave up and drank his tea.

'Not any more?' asked Helen after a while.

'Not as much, maybe.'

'Because of Lisa?'

'I suppose so. And because it's all just a day's work, now.'

They perched on the windowsill, knee to knee. Daylight growing. Bathroom lights coming on along the street. The sound of early car engines. Lisa spreadeagled in her cot, fidgeting to her own dreams.

Helen has kept that recollection like a photograph. It goes no further. She has no idea what day it was, or what happened in the following hours. It has its borders. It keeps its place.

Someone asks to share her table. The place is filling up and her coffee's gone cold. She consults her watch. Twenty minutes have gone by without her realising. She keeps doing this – losing track of time. Is it grief? Or is it the first stage of decline? Minutes here, minutes there… and gradually her interludes in the immediate world will grow fewer and shorter. One day she'll emerge from one of her reveries in a nursing home of faded armchairs and threadbare carpets, with only a blaring TV and a drooling geriatric for company. This, perhaps, is where they all go – the undead, with their loose jaws and hospital-bed rigging. Back to their own past, which looms behind their daily lives like a gothic mansion, intact, unchanging, with the door ajar.

Helen suddenly wants to vomit. She has to move, to do something. She forces her feet back into the shiny funeral shoes. It hurts like hell, which is exactly what she needs. She glances towards the fox woman. The archivist has gone again. It must have been a flying visit. Just long enough for a quarrel. The woman's getting up, preparing to go. Helen pays for her coffee and leaves the café just behind her.

She doesn't mean to follow the woman. At first they just happen to be heading in the same direction. It's stopped raining. The woman strides along in her high-heeled boots, cutting a swathe through the crowd. Helen falls into step and follows in her wake, mainly for ease of passage. She's never been able to walk like that, as though she had a right of way. She's always sidestepping, shuffling, apologising for being in someone else's path.

The woman takes her course past shoppers, office workers, street-hawkers – Helen sees the turn of her head as a man with a suitcase calls, 'Chanel for a fiver! Calvin Klein, the smell of it!'

Children and dogs bounce off adults' legs and skitter from the hiss of traffic. On they go, Helen and the fox woman, swerving, slaloming. Helen is mesmerised by the woman's quick footfall. She watches her plunge a hand into her shoulder bag without missing a beat and take out her mobile. Helen didn't hear it ring and can't tell whether she's receiving or making a call. She sees the woman's short denim jacket ruck up as she hoists the bag back into place and lifts the phone to her ear. A purplish patch of flesh is revealed at her waist. *Cover your kidneys, girl*, thinks Helen. It's something Nick used to say to Lisa.

They pass two foreign men arguing with operatic gusto. Dark, handsome, vibrant men. Helen enjoys the sight of them, enjoys the fact that, being sixty-four and invisible, she can look without inviting conclusions. The woman crosses a side road and so does Helen. They only just catch the last blink of the little green man, and a car bonnet revs at them impatiently. The woman's head moves in response and Helen catches part of her conversation.

'I know,' she's saying to the phone, 'I know. I told him. Yeah. Honestly, I think he's gone off his...'

A businessman is pacing towards them, coat tails flying, a conversation of his own pressed to his temple. He eyes the fox woman's exposed waist, lets his glance extend and linger, swivelling after her, as he talks: 'Forget it, mate, I'll print it out when I get there...'

He's acting two parts at once. And so is the woman – crossing roads, scowling at drivers, and discussing an entirely different matter with her friend, who's probably doing something else at the same time too. So many parallel worlds, and Helen sees them all, and remains unseen herself. She continues in a trance of clackety-clack, clackety-clack, until suddenly the woman turns in to a narrow road leading to a new housing estate. Helen carries on ahead and registers the full agony of her feet. She slows down. She begins to hobble. It's only when she reaches the hospital that she realises which route her screeching feet were on.

6

'Mum, let me know when you get back. Where are you? Oh, shut up, Mark! Sorry... Mark's being... give me a ring, anyway. Speak to you soon.'

Beep.

'Oh, hello, Helen, it's Nancy. Just calling to see how you are. Bit worried about you... I might just pop round when the Littles are in bed.'

Beep.

Helen's mouth curls. *The Littles*. Nancy's even been known to refer to herself and her husband as The Bigs. Helen picks the phone up then puts it down again. She doesn't want to put anyone's mind at rest just now. She wants to take off her shoes, take off her funeral togs, have a bath, have a glass of wine. But if she doesn't ring, Nancy's bound to come over.

'Damn you, bloody woman,' says Helen, dialling Nancy's number. As she listens to the ring tone she hatches a plan. She'll tell her Lisa's calling round. That'll put her off. And she'll tell Lisa that Nancy's coming. They're not likely to swap notes.

She lies chin-deep in bubbles. What a treat, finding bubble bath at the back of the cupboard. It must have been there for years. She wouldn't have bought bubbles while Nick was in hospital. It wouldn't have seemed right. She used to squat in two inches of tepid water and sluice herself with a flannel. It was a kind of solidarity with Nick, who had no idea he was being wiped clean in his bed every day. This evening, the water is piping hot, on the verge of painful. Steam soaks her face and the tiles around the bath. The radio natters affably in the background. The grouting around the rim of the bath is beginning to rot. She must do something about that. Ask someone. She doesn't feel up to doing it herself. Wouldn't have the first idea.

After Nick had filled his lungs with exhaust, Lisa went through all his files. He was a meticulous record-keeper. Helen wondered whether that had all been a bluff, and they'd discover an avalanche of debt, or a simmering case of fraud. But Lisa came to her with a sheaf of papers and said, 'You should be fine, Mum. He's got everything sorted. It's not a fortune, but it'll keep the roof over your head and pay the bills.'

He'd retired from the surgery the previous year. Helen had thought he might relax, after retiring; start to enjoy life. She'd thought work had become an ordeal for him, a prison sentence. But maybe when the cell door opened he just didn't know where to go.

I should be fine, thinks Helen. But I still don't know how to re-grout the bath. Or fix the cistern. Or where to find the water mains. She recalls a neighbour of theirs, when she and Nick were first married – a young woman whose husband fell off a mountain in Pakistan. Helen and Nick were self-conscious, offering hapless hands as the girl wept on her driveway.

'He always did all the driving,' she wailed. As if she'd be stranded there, from that day on. And such extraordinary grief left her young face streaked and flushed, like a child who'd dropped an ice cream.

'Poor girl,' said Helen, as she and Nick walked away.

'She'll be OK,' said Nick. 'She'll learn to drive.'

At the time Helen thought it a callous thing to say. Now, she reckons it was the simple truth. Forty years of allotted tasks leave her feeling a fool. But she'll be OK. She'll learn to re-grout.

Lisa calls round.

Helen is pink and glowing in her dressing gown, clutching a mug of hot chocolate.

'You look better,' says Lisa.

'I had a long, hot bath.'

'Good. Good for you. Have you eaten?'

Helen makes a face.

'How about,' suggests Lisa, 'I make us some toast?'

'That sounds lovely.' Helen looks uneasily towards the front door. 'Nancy might descend. I rang to put her off but there was no answer.'

'Don't worry. If she does come I'll soon see her off.'

Strange to think that Lisa used to be in and out of Nancy's house every chance she got.

'I'm just going to help with the baby,' she'd announce, importantly. There was always a baby to help with. Helen was touched with jealousy. Din, chaos, toys that squeaked underfoot, toddlers shackling Lisa's legs, orange mush to spoon into tiny mouths. By contrast, Helen and Nick's home was still and ordered, and that was no way to spend a school holiday. On Sundays, while Nancy's household conducted its processional of church and lunch and family visits, Lisa would be bored and restless. Nick would sometimes take her into the surgery to see the animals. Babies, pets – Helen could offer no such novelty appeal. So when the rift came with Nancy she couldn't help enjoying a sliver of satisfaction.

Lisa was away at university by that time. Nancy was between the second and third child, and many years off from the unexpected twins. She'd taken to popping round for coffee when the Littles had been packed off to school and playgroup. Helen didn't mind so much, then.

'I can't imagine what it'll be like,' Nancy said one morning, 'when the Littles fly the nest.'

'You've got a long time to go before that.'

'I tell myself I can't wait. But I know I'll be crawling the walls before the first week's out.' Nancy creased her forehead. 'You must miss Lisa so much.'

'It is a bit strange without her.'

Nancy studied Helen like a mathematician grappling with a conundrum.

'Have you thought,' she said eventually 'of going back to work?'

Helen laughed. 'Too old and out of practice.'

'I'm *sure* that's not true.'

Helen shifted in her seat. 'Middle-aged housewives don't get hired, whatever the law might say. And anyway the technology's overtaken me. Shorthand and typing are about as useful as stone-chiselling to your average office manager these days.'

'Then train up! Take a course!'

Nancy spread her hands, puzzled at Helen's intransigence. Helen made a sideways movement with her head, meaning, Who knows? Maybe… not a chance. She couldn't bring herself to confess how much she'd loathed every job she'd ever had, every jargon-spouting manager and every waspish colleague who'd ever whispered behind her back. She would never forget overhearing her name like a gunshot as she passed the photocopying room in her last post.

'Too good for the likes of us,' she heard. 'Thinks she's a cut above.'

Helen's mother had been a telephonist before her marriage. She had drummed into her daughter the importance of enunciation, modesty and deference to others. Plodding along the office corridor that afternoon, Helen had shovelled over her mother's memory every curse she could muster.

'I don't know,' was all she said to Nancy. 'I'll see.'

'It would get you out of the house,' urged Nancy. 'Seeing as Nick's working *so* hard, all the hours God sends.'

A fortnight after that, Nancy was on the doorstep, clamping a solution to her chest.

'Call me crazy,' she was saying as Helen opened the door, 'but Carl's mother had a litter – or, that is, her Pootles did…' she blundered past, toddler swinging, something wriggling under her arm… 'and I thought, well, let's give it a couple of weeks, see how you get on, because he certainly doesn't like the look of *me* – nipped my fingers more than once already...'

She hoisted the puppy into Helen's arms.

'What?' Helen squeaked. 'No, Nancy! I can't!'

'Don't be silly, of course you can. Look, he's taken to you straight away.'

The puppy was shivering violently against Helen's ribcage. Nancy waffled on about dog food, dishes, house-training, while steadying her toddler with occasional rebukes, and Helen thought: it's been taken from its mother. She wanted to bite Nancy too, to hurt her, sink dagger teeth through her skin and muscle. Because she couldn't hand it back now. It had been taken from its mother. Warmth blossomed over her thighs. The puppy had wet itself. It was terrified. It squirmed helplessly. *Wait*, Helen thought at it. *Wait till she's gone. Then we'll talk.*

Nancy deposited a box of dog snacks and a saucer and left. Helen transferred the pup's restless weight to one arm, harnessing its energy against her with the crook of her elbow. With her free hand she managed, with some difficulty, to release some brown lozenges from the packet. Then she lowered the puppy within sniffing range and gradually released her hold as it became absorbed in guzzling. The wet patch stuck to her legs. Its sour smell slapped her in the face. She hated Nancy for this – for robbing one mother of its young to fulfil another's need.

Nick greeted their acquisition with resignation and a hint of relief: even less reason to speak to Helen, now that she had other company. His only comment was: 'The house will stink, I'm warning you. Dogs and tramps. Same smell.'

He gave the puppy a businesslike scratch behind the ear and said, 'I'll give it a check-up tomorrow.'

Lisa came home for the weekend. She loved the puppy. She even gave it a name: Barnie. But she was furious with Nancy.

'A dog! I mean, did she stop and think? It's like putting you under house arrest!'

And when Nancy came to say hello, Lisa gave her a piece of her mind.

'You don't go round handing out dogs, Nancy! They're not

ornaments you can put on the mantelpiece when people come to call!'

Nancy was wounded.

'If you didn't want him, Helen,' she said, primly, 'you only had to say.'

'Of *course* she wouldn't say!' railed Lisa. 'That's what gets me – you make this great gesture to show how generous you are, but you're really forcing someone to do what you want...'

'Lisa!' Helen was appalled. Simultaneously, Nancy started to protest. Lisa charged on.

'...and if they *don't* do what you want, you take a major huff...'

Barnie squawked around Lisa's ankles, relishing the commotion. Nancy was welling up.

'All you have to do is say the word,' she quavered to Helen, 'and I'll take him straight back.'

'You'll do no such thing,' said Helen. 'Barnie is staying where he is.'

When Nancy had gone, Helen read Lisa the riot act.

'Where did you learn such rudeness? It certainly wasn't from us!'

'You're such a hypocrite, Mum!' yelled Lisa. 'You moan about Nancy all the time, but you're too wet to say anything to her face!'

'*You* might call that hypocrisy,' said Helen crisply. '*I* call it civility.'

'Yeah, the kind of civility that lets Nancy walk all over you.'

'Well,' said Helen, 'I'm a grown woman, thank you very much. I can fight my own battles.'

A sharp, succinct whistle came from the hall and Barnie shot out of the room. Shortly afterwards they heard the front door slam on their bickering as Nick and Barnie made their escape.

'Poor Barnie,' says Helen.

Lisa looks at her with curiosity, munching her buttered toast. They're sitting on the living-room floor by the gas fire. The lights are off and their faces are masked in red. Lisa swallows and says, 'What about poor Barnie?'

'I don't know, really.'

'Barnie did all right,' says Lisa. 'He couldn't have had a more loving home.' She takes another hanch of toast, chews for a moment, then adds, 'It was still a ridiculous thing to do.'

Helen laughs. 'I don't think I ever saw you that cross about anything.'

'Well!' Lisa puts down her plate to relive her fury. 'It was so…! I mean, it was like giving you one of her babies!'

Helen closes her eyes to the heat and returns to her task, trying to piece it all together. Was Nick more talkative with Barnie around? Was he worse, after Barnie was put down? She can see him, downcast and preoccupied, preparing to take the old boy to the surgery, kneading Barnie's silky ears, muttering, 'Come on, lad, good old lad, time to go.'

He hated putting any animal down. Of course he did. And she let him deal with it all, decide when the balance between happiness and suffering had tipped too far. He was the one who had to caress the woolly head with one hand and administer the injection with the other. Had that been the final straw?

Her eyes open. 'How soon after Barnie died did Nick retire?'

Lisa stares. 'Why?'

'Just wondered…'

'He was a vet, Mum,' says Lisa, as if addressing a dim-witted child. 'He had to do that kind of thing every day.'

'I know,' says Helen. 'I know. But maybe that's the point.'

She can't explain. She can't tell her own daughter how these things change, how the grim necessities, the caring and the culling, take on a new and terrible resonance as the years pass.

'An in-valid life.' That was how Nick had once described a cat brought to his surgery, grotesquely obese, half-blind, unable to walk. 'A life gone to waste.'

That kind of case would crush him, for a while.

Lisa retrieves her plate and pushes her finger around it, chasing the melted butter.

'We'll never know,' she says, and sucks the butter quickly from her finger. 'So there's no point trying.'

She's angry. She thinks her father was a coward. Thinks he gave up on life, bottled out. Perhaps he did, thinks Helen. But there's nothing particularly brave about carrying on.

7

She's in a bed, a single bed, in somebody else's house. A guest house, in France. She can tell it's France from the smell of soap and lavender, the bolster behind her head, the forget-me-not blue of the skirting board and window frame. The door opens and it's Nick, the way he was when she first met him, dark-haired and dark-eyed and giving her that demi-smile that twists her heart. She asks him, 'What's the name of this place?'

He says, 'Why are you so hopeless about names? You never know where the hell you are!'

She starts to panic, because she doesn't know what she'll see outside when she opens the curtains, and while Nick's talking to her his face is changing, contorting, stretching itself into elastic shapes, and she screams and screams and screams.

It's got to be Nancy. She must be leaning on the bell.

Helen scrabbles at the peg for her dressing gown and staggers downstairs.

'Oh, Helen – I'm so sorry – you were getting some rest. Quite right too. I'm so sorry. I was worried about you…'

'What's the time?' croaks Helen.

'Just gone eight. Look. You go back to bed and take it easy. I'll pop round in a couple of hours…'

As soon as Nancy's gone Helen takes the stairs two at a time and runs a shower. She has to get out of the house before Nancy comes to keep her company. Lie-ins and sympathetic chats are not the life she has in mind.

Forty minutes later she's on the bus into town. She hasn't got the faintest idea what to do. What *does* a widow do? Her own mother went shopping. Every day, as though she were working to a schedule, it was down to the arcades, where she'd browse and window-shop solemnly and finally pick out one more ghastly knick-knack to add to her growing collection. Hideously encrusted pill-boxes. Paperweights that snowed when shaken. Dung-coloured china dogs. On Sundays, when the shops were shut, she dusted them all. When she died, the clearance people took the whole lot for £300. That and the price of the tiny terraced house was the extent of her estate. Helen reckoned she must have missed meals for the sake of her trinkets.

Well, that's not going to happen to her. As Helen gets off the bus her head is swilling with alternative plans. She could do voluntary work. Ask at one of the charity shops. Even take Nancy's advice of seventeen years ago, and look for a job. They're supposed to be taking on older people. She doesn't have to be a secretary. She could sit at a till and – she walks faster and faster along the high street. As she passes the Argos windows, she catches sight of a grey-haired woman with sloping shoulders and a collapsed midriff. Surely that's not her? That's somebody else. Somebody whose future is already written off, somebody who's just killing time. She slows down in defeat. Taking money, pressing bip-bip keys, asking Sir and Madam whether she can help – it's all beyond her. All part of the other, visible world. She's one of the spectres at the edge, struggling with self-serve tills and moving their lips in an effort to remember their PINs. She can't step out of the shadows now. It's too late.

She's almost come to a halt. People are looking. She doesn't even know what clothes she flung on in her haste to leave the house. She glances at her feet: she's wearing her gardening shoes, awful squashed lace-ups with bruises at every joint and curve.

A voice says, 'You all right, love?'

'Yes, thanks,' she says. 'I'm fine.'

Oh God, she thinks, don't let anyone take my arm and try and help me across the road… here they come: chuckles. Or tears. She's not sure which. The threat of them propels her forward again. Without any conscious decision, she heads for the café.

She's sitting at the same table as before, to the side, near the window. This will be her table, then. She'll be the sad old lady who arrives at the same hour every day and sits for the same length of time, who doesn't have to order because the staff all know what she has. She'll be part of other people's landscape, a constancy in their busy days, a quirk, an eccentric, someone to add to their illusion of community. All right. That serves a purpose. That will be her value, for the rest of these dwindling years.

'Large americano, please.'

Helen's hands are starspread on the table. She looks at the rutted blue veins, the rucked skin over knuckles and finger-joints, the scar that she's had since a cat scratched her when she was eight, the squared-off nails, her wedding ring.

Helen Pascoe.

Sixty-four years old.

Mother of one.

Widow.

The waitress brings her coffee. Helen smiles too gratefully and watches the girl's slim back retreating to the counter. Doesn't even think about it, that girl. Doesn't wonder who she might be, how to account for herself. And neither did Helen, at that age. When she married Nick, when she kissed the envelope containing her letter of resignation, she didn't imagine that, forty years down the line, she'd be incapable of summing herself up.

'It's never too late.'

That's what she used to tell Nick, when he went through his periodic crises.

'I should have been an archaeologist,' he said, when he came home after putting Barnie down. 'I would have loved that: finding out about the past, constructing stories. Safer to deal with the dead. Less painful.'

Nick liked to read books about dredged-up artefacts and long-fallen cities. Even when he didn't read any more, he could sit, sullenly absorbed, as a TV expert resurrected the ghost of a face over an ancient skull. Helen found those programmes unsettling. She hated the thought of someone wrenching a body back to the light, just as it was merging into the earth. But Nick found it all compelling. Ironic, really, given all those months in the hospital, when he refused to be brought back.

'You could re-train,' Helen used to urge him, when he was still within her reach.

'Can't afford it. Anyway it's too late for that now.'

'It's never too late.'

She believed it, then. And she believed it these past two years, as she droned her news into his deaf ears. Keep trying. Keep hoping. It's never too late.

But it is, now, isn't it? She and Nick have had their turn, and squandered it. Helen's alien hands wrap themselves again around the warm mug. Outside, a woman shuffles along the pavement, her head and spine hooked over her shabby trolley. The tortoise-head turns to give the café window a bleary look. Helen chivvies herself: at least I'm not bent over like that. At least I'm not destitute. At least there's no war, no flood, no shifting and cracking underfoot as the ground gives way. The curved woman's head retracts and she totters out of view. Helen tightens her grip on the coffee mug, and waits. She doesn't know what for. She needs a signal, a reason to get up and go. She scrapes her chair back a little way, so that she can't be seen through the window. She's afraid they'll come searching for her – Nancy or Lisa. Maybe Lisa's gone to work – she hopes so. Carrying on may not be brave, but still it's the best way. Everybody dies, and in the meantime, everybody carries on. But today Helen feels as if she's slipped through a gap between the two. She's not dead yet. But she's forgotten how to live.

The café door opens. It's the man with the photographs. He doesn't scan the tables this time. He's not expecting to see anyone he knows. He goes directly to a table at the far end of the room, sits and immediately starts unloading his materials. Papers, card-framed photographs, notepad, pen. He must use this place as an office. He orders his drink, adjusts the position of his chair, considers his work and pulls his long hair free of his collar, bunching it with his hand in a gesture that, to Helen, seems graceful and feminine. He consults his papers and writes. The waitress, after serving his coffee, leans dreamily on the counter, gazing at the street. Helen observes them both and wills herself not to scream. If she doesn't move now, if she doesn't speak, there is nothing left. To find a place to sit, to tidy herself away, to keep her mounting insanity politely at bay – this will not do. It will not do. She stands up. The waitress looks at her. Helen says, 'Where, er, where…?'

'Door at the back,' says the waitress.

Helen stares into the mirror over the basins. There she is. The new Helen. The Helen she's had to get to know: grey hair, softened skin, a frown that no longer bears any relation to her frame of mind. The Helen who talks without expecting answers, who's a subject of concern but not of interest. She pushes forward against the basin rim.

'Never too late,' she says, doubtfully. 'Guess what, Nick,' she whispers, then discards the rest of the sentence and marches back to the café. She pays her bill and contrives to be putting on her coat near the photographs man. She pulls in a breath and says, 'That looks interesting. Are you doing some kind of research?'

He lifts his head and scalds her with a ferocious glare. Strands of hair fall across his face. He's not going to answer. Maybe Helen's already faded from the real world. Humiliated, she starts towards the door. Then the man says, 'Genealogy.'

It's a gentle voice, completely at odds with his expression. Helen turns, flustered, and says, 'Genealogy! Oh!'

He indicates a chart in front of him and adds, 'We all need to know who we are.'

At the bus shelter Helen perches on one of the flip-up plastic seats. She's shaking. It could be the after-effects of the funeral. Or it could be the effort of addressing another, living human being. But she reckons it's the man's reply that's agitated her. Uncanny. As if he'd read her mind. She searches for her purse and concentrates on slowing her breathing down. She's not behaving normally, she's aware of that. It's probably the grief. She dreads going home. Shutting the door on the afternoon. Waiting for Nancy's visit. Filling the kettle, switching on *Deal or No Deal*... No, thinks Helen. No deal. Adrenalin is pumping through her, making her clumsy with her coins; she nearly drops them all. Snub-nosing through the scrummage of traffic at the end of the road is the express coach to London. Lights change and the traffic exhales and halts. There's a poster stuck to the bus shelter: 'Return to London only £14.' Helen has a £10 note in her purse. A couple of two-pound coins in her hand. Is she the kind of person who goes to London on impulse? The day after her husband's funeral? She dismisses the idea. The lights change again and the traffic grunts forward. Then again, is she the kind of person who asks a stranger in a café what he's doing? Helen stands up and the plastic seat flips away. She gives a timid wave and the coach's yellow indicator flashes its response.

After buying her ticket Helen sits on the bus and counts through her cash. She promised herself, when Nick went into hospital, that she'd be careful, keep to a strict weekly budget. She set aside enough for her daily sandwiches and the bus fare and some basic groceries and that was that. Despite Lisa's assurances that Nick had provided for her well enough, Helen had a horror of the money running out. She'd hardly given it any thought for years, before that. The surgery was a going concern; they'd bought their house when houses were buyable, and paid off the mortgage. Occasionally, when Lisa was small, Helen would wake in a cold sweat after a nightmare about the heart attack or accident that would send it all into a tailspin. But only occasionally. On the whole, life seemed secure.

When Nick did what he did, he'd expected Helen to be out all afternoon. She had a hair appointment, and afterwards she was going to the optician's to get her reading glasses fixed. But the optician's was shut for refurbishment, so she came home early. She heard the chuntering engine from the bottom of the hill, and thought, 'What's the silly fool doing in the garage?'

As she approached, the smell of petrol swooned into her gut and skull, and suddenly she understood. When she clambered across him, keeping down the nausea, to thrust off the engine, his flaccid arm flopped down between the seats and she punched it, hard. Later she stood on the drive as paramedics busied themselves over him between the flailing car doors. The siren's blue reflection swept over them in slow, serene circles. Helen touched the back of her head, moved her palm down the freshly wire-sprayed hair to the gritty stubble at her neck. They began shifting Nick from car to stretcher. Someone put a blanket over Helen's shoulders and she was guided away like an abandoned child.

'Marble Arch,' announces the coach driver, 'for all you shopaholics!'

Helen thanks him as she disembarks and he says, 'Enjoy your splurge, love!'

She walks down Oxford Street. At first she has trouble falling into step with the crowd, and keeps bumping into people, but presently she finds the rhythm and adapts the air of a woman with somewhere to go. Shoe shops. Leather shops. Side-street stalls hung with Union Jack flags and bags and T-shirts… 'My boyfriend went to London.' A group of tourists ahead of Helen crosses the street and she follows. She goes into a department store and wanders among sparkling bays of jewellery and make-up palettes. A caving in her stomach reminds her that she hasn't eaten. She's already blown her daily budget. All around her, shoppers flourish their plastic cards and tuck away banknotes. Lisa would tell her not to be ridiculous: she's not that hard up. Nick has taken care of her. She's fine.

At the counter to Helen's left, a tall girl is applying lipstick from a tester and pressing her lips together at a minuscule mirror. Her bag is sagging open. Helen can clearly see the pouch of her purse, unencumbered, ripe for the picking. The possibility of it, the ease of it, sucks the oxygen from her brain. She sways slightly. No. It's a fantasy. She's not poor, she's not desperate; she wouldn't do it.

And besides – Helen's eyes dart upward – she's probably being filmed. She's aware, all at once, of the way she must appear to the nameless official in an upstairs room. Dawdling next to a customer with a gawping bag, checking shiftily for camera lenses – her fantasy takes on all the force of a crime. Helen lowers her head and leaves the store.

She continues up New Oxford Street and turns into Museum Street, towards the British Museum. On the pavement outside the railings, a fog of roasted chestnuts mingles with the fatty belch of a hamburger van. Helen enters the courtyard and approaches the grin of columns. Students and tourists sprawl on the steps and take pictures of each other. The relief of not having stolen a purse propels Helen up the stairs and into the Great Court. Voices rise and burst like bubbles under its glass sheath. There's a short queue at a self-service café. Helen thinks: *to hell with the budget*. She joins the queue and giggles quietly to herself. She buys tea and a ham sandwich and sits on a metal stool at a long white table. Clustered around the end of it is a group of French schoolgirls. They're spluttering over a magazine, heads together, brown and black, straight and curly. Their narrow hands flick and flutter over the page. At the next table a man snaps his *Daily Telegraph* irritably. But Helen enjoys their hilarity. Visitors progress past. Small children skip and leap, exhilarated by the space. Adults mull over gallery plans. In the central spoke of the Great Court wheel are shops brimming with paperweights and pencils and scarves and books and toys. Beyond the café tables, Helen can see a vast monolith, carved with symbols she can't quite make out. Nick would have loved it here.

She's sure of that. Why didn't they ever do this – hop on a coach, come to the British Museum? Too busy. Too tired. Too late.

From childhood, Nick had been known to his family as the sensible one. He had a brother who died young, before Nick and Helen had met. Patrick, he was called, after Nick's father, and apparently he was a chip off the old block. Reckless, quixotic, a loose cannon. Just like his dad. Except that, by the time Helen came along, Patrick Senior had grown purple and fat-nosed, and spent more time bellowing about his wild streak than demonstrating it.

'Dad changed,' Nick explained to her, 'after Pat.'

Nick's brother was fifteen when he launched himself off the bank of a railway line and tried to bound across the track before the fast train passed. The rules were – his friends told the coroner – wait till the engine's in sight, on the horizon; clear the line in three leaps. He nearly made it. After the accident they erected a high fence topped with barbed wire along the upper ridge of the bank. Nick's father was quoted in the local press, describing his late son as 'a touch crazy. Just the sort of lad to pull a stunt like that.' According to Nick, he said it with pride.

'He called it "spirited",' Nick said. 'I call it downright selfish. That train driver had to quit his job. Imagine what he went through.'

Nick's dad had a dog. He house-trained it by rubbing its nose in its own excrement. 'It's got to learn,' he'd say. Nick was horrified.

'Barbaric,' he said, adding, 'and yet they thought the world of each other, dad and his dog.' Nick was bewildered by the injustice of it all.

The afternoon is lagging. Helen isn't sure when the museum might shut. She gathers herself and sets out to wander through a couple of galleries. A group of people is semi-circling a display of grave goods. They're listening to a woman, a curator perhaps, who's telling them about the grave occupants: '…deeply superstitious,' she's saying, 'and hedged about with ritual.' Her voice is loud and strident; the vowels stretch and hover and descend over them like a sheet on a mattress.

Helen lurks at the back of the group. There was a time when Nick would have been enthralled by all this detail, about food and clothes and jewellery and pots. A man just in front of Helen interrupts the speaker: 'What's your evidence for that?'

Helen flinches. Coolly, the curator stays him with an outstretched hand while she finishes her sentence. Then she turns to look at him and address the group.

'A question about evidential basis. *Good* question. Let me tell you something about our methodology…'

Helen watches the back of the questioner's head. She sees, in tiny movements of his skull, how he bridles a little at being held off, and then how he succumbs to the speaker's praise. *Good question.* He feels clever, now. Feels like the school swot. Helen tries to tune back in to the curator's speech, but she keeps replaying that small and inconsequential episode. *People are so weak*, she tells herself. The way they bob and sway in the swell of other opinions. Always trying to prove themselves; always taking offence, unable to proceed through the most superficial exchange without monitoring their standing in the world's eyes. Suddenly she despises the whole crescent of sightseers, the subservient nodding heads, the spongy brains that accept everything this arrogant woman is telling them.

'Fascinatingly,' the curator is saying, 'the basic techniques were no different to those of contemporary craftsmen…'

'Different *from*,' thinks Helen, with real fury. She's inherited her mother's obsession with grammar. The curator talks on. Helen seethes. How does she *do* that? she thinks. How does she speak to whole groups of people, command their attention, stall interruptions with her traffic-control signals, deliver information with such unstinting confidence? Helen's colour rises and quickly subsides. No point railing at strangers, she castigates herself: *I'm* the feeble one here. She can't begin to imagine what it's like to give a talk, to expect others to listen. She remembers one of her mother's phrases, dealt out when Helen was a child, nagging at her side during the weekly shop: 'It's not *done*,' she used to say, with a look of pained distaste, 'to raise one's voice in public.'

Helen walks back to the bus stop from the museum and is pleased with herself for finding the way. She's never been good with directions.

You never know where the hell you are.

As she waits she fingers the return ticket in her coat pocket and rehearses the process of validating it on the bus. She's never had to do it herself, and is worried that she'll look a fool. On the way here the driver did it for her. During the journey she watched the other passengers as they lumbered up the bus steps and offered their tickets to the machine. The tickets seemed to know what to do, taking on their own momentum and leaping upwards until a heavy clack propelled them back into the passengers' hands. How difficult can it be?

Dusk is falling. Other people form a queue behind her. The bus arrives. Helen tries to feed her ticket into the machine. It remains stubbornly between her fingers.

'Other way,' prompts a young man behind her, and shows her how to do it. 'I'm always getting it wrong myself,' he says, to console her.

Helen takes a spare seat next to a portly man in a tweedy hat. *It doesn't matter*, she assures herself. *Everyone makes mistakes. It's not because I'm old and pitiable.* But she knows that all those daily irritants – dropping keys, stumbling on a loose paving stone, confusing one coin for another – are taking on a different character with age. And so is she, affecting a coyness, a dithery sweetness, as she did with the kind young man. The more she dreads their pity, the more she fosters it. She's a little old lady. Any previous life, loves, triumphs or tragedies count for nothing now.

'I do beg your pardon.'

The man next to her is tucking his coat closely around his girth, making sure there's no physical contact between them at all.

'Don't worry.'

'Busy,' he says, nodding towards the other passengers, who are still filing up the aisle, assessing free seats and potential neighbours.

'Yes,' agrees Helen. 'It is.'

'Always is, this time of day.' He's warming to a theme. Evidently likes to chat. 'I often travel at this time. Traffic's always a fiend – but I usually can't avoid it. Can't leave till I've finished the day's work, got to get there in time for the evening lecture.'

Reluctantly, Helen picks up her cue.

'Oh, are you going to a lecture?'

'Not attending it,' he explains. 'Delivering it.'

'Really!' Helen plays her part. 'How interesting. What's the subject?'

He gives talks on medieval castles. She can't quite make out whether he's a university lecturer or an enthusiastic amateur, and doesn't like to question him too closely.

'My husband,' she tells him, 'would have loved that.'

'Well,' says the man with ponderous gallantry, 'I should be delighted to see you among our number one evening. Newcomers always welcome.'

Helen smiles. *My husband* would have loved it, she corrects him silently. *I* wouldn't.

He drones on about donjons and murder holes all the way back. He insists on giving her his card before she gets off the coach. As the doors unfold behind her and the bus gears utter their seagull cry, Helen moves into the beam of a lamppost to squinny at his name: Arthur Ballantyne, MA DMS. DMS? She's never heard of that. Has he made it up? In smaller type it says 'Medievalist and Literary Consultant'. And charlatan, thinks Helen. She looks accusingly at the receding tail lights. It's quite dark now. Only a few shop windows are lit, and the rush hour has wilted almost to nothing. A couple of figures hurry into silhouette at the end of the road. A dog barks tetchily elsewhere. Helen wonders, with a surge of panic, how long she'll have to wait for the bus home. She knows she'll face the third degree from Lisa. In her head she practises a tone of careless confidence. I went to London. No reason – just fancied a day out. Yes, I hopped on the express…

A blow between her shoulder blades knocks her forward. Her left arm and hip collide with the lamppost. She steadies herself and turns to glare at the culprit. She meets a face, cavernous in shadow, inches from her own. Two eyes emptied of expression. She becomes aware of a furious grappling at her side. For a second she's baffled by the incongruity of that frenzied movement and this frozen face. Someone speaks, low and angry and not to her, and she realises that a second youth is trying to take her bag. At the same instant she registers a fine glint of blade held, still and eloquent, between the first youth's waist and hers. *Let them take it*, she's thinking, *let them take what they want and go*. But her fist is locked around the strap of her bag and her heart is hammering too violently to allow the thought to pass into action. Profanity erupts from the second youth like breaking sticks. Statelier words form in Helen's mind, words from another time and place. *Thank you for the mercy you show in the midst of your great power…* She directs them at the motionless youth, the knife-wielder, though she can't tell whether she's said them aloud or not.

They've gone. Running feet, a shout, and she's alone, leaning on the lamppost like someone in a comic song, clamping her bag to her ribs. The bus home is grinding into view, with its lights and its peopled windows.

'Madness! I mean – absolute madness!'

'I really, really think you should call the police, Helen. I really do.'

'Wandering the streets in the dark! Trundling off to London without a word! Madness!'

Round and round they go, flapping and cawing. Helen sits on her mother's old footstool, rocking on its dodgy leg, knotting her hands on her lap.

'I could speak to them for you, if you don't feel up to it, but I really, really think…'

'Sheer bloody madness!'

They're upset. They've been worried sick about her. She understands. But she wishes they'd shut up and go away. She wouldn't have told them, but they caught her off-guard. When she staggered back, hugging her handbag, her plan was to pour herself a drink and spend an hour calming down before ringing Lisa to let her know she was OK. But the lights were on in the house, there was movement in the window, the front door was opening to greet her, and for a moment she expected to see Nick. Instead, there was Lisa, hands on hips, strung out with anxiety, 'frantic', as she pointed out, trailing her mother up the hall, 'frantic with worry. I've been driving up and down, trying to think where the hell you could be…' up the scale she went, higher and higher… 'I even went knocking on Nancy's door, asking her what to do…' and then the scale was cut short, as Helen folded onto the footstool and caught a sob in her cupped hands.

They'd left the front door open, and Nancy appeared, drawn by the sound of distress. At first she and Lisa were tender, stooping over Helen, arms competing for her shoulders under a confetti of apology and wise words.

'It's been a tough time,' they were saying. 'With the funeral, the grief…'

Helen exploded: 'It's *not* that! I was *mugged!*'

And that set it all off again: the cycle of rebukes and exhortations. She wishes she'd kept it to herself. Why *did* she tell them? Not to share the burden, not to spread the shock. It was more a matter of self-defence. They had to know Helen wasn't beaten by plain old, ordinary old grief. And now Nancy is pecking at a phone, and Lisa is talking about moving in.

'I'd say come to ours, but I know you wouldn't, and besides there isn't the room, but there's plenty of room here for me, just me, I wouldn't bring Mark, just you and me for a couple of months, it would be…'

Helen stands. Something in her manner, her resolve, stops them both in their tracks. She's dry-eyed and thin-lipped, and she pauses like an actor before delivering her lines.

'Listen to me,' she says. 'I'm not calling the police.'

'But…'

'I'm not calling the police. I didn't see anyone, not properly, and I've still got my bag, and I'm fine.'

Lisa and Nancy look meaningfully at each other.

'And Lisa,' Helen goes on, 'you are not moving in here.'

'Only for a few…'

'Not at all. I'll let you know if I need you. Both of you. At the moment, I'm tired, and I'd like to go to bed.'

They shuffle towards the door. Thank God. If they'd put up a fight, thinks Helen, they'd have won.

Lisa waits until Nancy's left, and studies her mother's face.

'Mum, please, will you promise not to do this kind of thing again?'

'What kind of thing?'

'Galloping off here and there without a word, wandering the streets at all hours…'

Lisa shrugs at a vast range of inappropriate behaviour.

'Once upon a time,' Helen reminds her, 'you had a go at Nancy for putting me under house arrest.'

'Oh, Mum, come *on…*'

Helen holds out a tremulous hand, palm up.

'I'd like the spare key back, please.'

Lisa stares. Helen relents immediately and drops her hand. But she adds, 'How would you feel if I let myself in to your home whenever I liked?'

Lisa's mouth works silently then shuts like a trap. She leaves, slamming the front door hard. Helen makes a fist to stop the trembling. That was cruel of her. Lisa is grieving too. She's lost a father and is doing her best for her mother. She doesn't deserve such coldness. But Helen can't afford to lower her shield. If Lisa sees how scared and weak her mother is, it'll be the beginning of the end.

8

Helen turns a page. Dozens more small ads. This would have been so useful at the hospital. She experiments with reading aloud: *This elegant hand-crafted ornamental plate can be yours for only...*

but her voice rasps in her throat. This is what happens when you don't speak for seventy-two hours: you forget how it's done. She coughs. It's nobody's fault but her own. She asked for space and she's got it: the space between the walls of her house, stale with her own breath and meandering thoughts. She's alienated the only two people who care one way or the other. And here she is, in self-imposed solitary, reading the *Radio Times* for the seventh time.

Maybe she should get another pet. At least she'd have an excuse to exercise her vocal cords. It would have to be a cat, this time; she's been nervous of leaving the house since the mugging, and at least a cat takes care of itself. Then again, it would need feeding, and she can't even do that much for herself at the moment. She hasn't eaten for a day and a half. She's been checking the doors three times over every night, to make sure they're secure. She never does that sort of thing – never. Nick used to complain about it.

'Helen, you've left the door on the latch again. Why don't you just put up a sign saying "Burglars Step This Way"?'

That was one of the symptoms – Helen supposes she must think of them as symptoms – of his deterioration. First he became more paranoid – double locking the door, constantly checking the windows, testing the handles; then he stopped bothering altogether, and that was when things really started going downhill.

Helen wonders whether she's destined to mimic Nick's decline. With nobody around to serve up food or nag her to her feet, it would all be a lot quicker, wouldn't it? That's what I'll do, decides Helen. I'll just sit here, and waste away.

Lone Widow Left to Die.
Found decomposing over three-year-old Radio Times.
Next-door neighbour protests: 'She said she wanted to be alone!'

She would have found that funny last week, but giggling is another knack she's lost.

Sobbing daughter tells of family feud: 'I never thought it would come to this,' says distraught Lisa, 36.

It won't.

It won't come to this.

From nowhere, a tornado of indignation whips her out of her torpor. Two scraggy, pathetic youths, with a blade in place of a life. She's damned if she'll let them slash through whatever future she's got left. And besides, she's wounded Lisa enough. The least she can do now is live.

A child's mournful eyes meet hers. A grubby child, in adult clothes, staring from a full-page advert on the back of the *Radio Times*.

Say hello to your great-great-grandmother!

There's another photo overlapping it, of ludicrously whiskered men arranged in a stiff-spined group. *Meet the relatives!*

It's an advert for a genealogy magazine. *Grow your own family tree!*

Helen thinks of the strange man and his gnomic comment in the café.

That's what people do, isn't it? When they can't see what's ahead. They explore the past instead.

Helen's feet are cold. She needs to move. Well, this is as good a reason as any. The magazine slides to the floor as she heaves herself out of the chair. She pulls open a drawer in the sideboard and takes out the local directory.

Acupuncturists…

Aquariums…

Archives.

Part Two

9

This is a building that takes itself seriously. A hammy Victorian building, cobbled with stone flourishes and curlicues. Chiselled over the original entrance are seriffed capitals: DIOCESAN RECORD DEPOSITORY. Recently there's been an effort to lighten up, and a glass-walled extension has been wrapped around it to house the reception and reading room. A new title is sandblasted sleekly across one wide pane: THE ARCHIVE.

Helen stands outside. She can see people in there, walking between tables, taking up places at computer screens, passing to and fro under spaceship lights. Behind her, a slim row of trees between the car park and the road shakes off a breeze. It's chilly. She'll have to go in – or go home. She can't hang about. She won't let the evening catch her up again.

'I don't really know where to start,' confesses Helen. The receptionist summons a gangly man in specs, who tells her about research methods, the internet, letters and diaries, parish records, wills and deeds. He gives her some leaflets, and advises her not to underestimate the value of memories and family tales. He talks in a floating tone which brings to her mind the doctor who first broke the news about Nick's coma.

'Do you have,' asks Gangly Man, 'any older relations who might know some anecdotes, or…'

'No,' says Helen. 'All my older relations have gone. I'm at the head of the queue now.'

She laughs feebly and Gangly Man pinches the arm of his spectacles.

'I see,' he says. 'Well, often the best way to start is by jotting down anything you know about your family – parents, grandparents, aunts, uncles. Anything you know and anything you think you might know. And take it from there.'

Helen sits at a long table with a sheet of paper and a stubby pencil, both provided by Gangly Man. There's an atmosphere of quiet industry, occasionally punctuated by the phone at the reception desk, or the whirr and thunk of a drinks machine in the far corner. Helen monitors the heaving shoulders of the trees outside. It's hard to tell how light it is, through those smoky glass panes. She keeps checking her watch. She must reach the bus stop well before dusk.

Following Gangly Man's suggestion, Helen writes the youngest relation at the top of her page. LISA VERONICA PASCOE. She draws a horizontal line, then hesitates. Mark and Lisa haven't married, but… She mulls it over, then decides against entering his name. If she did, and they split up tomorrow, Helen would blame herself. Under Lisa's name she draws a vertical line and writes: HELEN AMELIA PASCOE, née MURRAY.

Line.

NICHOLAS BENJAMIN PASCOE.

She should be adding brackets and dates. She'll come back to that later.

Helen rests her chin on her hand and considers her surroundings. They remind her of primary school afternoons, when Miss Warriner would let them draw while she loitered at the window, waiting for the weekend. Helen remembers her excitement as going-home time approached, mingled with the fear that her mother wouldn't be there at the gate, that darkness would fall before she came. And here she is, sixty years on, still fretting about the dark.

A movement in the reception area beyond the reading room distracts her. Someone's talking earnestly, decorating his words with his hands, making small, precise circles and strokes in the air. His hair jolts with every emphasis. It's the archivist from the café. He's addressing a lugubrious-looking man in a zipped-up anorak. He ends his lecture with a sharp jerk of the head and swings round to leave the building. As he's opening the glass door Helen senses that their eyelines are about to collide, and dips hastily over her list.

10

Now that she's up here, Helen realises the enormity of her task. She balances on the steel ladder, holding the hatch door open above her head, regarding the chaos of the loft with dismay. Somehow, over the years, she convinced herself that she had very little clutter; that she was a clearer, not a hoarder. She presses her legs against the cold rungs and confronts the extent of her delusion. Cardboard boxes spewing papers, letters and files; photograph albums from another age, their covers curling and bulging as the images between them slowly combust. Old curtains spilling from a hamper. She has an electric shock of memory: she and Nick hauling them from the curtain rails and Nick saying, 'Better keep them just in case. They might come in handy'.

They'd just moved in. Helen said, 'This is *our* house now. I don't want someone else's hideous green curtains in it.'

But Nick insisted, and they lugged them up here together, Helen going backwards up the ladder to steer him, and Nick balancing the great fat gloop of green velvet on his head.

Helen climbs the last few rungs and steps into the attic. Dust rebounds from the slamming hatch door. She can hardly breathe in here. She clambers over a plastic crate of Lisa's schoolbooks and opens the dormer window. Craning to look over the ledge, she catches sight of Nancy packing two of her children into the back of her car. School run. The daily accumulation of strata is taking place in that household too: pictures, photographs, first attempts at joined-up writing, sums, times tables…

She squats over the plastic crate and extracts a book at random.

Causes and effects of the French Revolution. She plunges her hand further into the crate and pulls out a soft exercise book with DIARY written on the cover in careful, round letters.

On Saturday Daddy and Mummy took me to the playground. I went on the roundabout and I did a head first on the slide and Daddy caught me.

The words are traced in ink over a pencilled first draft, and spattered with blots. Helen tries to attach them to a specific occasion, but she can't: it's just one Saturday, after all, among so many. Anyway. She's putting things off. She's up here for a reason. Helen starts to negotiate her way through the ragged cityscape of boxes. She recognises a tightly packed container of pastel-coloured albums: pictures of her and Nick and Lisa. Too recent. The stuff she's after is right at the back, shoved into the lowest corner of the roof to make room for a new generation's detritus.

A wooden box of jaundiced envelopes, handwritten documents, thinner albums with small, monochrome photographs. Underneath all these layers, which Helen inherited from her mother, are the sparser legacies of her grandparents' lives: brown photographs, posed with solemnity and pasted onto thick card. She knows they're here, but she hasn't laid eyes on them for decades. They've just been a murmur, a receding shadow, hidden away behind a hatch door.

She leafs through the albums first. Each shot has its own caption on a strip of paper, neatly scissored and pasted underneath. The glue is drying and flaking, now, and some of the captions flutter onto the floor as Helen turns the pages. She tries to match them up to the pictures, frowning as she deciphers her mother's spidery hand: 'Mrs Cartwright at Number 42' – a woman with curlered hair and no teeth, sitting on a deckchair in a garden.

'Rowena and Skipper' – a dark-haired girl holding a spaniel on her lap.

Helen doesn't recognise any of these people. She sets the albums aside and ferrets about in the box. She fishes out an old school photograph and spots her mother sitting cross-legged at the front, next to a girl holding the slate: CLASS TWO 1930. She scans the rows of children with little interest. All this hoarding of images and jotting down of memories strikes her, in truth, as a waste of time. Every one of those thumbprint faces in Class Two 1930 will disappear from sight and mind in due course, and so will everyone else, much sooner than we think.

There's a pompous studio portrait of her grandfather: she remembers it from her childhood, framed and displayed on her mother's mantelpiece. On the back there's a date: 1919. Edward Blake sneers at his granddaughter from his high-backed chair. Hooded eyes, wavy hair, a rather unimpressive moustache. The arrow collar looks as if it might slice his neck. Helen has no recollection of her grandfather; he died before she could talk. But she does remember the way her mother's chin jutted with pride whenever she quoted his sanctimonious aphorisms, or harked nostalgically back to his strict disciplinary regime. ('If I stepped out of line, three strokes of the birch, no questions asked, and I'm none the worse for it today.') Helen glares back at the dead tyrant.

'Bully,' she says. With the casual power of the living, she flings his portrait back into the box.

11

Helen doesn't really know why she's come back to the Archive. Maybe it's something to do with having people around her – like the café, but not as pricey. She certainly hasn't come to pursue her ancestry: she hasn't added anything, yet, to the upper branches of her tree. She wonders vaguely whether anyone comes round to check that people are doing what they should, and returns to her page. She draws a vertical line under her own name, then realises that she's been doodling in the margin. She's drawn a face with zigzag hair and sticky-out ears. She used to do this in her schooldays, during the most tedious lessons. A rumour of a smile nudges her mouth. The woman sitting diagonally opposite nods at Helen's paper.

'Found a funny one?' A large woman with a great guffaw of hair and a voice like a bear-hug. 'I've found a few jokes in my lot, I can tell you!'

She laughs with her entire body – a delighted, bronchial, tidal laugh that lifts Helen up and rolls her to the shore.

Helen says, 'I haven't got very far. I've only just started.'

'And already you've found the family clown, huh?'

Another crash of surf. Helen looks down at Nick's name and is jolted by a single hiccough.

'No… not exactly a barrel of laughs,' she ventures, and blushes at her own disloyalty.

The woman jabs her biro at the notebook in front of her.

'I'm taking a break from mine.' She winks. 'They're giving me the 'ump.'

Helen isn't sure how to answer, so she makes a face.

Ambling towards their table is the man in the anorak, who was speaking to the archivist the other day. Laughing Woman turns to greet him.

'Hello, darling,' she says. 'Come and join us.' The man hovers next to Laughing Woman's chair, hands in pockets.

'How ya doing, Barnaby?' asks Laughing Woman, reaching out to pat his arm.

Barnie, thinks Helen. She sneaks a glance at him. Beady eyes, fleshy nose, a bumble of grey hair – yes, it could be Barnie reincarnate in an anorak.

'I was just saying to this lady,' says Laughing Woman, 'I've had enough of my lot for today'.

'Had a gutful, have you?'

'Had a gutful, Barnaby. Shouldn't say so, to a lady just starting out, should I? Don't want to put anyone off…'

Having towed Helen into the conversation, Laughing Woman introduces herself. Her name is Latisha, which sounds like laughter when she says it.

'We're old hands, me and Barnaby,' she tells Helen. 'He's got as far as – where've you got to, Barnaby?'

'Sixteen-forty.'

'He's got to 1640, can you believe it? Civil war, right, Barnaby?'

'Mmm. Tricky period.'

Barnaby is a shy man. As he speaks his pebble-eyes skim along the seams between ceiling and walls.

'Yeah, tricky old thing, civil war!' Latisha quakes and sizzles. 'And there's me, still stuck in the nineteenth century.'

'You get waylaid,' Barnaby tells an electric socket.

'Yeah, well, I'm into *family history*. Not just names and dates. I want to know what they've all been up to!' She leans across the table confidentially. 'Barnaby's a vertical man. Me…' she performs a breaststroke – 'I go for *broad!*' Then she's hurled backwards by a fresh wave, provoking a ripple of tutting and dirty looks along the room.

Helen consults her watch again and starts folding her pointless piece of paper.

'I'm afraid I've got to go.'

'Already? Haven't scared you off, have I?'

'No, no,' says Helen politely. 'Of course you haven't.'

'Ah, well then,' says Latisha. 'See you tomorrow,' so naturally, that Helen automatically replies: 'Yes, see you tomorrow.'

Helen walks quickly to the bus stop. It'll be light for another hour, but she can't take any chances. As she hurries past the magistrates' court and the library, she catches sight of a person on the other side of the road, standing in the shadow of a tall hedge. She yelps with fright and almost trips over her feet. He steps forward. Not the knife-wielding youth after all, but the archivist. He sees her, gives a minimal nod of recognition and turns away to scrutinise the street. Apparently he's waiting for someone else.

*   *   *

Helen fiddles with her front-door key, trying to get a purchase. Next door, Nancy's curtain shifts.

Helen lets herself in and tries to revive the house, switching on lights, radio, heating, kettle. She puts a couple of teabags in the pot and then remembers that she's out of milk. In fact she's probably out of everything. She opens the fridge door. Parked in the middle of the near-bare shelf is a full pint of semi-skimmed, emphatic as a kiss.

12

LISA VERONICA PASCOE

|

HELEN AMELIA PASCOE —— NICHOLAS BENJAMIN
née MURRAY   PASCOE

AMELIA CATHERINE —— FRANCIS MURRAY
BERWICK MURRAY née BLAKE   (1916 – 1989)
(1924 – 1995)

She can manage her parents' dates easily enough. The rest can wait.

Her mother hated 'Berwick'. It was a family name, apparently, inherited from her mother's line and tucked discreetly towards the back. She imagines her mother's childhood friends taunting her in hooting accents: 'Lady Amelia Catherine Berwick-Blake! How frightfully honoured to meet you!' Helen thinks of the school photograph, and little Millie Blake in the front row. Greasy hair, thick woollen stockings corrugating over lace-up boots. That name was a gift to the school satirists.

Helen lifts her plastic mug of coffee by the rim and takes a tiny, bitter sip. She's not cut out for this family history lark, that's obvious enough. But the coffee's cheaper here than in the café, and it's somewhere else to be. In her anxiety to keep ahead of the dark she's come early today. In fact the receptionist was opening up when she arrived. Nevertheless others were waiting at the door, and are now already huddled over their work. One or two have been admitted into a mysterious anteroom leading into the stone core of the building. This room has to be unlocked by a member of staff and contains – as far as Helen can see, in the fleeting moments of entry – rows and rows of slim, metallic files.

'Not given up yet, then.'

Barnaby takes a seat. He's wearing the anorak again, and it's still zipped up.

'Not yet,' says Helen. 'But I'm very slow.'

Barnaby shrugs. 'I take it there's no rush,' he says. He spots her plastic mug and shifts uneasily. 'Er… strictly speaking it's no consumables at the tables.' He throws a look over his shoulder. 'But I suppose it doesn't matter as long as you're not working on anything…'

'Only a piece of paper,' says Helen, apologetically. 'And not much on that. I don't even know my grandparents' dates.'

Barnaby looks into the middle distance. 'Easy enough to find out. I'll show you how.'

When Latisha appears, an hour later, Helen is seated at a computer terminal, navigating a database, and Barnaby is stationed at her side.

'Woah!' bellows Latisha. 'It's Captain Kirk and Mr Spock! Live long and prosper, guys!' She leans over to examine the screen, her vast breasts cushioning Helen's neck.

'A-ha-ha! Ordering certificates, huh! You're on the trail, lady.' She squeezes Helen's shoulders between her hands. 'You'll be hooked, believe me. All those rellies out there in the dark, waiting for you to switch the light on…!'

Helen swivels her chair round to disengage herself. 'It's quite disconcerting,' she says 'how little I know, even about my grandparents.'

Latisha flings out her arms. 'Hey, don't give yourself a hard time! I mean, we all know our birthdays and stuff like we know the colour of our eyes. But you go back a couple of generations and half of them don't know how old they are. Some of them don't even know what they looked like, ten years back! Only what the mirror says, one minute to the next. And if you saw some of my lot, you'd know they don't spend a lot of time with mirrors!'

Helen is confused. She wonders whether Latisha's referring to her current family. Then Latisha continues: 'You come and have a squint at Alfie. Then you'll see what I mean.'

A force-nine laugh rattles the room and its occupants. Barnaby looks about him sheepishly.

'We'd better go to the Canteen,' he says.

'Breakfast! Great!' yells Latisha. 'I'll get my trolley!'

The Canteen is a dowdy tearoom tacked on to the back of the magistrates' court, next door. Latisha parks her shopping trolley next to their table, while Barnaby queues for tea and buns.

'My filing system,' she explains to Helen. 'Shouldn't really take it into the Archive but they let me leave it at reception.' She dives into it and resurfaces with a folder stuffed almost tubular with papers and held fast with a piece of string. 'You'd think,' she hollers 'they'd be checking I haven't got a bomb. 'Specially in *here!*'

At a table on the other side of the Canteen, a grey man reeking of dead alcohol is spitting smoke from his cigarette while a woman in a suit speaks to him with muted urgency.

'Can't tell the villains from the briefs in here!' comments Latisha. She releases the string and her file explodes, shedding papers onto the table and floor. Her laughter peaks as she gathers it all together.

'Here it is!' she cries and flaps a photocopy at Helen, who straightens her reading glasses and concentrates. She assumes, at first, that it's a page copied from a photo album. But these are portraits, arranged in dour ranks, challenging the lens, resenting it or – in some cases – fearing it. Even in black and white, Helen can see the grime embedded in their skin, the lines that mock their youth. These are children. Urchins. The word slips unexpectedly into her mind.

'You can tell which one is Alfie,' says Latisha, still reaching for stray papers. 'He's the only one with a smile!'

Sure enough, one scatter-toothed grin slits the middle of the page. There's a name written under it in tiny copperplate. Helen makes out an 'A' but no more.

'Hard one to pin down, was Alfie,' says Latisha. 'But worth it.'

Alfie is Latisha's great-great uncle. His broken smile and jester-cap tufts of hair propel him into the present tense. His paper eyes crinkle with mischief. Helen can't believe he's grown old and rickety, died and crumbled away in the years that lie between this photograph and her first sight of it. Latisha tells her about Alfie's troublesome youth. Stealing, gambling, pimping, fighting, living off his wits. In and out of the police cells, on and off the genealogy radar.

'Look at the rest of them,' she says, wagging a finger at the mugshots, '...don't know what to make of it all. Like the camera's a trick to catch them out. But our Alfie – get a load of him! Thinks he's a movie star!'

It's 1892, and Alfie is 12 years old.

'Start of a long career,' says Latisha. 'Always was a no-good, all his life. I s'pose he'd mellowed, though, by the time I knew him.'

'You *knew* him?'

Helen blinks from Alfie to his great-great niece.

'Oh, sure. Old man by then, of course. Lived to ninety-four. Skinny as a whippet to the end. Smoked like a chimney – couldn't see him for smoke sometimes. Drank like a fish. Still tottering down to the bookies every chance he got. But he made it, didn't he? Did his last stretch inside in his 50s, never went back to it. Good old Alfie. Lasted the course.'

Helen is staring hard at Alfie, as if he might have something to tell her.

Barnaby lays out the tea and buns. Latisha starts decanting her papers back into the trolley.

'Drives him up the wall, my filing methods,' she says, tipping her head at Barnaby.

'Each to his own,' says Barnaby.

Helen returns to the mugshots.

'Scallywags and slaves,' Latisha says. 'That's where I come from!'

Helen sips her tea. She's drinking far too much tea and coffee these days. But the strength of it, the tinny taste, gives her a boost.

She says, 'I doubt I'll find anything half as interesting in my family.'

'Don't you bet on it, lady!' Latisha rocks and rumbles.

Helen turns to Barnaby, who still hasn't undone his anorak.

'I recognised the young man talking to you yesterday,' she says. 'Long dark hair. I've seen him before.'

Latisha's cackle stops abruptly. 'Huh! Marcus Edwards. Lord High Pretentious.'

'A very thorough man,' adds Barnaby, watching his teaspoon stir his tea.

'Yeah, a very thorough pain in the backside.'

'Exacting,' Barnaby tells the salt cellar. 'A perfectionist.'

'In other words, nothing's ever good enough for His Lordship. What was he bending your ear about this time, Barnaby?'

'Oh, something he wants is being rebound. I think that was it. He was rather annoyed. But I wasn't really listening.'

Latisha takes an enormous bite of bun and rolls her eyes in ecstasy.

'I'd have two of these,' she says through her mouthful, 'if I didn't have to get back and get on with it.'

Helen holds her own bun primly, nibbling at the icing. She's never been able to take that kind of wholehearted, sensual pleasure in her food. Latisha munches in a delirium. 'Lots to do today. And I'm on the road tomorrow.'

'On the road?' Helen pinches out a manageable portion of pastry.

'Going to Kew. National Archives. Got some goodies on order.'

'They keep one on the hop a bit,' says Barnaby, 'one's ancestors.'

'Yeah, to and fro, up and down… nice to touch base at the Archive when we can, eh, Barnaby? Hey! Helen!' Pastry crumbs spray across the table. 'Why don't you come along?'

Helen flushes deeply.

'I'll show you the ropes! Why not?' Latisha spreads her arms to embrace Helen, Barnaby and the whole Canteen, including the defendant and his lawyer.

'Come on! We'll have a laugh! Unless you've got other plans?'

Helen's heart is racing. She can't think of a way to refuse.

'No', she says. 'No other plans.'

* * *

'Just chuck 'em behind you. Anything that's in your way, sling it in the back.'

Latisha's car bucks over the kerb as she manoeuvres away from Helen's house. Steadying herself with an effort, Helen lobs between the seats a paperback, an unopened bag of mints and a tube of lipstick, all of which hurled themselves into her lap as Latisha turned the wheel. The back seat is a tumult of cassettes and CDs, books and maps, scarves, umbrellas and soft toys. Something nuzzles against Helen's ankles and she retrieves a threadbare toy rabbit from the floor.

'Your children's?' she asks.

'Not mine. Nephews and nieces. I've got a million of 'em.'

Helen grooms the rabbit's ears. It must be lovely to have Latisha as an aunt.

The car is a big old boxy saloon that chatters with Latisha along the motorway. Helen settles into her seat with the rabbit under one arm and her handbag under the other. She feels safe. Latisha witters away about her interest in family history, and how it began after her mother's death.

'We all came together – gazillions of us – brothers and sisters and cousins and kids and grandkids – 'cause she was a real character, my ma, and everyone adored her, even if they'd hardly even met her. Once was enough. You know?'

Helen says yes, she knows, although she can't imagine how that might be.

'And I'm checking out this crowd of people,' continues Latisha,

73

'and all the family resemblances – you know, who's got Grampa's nose, who's got Ma's smile – and I'm thinking: what's this all about then? Oh, get a wiggle on, lady...'

The car veers into the outside lane to overtake a mini. Helen clutches her seatbelt and the rabbit makes a break for it onto the floor.

'I mean,' Latisha resumes, guiding the car back into its lane with one fluid swing of the wheel, 'what is it that connects all that lot, and me, any more than any old bunch of strangers in a room? Plus, I'd lost my job, and I needed something to do.'

She shimmies and shakes as if losing her job was the funniest experience of her life.

'Oh...' she interrupts herself, freeing one hand from the steering wheel to give Helen's arm a reassuring pat – 'I didn't have my fingers in the till, nothing like that! Redundancy. Surplus to requirements. So I thought, right, well, I'll take a year off. What do they call it? Something churchy-sounding.'

'A sabbatical?'

'That's the one. I'm taking my sabbatical, to do some research!' She flings her head back to laugh and almost leaves the road. 'I love it,' she adds, eventually. 'It's fun. Basically I spend my whole time nosing around, minding everyone else's business. Here comes the rain.'

The windscreen wipers start their jerking dance. Helen watches the rhythmic splash of overspill.

'What about you, Helen?' asks Latisha. 'What set you off on the trail?'

'Oh... er...' Helen feels caught out. She doesn't really consider herself to be on a trail. 'I suppose I've got time on my hands,' she says, lamely. Then, by way of an apology, 'My husband died recently.'

'Oh, I'm sorry to hear that.'

'In fact,' adds Helen, with surprise, 'it was less than two weeks ago.'

'Oh, God!' says Latisha. 'You must be in a daze.'

'I suppose I must be...'

Helen looks at the rain strafing the passenger window. She's glad she left that message this morning, even if it was rather stilted. Hello,

Lisa. It's Mum. Just to let you know I'm going to Kew today. With a friend. So don't worry if you call and I'm not in. Thank you for the milk.

She should have asked after her. Should have asked if she wanted to come round, if she needed a hug. She's sure that's what Latisha would have done. But somehow it seemed more important to mention her 'friend', who was taking her to Kew. Still. At least she rang. That was something.

'It's often *the way*,' Latisha is saying, 'that people get into this game after a loss. Making connections, I suppose. Keeping hold of something.'

'Mmm,' says Helen. 'Maybe that's it.'

They drive on and leave the rain behind. The sun comes out and sequins the tarmac, the cars and the rushing fields.

'I dunno, this weather,' says Latisha, 'you never know what mood it's in. Like me – going through the change!'

Helen wants her to say more, but doesn't know how to prompt her. She's never had the gift of quick intimacy. She was always taught not to be curious. Keep yourself to yourself, her mother used to say. All kinds of innocent enquiries or observations were ruled out. Never talk about Government or God. Never refer to someone's appearance, even with a compliment. 'It's vulgar,' Amelia Catherine Berwick Blake would say. 'It's not done.'

So Helen has made it through life so far without ever telling anyone, friend or foe, how nice they look today.

'Shall we have the news?' offers Latisha, and switches the radio on. *She thinks I don't want to talk*, Helen tells herself, and says, 'Yes, all right.'

There's music leading up to the hour. Latisha starts singing along in a tuneful, husky voice. Helen sits back and lets herself be lulled by their journey, the pulse of footbridges, the cryptic code of arrows and markings and signs that she's never had to learn. Helen likes motorways. She likes their promise of a new destination. She likes their timelessness, the way they interrupt and link life's disasters and banalities. An interval in the play.

Nick hated cars. He called them killing machines. He winced at every sight of roadkill, even when the mess of blood and fur had almost become part of the road. Once they saw a small deer, limp and twisted on the verge. It was clearly dead, but Nick stopped the car and went to stand over it. Watching him in the wing mirror, Helen wondered whether he was saying a prayer. She didn't think he was religious, but she couldn't be quite sure. Never ask about Government or God. When he got back into the car she just said, 'Why do they go on crossing the road?' and wished she hadn't; it sounded like a feeble gag. Nick tugged the door shut and fumbled with his seatbelt.

'I don't know,' he said. 'Migration routes, breeding territories – maps and routes that are etched into their genes, I expect. They can't help it. We slam a road down, aim a car, and they're done for. Trapped.'

It occurs to Helen now, as they race along the motorway, that doing what Nick did – choking on car fumes in a garage – may have been his warped idea of justice.

The news comes on. Latisha greets every headline with a groan or a cry.

A Home Office report has concluded that…

Ha!

In Baghdad, a car bomb has…

Oh, God…

As soon as the news ends Latisha switches the radio off.

'Depressing,' she says. 'Don't know why I listen to it. Never mind – nearly there now. And we can forget current affairs and concentrate on over-and-done-with affairs instead!'

Her laughter propels them up a slip road and away from the motorway's blare.

Latisha is tracing one of great-great uncle Alfie's older brothers.

'He was the youngest of thirteen,' she explains, 'and I can't pass any of them by. That's what takes me so long!'

This particular brother, Harold, ran away to sea and was never heard of again. Latisha is searching through nineteenth-century lists of burials at sea. As her gloved finger slides down the columns of names, each one registers on her face as if it's someone she recalls.

'Who knows,' she muses, 'what kind of exotic places the old boy got to see? Bit of a change from the back-to-back in Walsall…'

She runs through another column, then says, 'On the other hand, he might have spent the rest of his natural throwing up below decks.'

Two more columns. Then: 'I hope he had a good time.'

Helen nods, but she's perplexed. Latisha's great-great-uncle Harold died long ago, in another world. A world of steamships and horses and carts, a world without computers or radios or electric lights or mobile phones, where an illiterate son could just hop on a ship and disappear. Helen hasn't the remotest shred of connection with this man, and neither – as far as she can make out – has Latisha. Great-great-uncle Harold lived out his days with no conception of the possibility that, 150 years on, his family might finally hunt him down.

Latisha continues through the roll-call of names with tears in her eyes.

'All these young lads,' she says. 'All these mothers' sons.'

She doesn't find Harold.

'You don't seem too disheartened,' comments Helen, as the saloon rollicks back a few hours later.

'Got to keep at it!' says Latisha. 'The further back I go, the harder it'll get. 'Specially when I start on my dad's side. Then we're into Colonial Office stuff, Plantation books – and with a bit of luck, a whole gang of new relatives, all desperate to invite me over to the sunny Caribbean shores!'

'Your family,' says Helen, 'sounds amazing.'

'*All* families are amazing,' says Latisha. She looks quickly at Helen's profile and back to the road ahead. 'What about you? Any family?'

'One daughter. Lisa.' Helen's throat is tight.

'How's she coping?'

'She's very…' starts Helen, then coughs and tries again. 'We knew it was coming, you see. Nick was in hospital for quite a while.'

Latisha considers this for a moment, then says: 'Well. It's good you've got each other.'

'Yes,' says Helen, adopting the same sentimental inflexion. 'Yes, it is.'

13

CERTIFIED COPY OF AN ENTRY OF BIRTH
Pursuant to the Births and Deaths Registration Acts, 1836 to 1929.

When and Where Born: 12 January 1924, 4.10 AM
Abbey Cottage Hospital, Forbridge
Name, if Any: Amelia Catherine Berwick
Sex: Girl
Name and Surname of Father: Edward Blake
Name and Maiden Surname of Mother: May Jones
Rank or Profession of Father: Clerk

Well, thinks Helen. That doesn't tell me anything new. She fishes a
second document from the envelope.

CERTIFIED COPY OF AN ENTRY OF MARRIAGE

When Married: 14 May 1923
Edward Stanley Blake, 23, Bachelor; May Jones, 17, Spinster
Groom's Rank or Profession: Clerk
Groom's Residence: 14 Dover Way, Forbridge
Bride's Residence: White Hill House, Forbridge
Groom's Father: John Blake, Tradesman

After a cursory glance Helen replaces both copies in their envelope.

She was meant to have ordered more: death certificates, her grandfather's birth certificates... but she was worried about the cost, and in truth it all seems fairly pointless. Names and dates and names and dates. She can almost hear their accumulating babble, thickening the atmosphere as the dead thicken the earth.

The phone rings.

'Hi, Helen. It's Mark.' His voice springs along the line, unnaturally jaunty. 'I'm being despatched to do the weekly shop, and I just wondered whether there's anything I can get you while I'm there.'

Lisa's presence fills the interval before Helen's reply.

'That's kind of you, but I think I'm all right at the moment.'

She and Lisa have spoken since their row. Lisa returned the answerphone message while Helen was at Kew. She hoped it had been a good day and – with laboured playfulness – hoped this 'friend' was someone she'd approve of. So that evening Helen called her back and told her about the Archive and Latisha and Barnaby, and Lisa said it was a good idea to get involved in something like that. It would keep her occupied.

Helen knows this is only a working truce. It'll take more than one chirpy phone call to mend the rift she's created. Before Mark rings off she asks him to tell Lisa about the certificates.

'She might be interested to see them,' she suggests.

'Oh, this is the ancestry thing? Yes, I'll tell her. You never know, you might find out you're royalty or something!'

They round off the phone call with mutual relief. Helen has a flashback of Mark's first meal with them as Lisa's official partner. The four of them sitting round the table: Mark red-faced and rigid, Lisa retreating behind her hair, Nick feeding scraps to the dog, Helen frantically casting around for another friendly phrase to spoon out with the peas. Afterwards, when Lisa and Mark had made their escape, she served up tentative impressions to Nick.

'He seems very nice... very eager to please... I think she's serious this time... maybe there'll be wedding bells...'

Nick cocked an eyebrow and Helen blushed. When did she turn

into a sit-com caricature? She struggled on.

'I think they'd be happy, if they did get married. I think he'd be good for her.'

'Good for her!' The sound of Nick's voice made Helen start and Barnie's tail thump against the linoleum. 'Marriage for medicinal purposes,' he grunted, and led Barnie away for his walk.

'Well, well,' says Barnaby. 'Well, well, well, well, well.' He looks from one facsimile to the other and shakes his head. 'Well, well, well...'

Helen takes more squirrel-bites of her iced bun and waits. She had hoped to find Latisha at the centre, but Latisha, according to Barnaby, is 'on the hoof'. So Helen and Barnaby have retreated into a corner of the Canteen, and Helen is trying not hear the muttered note-swapping of two solicitors, a couple of tables away.

'Well, I never,' says Barnaby, and Helen decides enough is enough.

'I'm afraid I couldn't see much of interest, myself. But then, I'm...'

'Oh!' says Barnaby, forgetting himself and looking her straight in the eye. 'Oh, there's a *very great deal* of interest here, if you don't mind my saying.'

Helen simpers politely and braces herself for a short talk on demographics.

'Did your mother ever mention,' he carries on, his doggy eyes bright with interest, 'whether she was a premature baby?'

Helen wrinkles her forehead.

'No... it's not really the sort of thing she used to talk about.'

'Was she a small woman? Delicate?' Barnaby seems to be interrogating the certificate itself.

'Not delicate. I wouldn't say delicate. Short of stature, yes, but she had a robust constitution.'

To the end of her days, Helen's mother would kneel to scrub the hearth – though she would have liked the world to believe someone else was paid to do it. Helen can see her clearly: solid shoulders, curling in latter days to a widow's hump. Red knuckles. Square buttocks, pivoting in time to the effort of her arms. Pared-down fingernails, always immaculately cleaned and buffed in denial of the rough and tussocked flesh on her old hands.

'No, definitely not delicate.'

Barnaby holds the two copies up to face her and quotes: 'May Jones. Married in May 1923.'

'Yes, rather romantic, I thought,' says Helen.

'Amelia Blake. Born in January 1924.'

Barnaby takes both certificates in one hand and counts the months on the fingers of the other. 'May... June... July...' Helen nods sagely, without following. '...January 1924. Eight months after the marriage.'

Gradually Helen's posture alters as she registers his meaning.

'Oh! You mean...'

'But she may have been premature. It's possible.'

Helen thinks of the hangdog little face in the school photograph. Three rows of Class Two 1930 start to rustle with rumour. A shotgun wedding. It was probably common knowledge. *Here comes Lady Amelia Catherine Berwick-Blake. How frightfully honoured to meet you!* Across the decades, that taunt develops a sharper edge.

Barnaby hasn't finished. He's found more clues in those few bland facts. The absence of May Jones' father from her marriage certificate might indicate that she herself was illegitimate. Helen purses her lips. *So*, she thinks: *I come from a long line of bastards.*

'A blank space is like a silence,' says Barnaby. 'Hides a wealth of detail.'

Apparently even May's address is worth further investigation, though he doesn't say why.

'And another thing,' he concludes, handing the copies back. 'I think your mother may have had a twin.'

14

'Your mother had a twin? How does he make *that* out?'

Lisa regards the certificate with scorn. She turns it briefly, as if there might be a clue on the other side. Helen shrugs.

'Apparently it's something to do with the time. They've recorded the time of Mum's birth – see?'

She points to the column: 4.10am. The end of a night's struggle. Blood and tears and the first fragments of a dawn chorus.

'So?'

Helen explains, borrowing Barnaby's air of patient authority, that a precise time of birth was usually only given in the case of twins.

'But there's no one else on here,' Lisa protests, shaking the certificate impatiently.

'According to Barnaby, that might mean the other baby was stillborn.'

There's a pause as the phantom of tragedy wafts between her words. Then Lisa says, 'Well, why bother recording the time of birth, then?'

And Helen can't answer that.

Lisa is standing in the hall. She hasn't taken her coat off: she's on her way to work. She rang the doorbell and checked, with pointed formality, that it was all right to come in and see how Helen was. Now she's standing here like a stranger, saying she won't stop long. But she's here. And that's a step forward.

Helen takes the certificate back and tries not to sound crestfallen:

'I thought it was quite intriguing.'

Lisa sniffs. She's got a heavy workday ahead and she and Mark had a big argument about who should take the car. She says, 'Weird name, Barnaby. For a man.'

'Weirder for a woman,' says Helen, hoping to make her laugh, but Lisa just rolls her eyes and says, 'So, you're going to carry on with this mullarky, then?'

Helen looks at the certificate and says, 'I'll do a bit more. See what comes up.'

'Well, Mark thinks it's a great idea.' Lisa takes the car keys from her coat pocket and tests their weight. 'Anyway. I've got to go. Can't be late for this bloody meeting.'

'I hope it goes well,' says Helen, vaguely. Lisa dawdles on the doorstep, eyeing a streak of bird shit on her car window. She says, 'So… like I said, I'll be popping out at lunchtime to pick up all the stuff Mark forgot. If you think of anything…'

'Yes. I'll let you know,' says Helen, adding, 'Thank you,' and hoping it sounds like 'sorry.'

They stand there for a moment. Helen bolsters herself against a tidal pull of weariness. Lisa looks tired too, she thinks. And then, as if at a signal, they both rally and return to motion. Lisa points her key fob and the car tuts.

'Good luck with the meeting,' says Helen.

Halfway along the path Lisa turns and says, 'Are you only doing your side, then?'

'My side?' says Helen, and Lisa waves dismissively.

'Never mind. Give me a ring if you remember anything you need.'

Helen watches the car until it's turned out of the road, then shuts the door and looks again at her mother's birth certificate. She pretended not to understand, but she knew exactly what Lisa was asking. Why trace her own family, when all her questions are about Nick?

It strikes her that, as far as Lisa is concerned, Helen and Nick are the same family. Actually, though, Helen knows even less about Nick's than about her own. She's heard it said that suicide runs like wire through the generations. And depressive tendencies – yes, of course, she knows all about that. She remembers how Nick's parents shuffled around in their prison cell of routine – his father drinking, lying on the couch with the dog to rage at the telly; his mother always in the kitchen, cleaning bare patches into the lino, or sitting on her pine chair, smoking, brooding. Helen never thought of them as depressed: that's just the way they were. If their world seemed stifled and melancholy, she put it down to young Pat's death. Maybe she should take a broader view, look further into it, hunt down connections, follow trails of mood and catastrophe into the past. But what if she finds nothing? What if there's no pattern, no magic DNA code to explain why Nick did what he did? What if the only trail leads to Helen herself?

Helen returns to the kitchen, where she's been making notes about her mother.

Time of birth: 4.10am.

Amelia Catherine Berwick.

Did they pick a name for the other child, or was it only ever a blank space?

Helen is beginning to understand why Latisha shed tears over those endless columns of names. She sits at the table and seems to heave somebody else's sigh, a sigh that could be profound suffering or profound joy. She picks up her biro and resumes her work, jotting down some of the points that Barnaby made, copying out times, date, address, name, reducing and soothing an age-old sorrow into words on a narrow-lined page.

15

Tears are coursing down Latisha's cheeks. They branch into narrower tributaries and trickle under her ears and around the gutterings of her nose and lips and chin. Helen and Barnaby watch across the Canteen table. The line of Barnaby's mouth extends fractionally into a smile. Latisha's head lolls back and her chest heaves. A soundless momentum builds until, finally, she lets rip a great hoot that frightens the teacups.

'Oh,' she gasps, as her body subsides and steadies, 'oh dear, oh dear, oh dear… you're a caution, Barnie-boy!'

She gropes up her sleeve for a tissue and wipes her entire face in one move, before blowing her nose with extravagance.

'It was rather amusing, I thought,' concedes Barnaby. He's been telling them about the confusion caused by a portrait of one of his forebears, swathed in classical drapes and long thought to be one William Head, until the square features and heavy brow turned out to belong to William's sister, Anne.

'Oh dear,' says Latisha again. 'I've got to say, it's a treat to hear a funny story for once. Most of the tales you find in this game are doom and disaster. Enough to make you slit your throat sometimes.'

Helen casts an apologetic look at the Canteen's other customers, still reeling in the shockwave of Latisha's outburst, and as she does the door opens and a woman peers in, evidently searching for someone. She catches Helen's eye. It's the foxy woman from the café. Helen begins a smile of recognition, but is frozen by the woman's expression of outrage and disgust. It's directed straight at Helen herself, with the force of a physical blow. Foxy Woman turns on her heel and leaves, banging the door shut behind her. Somewhere in the Canteen a voice says, 'Jesus, what's got into everyone today?'

Barnaby raises his eyebrows.

'That,' he comments, 'is what I call an old-fashioned look.'

'Meant for me, probably,' says Latisha, blithely, 'and my foghorn gob,' then: 'Right, then, Helen, drink up, lady, and we'll go fetch those books!'

The dregs of Helen's tea are cold, but as she drains her cup she feels a slow flush of heat spread from her ribcage to her forehead. She's remembering the day of Nick's funeral. The day she left that café behind Foxy Woman, and followed her halfway across town. Foxy must have seen her. Helen cringes. What was she thinking? She puts down her empty cup and glances from Latisha to Barnaby. They don't seem to have noticed that Helen's face is still smarting from the smack of Foxy's glare.

'Before we go,' orders Latisha, 'a quick trip to the loo. Barnie, keep an eye on our stuff.'

Helen follows her obediently, disguising her deep embarrassment. She was taught to leave a room discreetly and return unobtrusively, to murmur, 'excuse me for a moment,' without mentioning any feral urges. Even euphemistic phrases – 'call of nature', 'spend a penny' – were regarded as vulgarities in Amelia Berwick Blake's house.

Latisha bursts into the public toilets like a bandit entering a saloon. Helen pads towards a free cubicle at the other end of the row. There's no lock on the door, and the last of the paper is straggling from its holder into a soggy 'S' on the floor. Helen considers propping the door shut with the tampon bin, but it's full to overflowing; several leavings are bulging from its plastic mouth and threaten to erupt out of it if disturbed. From the far end of the cubicles, Latisha's voice rings out: 'Got to start cutting down on all that tea and coffee...'

Helen shudders and leaves the cubicle. She'll do as she was always told to do: hold it in. Nevertheless, she feels the need to wash her hands. Two of the sinks are blocked with hair and paper. The other has a tap that won't turn off. Helen decides against the dirt-cracked pebble of soap and waves her hands under the broken tap. In the mirror she sees one of the cubicle doors open and Foxy Woman comes out. Helen sees her own quick, reflected blush. She turns towards the towel, which is hanging limp and sodden from the dispenser. Behind her, a flinty voice says, 'Give your spymaster a message from me.'

It could almost be a radio transmission. Helen's shoulders contract, but before she can react there's a commotion at the end of the room and Latisha is there, bellowing, 'Not exactly deluxe facilities, are they?'

A flurry of hair and anger, and Foxy has gone.

'Hey,' says Latisha, shaking her wet hands over the sink. 'Wasn't that hatchet-face again?'

'Actually,' says Helen, failing to sound nonchalant, 'I've seen her a few times before. I think she's a friend of that man – what's his name? With the long hair…'

'Marcus Edwards!' Latisha's hands fly up, showering the mirror. 'Pah! That explains the permanent stink under her nose, then.' Something about Helen's posture makes her pause and change her tone. 'You all right? Did she say something to you?'

'No! No,' says Helen, forcing her most social smile. 'I don't think she recognised me at all.'

*   *   *

'Turning the Key: A Guide to Family History… Growing Your Family Tree… Beginners' Guide to Genealogy…'

Latisha moves along her bookshelves, tipping out a volume every so often and adding it to the pile on the floor.

'I'm not sure I'll ever get through all those…' says Helen.

'Oh, they're all handy for dipping and skimming,' says Latisha, without pausing in her progress. 'Specially if you're not on the internet. Here's a good one – *The Women in your Past: How to Trace the Female Line…*'

Not on the internet. Helen is ashamed. She feels like a child among adults. Everyone else is engaged in a conversation far above her head.

'I suppose,' she says doubtfully, 'I should do something about that…' But she doesn't even know what she means. Lisa has often urged her to 'get email', but Helen hasn't admitted to her, yet, that she doesn't know where to get it.

'Park yourself wherever there's a space,' urges Latisha. 'I'll put the kettle on in a minute.'

Not more tea, thinks Helen. Her stomach sloshes as she turns to find a seat. Latisha's house is, like her car, a pandemonium of toys, newspapers, discarded shoes and items of clothing. Helen unearths an armchair, clearing away a baby's rattle, a plastic tennis racket and a colouring book.

'You must have your nephews and nieces round a lot,' she observes.

'They sure leave a trail, don't they, the little buggers!' says Latisha, squatting to examine the lowest shelf.

Helen considers the rattle still puttering in her hand, and remembers the way Latisha spoke of her great-great uncle Alfie, the grinning twelve year old of 1892 – *Our Alfie – get a load of him!* – with the same brusque affection.

The pile of books is growing.

'Gosh,' says Helen, with alarm, 'you're being far too generous.'

'Hey,' says Latisha, 'I can spare 'em!'

The bookshelves cover an entire wall of Latisha's small sitting room, from ceiling to floor.

Helen asks, 'How do you reach the top shelves?' – and immediately regrets it. There may be even more required reading up there.

'I've got a proper library ladder in the shed,' says Latisha, proudly, struggling to her feet. 'I'll show you if you like.'

'Oh, no, no, don't trouble,' says Helen, and the rattle in her hand chatters nervously.

'Got it on eBay,' adds Latisha. 'But to tell you the truth I've never used it. I love my books, but once I've read 'em, that's it. Never go back!'

She steps into the middle of the room to survey her library, nearly falling over a bright yellow water-gun.

'My eldest put these up,' she says. 'Eldest nephew, I mean. Twenty-one, he is. Can't believe how fast they shoot up. He's a dab hand with a hammer, my Grant. Put all the books up for me, too. Only did it last year. Before that they were all in boxes, all over the place. Right. Kettle!'

Helen pictures the room without Grant's handiwork. *My eldest*, she thinks. *My Grant*. Does his mother bridle, when Latisha slips into these proprietorial terms? Helen imagines what her own reaction would be, and recalls her old jealousy of Nancy. But that's different, she tells herself. And anyway, Latisha seems to lay claim to everyone she likes. *My love, My darling...* even the ancestors she traces are 'one of mine'.

Latisha brings tea in mugs and finds room for them on the floor. Helen has hers black – somehow it seems more solid that way, and easier to digest. She can't bring herself to decline altogether. Helen was brought up never to refuse the hospitality of a host.

After tea Latisha disappears to find a container for the books. She comes back carrying a shoebox.

'I don't think we'll fit them in there!' says Helen.

Latisha perches on the arm of the chair and removes the box lid.

'Thought you might be interested,' she says. She's unusually bashful. 'Some people would say it's morbid, but – well, see what you think.'

She hands Helen the box. Inside are several pieces of card. Helen takes one out and reads aloud from the back: 'Perkins and Son. Old Kent Road, 1878. *Cartes de Visite*. Prices per dozen on request.'

She turns the card around and studies the photograph pasted on the front. A small girl, perhaps about three years old, sleeps peacefully among satin folds. Reflected light speckles her fair, curly hair. Her lips are fractionally parted. Her hands lie on the sheet, fingers loosely entwined. Latisha waits while Helen takes in the details, then explains: 'It's a post-mortem portrait. They were all the rage back then.'

Helen struggles against a wave of nausea – due mainly, she reckons, to excess of tea.

'You mean,' she says, 'this little girl is dead?'

'She looks really tranquil, doesn't she?' says Latisha. 'Serene. That was the point – it's comforting. You know? Like, well, she's gone, you've lost her, but she's OK. She'll never be in pain again.'

Ants are scurrying across Helen's flesh. Maybe it's not just the tea. She takes out another picture. A baby, this time, with impossibly small hands and a round, bonneted face. She hears a strange, guttural sob and realises it's come from her.

'I know,' says Latisha, tenderly. 'They get to you, don't they?'

Helen draws in a wide breath and holds it, dreading the return of the giggles. Latisha leans over her with great concern.

'Oh, God, Helen, I'm such a stupid mare. What a thoughtless cow. I could kick myself from here to the high street. Look, let me…'

She tries to take the box back, but Helen keeps a firm grasp, and masters the urge to laugh.

'Nonsense,' she says. 'It's not thoughtless at all. It's got nothing to do with… it's very interesting. Really – I'm very interested. Tell me more about it. Please.'

So Latisha tells her about the custom of portraying the dead – a brief vogue, a quirk of the photographic age, which petered out with the coming of war, when death ceased to be a domestic affair, and not even the most skilled technician could light and position the torment out of the picture.

While Latisha talks, Helen carries on taking out the cards, noting their oblivious subjects and the prices quoted for enlargements and copies by the dozen. The oldest child is no more than seven or eight. The youngest is probably only a few hours old. Helen asks, 'Do you know who they are?'

'Nope. Not one. That's sort of why I've got them.' Latisha adjusts her weight, making the chair groan. 'It's like, like I'm…'

'Taking them under your wing?'

Latisha laughs, but this time it's a muted, uncomfortable sound. She says, 'I just think there's something sad about it. You know. All those little lives gone by, and nobody remembers who they were. I find a lot of them in markets. Junk stalls. That kind of thing.'

Helen thinks about her mother's twin. But these photographs are all Victorian – too old.

'Did they take pictures of adults, as well?' she asks, and has to resist a memory of Nick crumpled in the driver's seat.

Latisha says, 'Oh, yeah. Adults too. But I don't go for those.'

16

A large ginger tomcat emerges from under the dripping leylandii and makes a dash for it across the lawn and over the fence into Nancy's garden. The neighbourhood cats have been a pest since Barnie died. Come to think of it, though, Barnie never was much of a deterrent: the cats regarded him in the main with cool contempt. Helen watches a bare patch of soil bubble and foam under the relentless drizzle. If it doesn't stop soon the whole garden will be saturated. Not that Helen particularly cares. She's never been very interested in flowers and shrubs. Luckily, Jim the odd job man comes every three weeks to keep everything trim and tidy, and stave off the signs of dereliction. Nancy's husband used to pop over and mow the lawn, when Nick stopped bothering; and then, when Nick went into hospital, Nancy asked around and found Jim. One less thing to worry about. Helen tries to recall what Auntie Fay said at the funeral: something about it being an afterthought. This has been a widowhood in stages.

She turns a page in the book she's pretending to read. *Family History for Beginners*. Another three books are piled ready on the kitchen table, and Helen's made a few cursory notes in her writing pad. But it's hopeless. The text swims in the hiss of steady rain.

The doorbell screeches. Nancy, in a yellow raincape and sou'wester. She avoids Helen's eye.

'Sorry to trouble you,' she says icily, 'but I thought you might want to know that the cats have dug up your geraniums.'

Helen reins in a smile.

'Yes, I noticed that. Thanks for letting me know…' She's tempted to shut the door again, just for the hell of it. But they haven't spoken since the day of the mugging, and this is Nancy's peace offering, and Helen steps aside and says, 'Why don't you come in for a coffee?'

Nancy goes into a dervish-whirl of disrobing. She flaps out of the cape and sou'wester, showering Helen and most of the hall, levers off her wellies and reverses out of a gargantuan home-knitted jumper. She sheds her frostiness with them and makes for the kitchen, crying, 'Helen! All those books! It's like something out of Harry Potter!'

Reluctantly, Helen cranks up her apology as she boils the kettle.

'I'm afraid I was a little short with you when…'

'All forgotten!' Nancy shakes her hedge of hair and starts clearing Helen's work to one side. 'All forgotten, Helen. You know me. I'm never one to bear a grudge. And you've been under such a strain.' Her eyes and voice grow soggy, merging with the drizzle: 'I *completely* understand.'

Helen says, 'Well, you're very kind.'

'Nonsense. What are friends for?'

Helen finds some stale Jaffa Cakes. She sits opposite Nancy and listens to her accounts of Finn's new glasses and Della's boyfriend, and the various shortcomings of teachers, vicars, husbands. It's a relief, of sorts, to hear another voice compete with the drone of the rain.

'And what about you?' Nancy's suddenly saying. 'You seem very busy, with your books and your trips… not that I'm inquisitive; you know me, I keep myself to myself…'

Helen says, 'Oh, nothing much to report. I've been looking up some family history. As you can see.'

Nancy examines the book spines as she bites at the chocolate edging of her biscuit.

'It's quite absorbing,' lies Helen.

Nancy waggles her head. 'Aaaa… I think it's *wonderful*. To have a hobby. Well done you, I'm sure it's *just* what you need.'

'For some people,' says Helen, more defensively than she intended, 'it's almost a profession.'

'Mmmm, I'm sure. People do get obsessed with all this, don't they? How far back have you gone?'

'Well, I – I've only just started…'

Nancy nods sympathetically. 'Of *course* you have. It takes *time*, getting to grips with something new. And you've got a lot on your mind…' her eyes crinkle with emotion. 'But I think it's *fantastic*, that you can find an interest like this. It's so *brave*. And it's so important, isn't it, to make the family links, at a time like this? I mean, I'd do it myself, if my hands weren't so full with the Littles.'

Helen lowers her eyes and Nancy coughs, realising the implication: she has too much of a present to be worrying at the past. Helen sees her embarrassment and feels sorry for her. She knows Nancy means well. She says, 'Yes, well, it does keep me occupied, you're right about that. And I've met some nice people, who are helping me find my feet.'

'Good for you,' says Nancy. 'I do admire you, Helen. Battling on. Despite everything.'

They both jump at the sound of the doorbell.

'Lisa not at work today?' asks Nancy, but Helen knows it's not Lisa. Too hesitant for her. She opens the door to a hooded figure, zipped so firmly into an anorak that only his pebble-eyes are visible. For a split second she's gripped with terror; then he tugs the zip down to reveal his mouth and she recognises Barnaby. He's very sorry to have called by without warning. He was in the area, and…

Barnaby stutters to a halt and Helen knows that Nancy must be standing behind her. Helen introduces them, noting the tremor of Nancy's expression at his name. Nancy says, 'Don't mind me. I'll have to be off soon.'

Helen herds them into the kitchen and Barnaby sits uneasily. He's been doing some detective work, he explains, on Helen's certificates. He regards the damp knees of his trousers.

'Maybe…' he falters, 'maybe I should…'

'That's quite all right,' interrupts Helen. 'Carry on. I don't suppose Nancy will be shocked by any skeletons in my family cupboard…'

Barnaby doesn't seem so sure. Helen becomes nannyish with him:

95

'Please, do take off your anorak and have a coffee with us. You're not disturbing us at all, is he, Nancy?'

'Not at all,' says Nancy. 'And anyway, I won't be stopping long.'

Barnaby clears his throat.

'As you know,' he tells Helen, 'I was minded to follow up one particular item of information on your grandmother's wedding certificate.'

'Her place of residence,' says Helen, triumphantly.

'Quite so. Bride's residence, White Hill House. That, I thought, was intriguing.'

'Yes, I remember you saying so.'

Nancy looks from one to the other, eyebrows arched.

'I checked it,' says Barnaby, and gazes into the garden, apparently in search of an escape route.

'Go on,' says Helen.

'It's as I thought,' continues Barnaby, with a quick glance at Nancy. 'Not a private household – neither hers nor an employer's. She was living at a workhouse.'

17

'Look at them. They're so *serious*.' Nancy brushes a finger along the row of Class Two pupils. 'Compare this with the Littles and their pals in the school photographs – all beaming away fit to bust, bless 'em…'

'A school photograph,' says Barnaby, 'was a very solemn matter indeed.'

'Talking of school…' Nancy checks her watch and scrambles to her feet, nearly smashing her head on a roof beam. 'Oh, cream crackers! I'll miss the school run!' She stoops and scuttles to the hatch door. 'Sorry, Helen, I'll have to dash, nice to meet you Barnaby, must be…' and she's clanking down the loft steps, leaving a small whirlwind of dust in her wake.

Strangely enough, Helen is quite sorry to see her go. She's been grateful to Nancy this afternoon. Grateful for her interest, and for her response to Barnaby's revelation about the workhouse: 'No shame in that.'

She was grateful, too, when Nancy declined to join their trawl of attic archives, saying, 'You know me – I don't like to go nosing into other people's business,' – and grateful that, in fact, she did.

She and Nancy and Barnaby have been in the loft for over three hours, sifting through pictures and documents under Barnaby's methodical guidance. And Nancy has been genuinely helpful, asking questions, providing comments about every line and character they've encountered: Who's this little boy? These must be brother and sister – same nose. Oh, look, that's Mrs Wotsit from the garden… And so on and so forth, pummelling Helen's mind out of its stupor. Helen has even started to dredge up stories her mother told her – stories she'd forgotten, or thought she had; stories that must have lodged deep in her brain and lain there waiting for excavation. Her grandfather had died young, but she was vague about the cause. 'I suppose,' she confessed, 'I should have checked that out already.' In her imagination he had grown gaunt and tragic, expiring poetically in the grip of some obscure disease. Long before she developed her adult opinion of his character, Helen had revelled in her mother's tales, in which he was always a hero.

'A war hero?' prompted Barnaby.

'No... not war...' An image fizzed before her, obscure as a badly tuned TV, of her mother in a chair by the gas fire, sewing; and Helen saw herself, sitting on the floor, arms roped around her knees, breathing in the home smells of soap powder and stew. Another picture appeared – clearer and more vividly coloured: a picture from Helen's own childish imagination, conjured to fit her mother's words. A man, a towering, beautiful man, with magnificent whiskers and a silver sword at his flank...

'A *romantic* hero,' she told Barnaby and Nancy. 'A hero who rescued a maiden in distress.'

It didn't seem to Helen to get them very far – a child's fancies, reconstituted half a century on. But Barnaby was adamant that she should write this down, along with every other scrap of ill-digested fact or incomplete fantasy that she could reel in from her youth.

'They're all clues,' he told her. 'All worth keeping at hand.'

Nancy nodded fiercely, giving herself a halo of dust.

The three of them have amassed a treasury of material, all sorted by Barnaby into different piles. Helen has made hurried notes of vague memories and possibly misheard names. And now Nancy is thundering down the stairs, running late for the Littles, and Barnaby is easing his legs out of their cramp, and wet sunlight is craning through the dormer window, and Helen's throat is dry, and she really would like to know how her grandmother ended up in the workhouse.

She and Barnaby have tea in the kitchen. Helen opens the window to let in the scent of finished rain. A fretwork of birdsong is greeting the sun, and the garden steams and shines. Helen feels tired, as if she's physically exerted herself, and she savours her tea while she and Barnaby watch the changing weather. Then Barnaby says, 'Nancy told me about your late husband. My condolences.'

'Thank you,' says Helen. One more reason to be grateful to Nancy. Someone had to broach the subject sooner or later, and Helen's glad it didn't have to be her. She heard the tail end of that exchange, as she returned to the attic from the loo – Nancy's lowered voice, sinking through the open hatch door – 'Terrible thing. No note or anything,' – and the switch to higher-pitched banality as Helen's foot on the rung set a metallic alarm vibrating up to the loft.

Barnaby doesn't pursue the subject, but after a few moments he says, 'I lost my wife five years ago.'

He states it as a simple fact – one more piece of information for the family tree. Helen says, 'I'm very sorry to hear that.'

'It was expected,' says Barnaby. 'She'd been ill, on and off, since childhood.'

'Oh,' says Helen, and isn't sure what to say next. *That's all right, then?* She manages to keep a straight face.

'Yes, so we always knew.' Barnaby is still monitoring the sky. 'When we married – we knew. Rather like genealogy, I suppose.' He meets Helen's eye fleetingly, and looks back to the window. 'One knows the end before the beginning.'

Helen says, 'Well, you could say we *all* know the end, don't we?'

She blinks rapidly. She wouldn't normally come out with something like that. It sounds rather heartless. Smug, even. But she knows Barnaby won't take it that way. He smiles – one of his small, zipped smiles – and says to a blackbird hoisting worms from the softened lawn: 'That is true, of course.' He drinks more tea, then adds: 'We had longer than we'd expected. Which was a blessing.'

He doesn't seem to require a reply, so they settle into silence. Helen thinks again about her grandmother, and about her mother and her sewing stories, and the dashing hero of Helen's young imagination. She thinks about Barnaby on his wedding day, with his new bride and her preordained future. Her thoughts fall and spread and evaporate like afternoon rain, and Helen feels no need to talk.

18

'Something smells delicious,' says Helen. She fastens the top button of her blouse, and Lisa says, 'Leave it be, Mum. It looks better undone.'

Helen feels awkward. She always feels like this in Lisa and Mark's flat. Like a guest from the wrong period. Wrong clothes. Wrong language.

They've done the place up well – stylishly, she tells herself. Clean lines, plain, wooden table, charcoal-coloured sofa, right angles and neutral shades and no superfluous flourishes or frills. Their places are laid in regimental symmetry: polished slate 'place mats'; cool ranks of cutlery; ice-white wine in slim glasses. Helen smooths her flowery skirt and feels like an overstatement.

'What are we having?' she asks. They can hear efficient clinks and clangs from the kitchen. Lisa says, 'He's doing something clever with a chicken.'

'You're so lucky...' starts Helen, then changes her mind and reaches for her wine. Lisa gets tetchy if Helen praises Mark's culinary skills. She says things like *We don't have to fall to our knees and give thanks any more, Mum, just because men have found out how to turn the cooker on*, and Helen says *You would if you'd had to dish up everyone else's meals all your adult life*, and then the row begins. Helen understands exactly why Lisa finds it so annoying. She remembers how galling it was to see her mother's bemused, averted face, whenever Nick changed Lisa's nappy or gave her the bottle. Fathers laid down the law, and mothers did the rest.

That was the natural order according to Amelia Catherine Berwick Murray, née Blake – despite the fact that her own husband was a silence behind a newspaper, and Helen's mother had been both carer and law-giver from the start.

'Is the wine too dry?' asks Lisa.

'No, no, it's lovely. Very nice.'

They smile at each other. Lisa retrieves a discarded conversation.

'So – you really had no idea about this workhouse business?'

'None at all. It's possible my mother didn't know about it herself. And if she had known, it's not the sort of thing she would have mentioned.'

'No. Gran was always a bit of a snob, wasn't she?'

Helen is taken aback. She's never thought of her mother in such stark terms. Lisa notices the flinch, and persists, 'Well, she was, wasn't she? Always going on to everyone about my degree. It was embarrassing.'

'She was proud of you,' says Helen. 'That kind of thing was important to her.'

'Yes, well, exactly. That's what I mean. And Grandad used to say, "Millie, don't go on…"' She catches her grandfather's weary inflexion, and they both laugh. Helen says, 'He never got much of a word in, poor Dad.'

She looks away quickly. What fond reminiscences will Lisa pass on about her own father? *Damn you Nick*, she thinks. *Damn and blast you to hell.* Maybe Lisa's thinking along the same lines, because after a moment she says, 'It's all a bit weird, though, isn't it, this family tree stuff.'

'Weird?'

Lisa is topping up the wine; Helen places her hand over her glass. More than a glassful makes her bloated and hot.

'Well,' says Lisa, 'it's all pretty pointless, isn't it? When you think about it. Sea levels rising, ozone layer fizzling away, we'll all have drowned or cooked in a couple of hundred years' time, and that's that. All this obsession with names and places and birthlines and so on…

phhht!' She flicks her hand to suggest a bursting bubble. 'All gone.'

Helen thinks: *I hope she's not going to drink too much.* She says: 'By that logic there'd be no point to anything at all.'

The words drop like stones between them. Will there ever be a time when Helen can pass inconsequential comments, without seeing them sink under the weight of Nick's memory? Lisa gulps at her wine and struggles to keep the exchange afloat.

'That's what I say to myself when I'm stressing about work: it doesn't really matter in the scheme of things...'

'That's right,' says Helen, and then Mark comes to the rescue, bringing dishes and reviving the safe topic of food and recipes and what a difference organic ingredients can make.

Mark really is a good cook. Helen realises as she eats how rarely she enjoys a filling meal. Nick was never very interested in food, even before his despondency took hold. He was a vegetarian when they first met; Helen spent a panicky day after their first date looking for meatless recipes, unable to find anything, in those days, more exciting than cheese flan. In his last years, Nick stopped noticing what was on his plate altogether. Maybe *that* was when it started – that day when Helen found him in the kitchen taking a bite from her ham sandwich.

'Nick,' she said, astounded, 'there's meat in that.'

And he just shrugged and said, 'I'm hungry.'

Years of Nick grazing on whatever was on hand. Then barely eating at all. Then years of flabby sandwiches from the WI ladies at the hospital kiosk. Occasional pasta boosts from Lisa. And now, the widow's empty fridge. Old Mother Hubbard. No wonder Helen is fuelling herself with such relish on Mark's clever chicken dish. Mark spoons more veg onto her plate, and Helen doesn't object. Lisa says, 'It's good to see you've got your appetite back,' and pushes her own food to the edge of her plate to create a deceptive space.

Mark chats about his family. One of his two older sisters has recently started a new job nearby.

'Not that you'd know it,' grumbles Lisa. 'We never see hide nor hair of her.'

'Well, you know how it is,' coaxes Mark. 'New job, new flat, she's probably up to her scalp at the moment.'

'Yeah, right,' says Lisa.

It's obviously a well-worn argument. Lisa longs to be embraced as an honorary sister. She's pictured girly shopping trips and heart-to-hearts over coffee, and she resents the indifferent breeziness of Mark's clan. Helen licks the lemon sauce on her lips and says, 'Mark's right, sweetheart. You know how difficult it is when you're settling in.'

But Helen is aching on her daughter's behalf. She was an only child herself; she recognises the yearning for sibling secrets and in-jokes. She remembers her consuming envy of her schoolfriends' large families, with their long-running squabbles and spontaneous affections, all played out in the diffused glow of shared experience. Helen always vowed to have a big brood. But it didn't happen. Nick resisted any talk of tests or adoption, and Helen never really pressed the point. It was one of those many subjects one didn't pursue.

'…a pain in the neck,' Mark is saying, discussing his other sister's son, 'and completely out of control.'

'Oh, come on,' protests Lisa, 'he's not that bad. Just a bit hyper, that's all.'

Here's another subject Helen can't raise: Lisa and Mark, and families, and plans. What their status is, whether she's ever likely to be a grandparent – these matters used to be so clearly signposted, hung about with rings and announcements and family gatherings. Now couples don't have to conduct their lives to other people's rules, and Helen is glad about that – as glad as anyone. She sometimes wonders whether she and Nick, if they hadn't been bound by an older generation's conventions, would have found a better way. So she's all for it. But the old forms did make life a little simpler for everyone else concerned. That's all.

'He'll calm down,' Lisa is saying, 'when he's got brothers and sisters to play with.'

'Or get even worse,' says Mark. 'Personally, I think she's a glutton for punishment…'

On they go, speculating and theorising about Mark's sisters' lives, and Helen goes on eating and thinking of a time when Lisa was small and the future was unwritten. She can see herself – young and fraught and smelling of motherhood, balancing Lisa on her hip in her mother's parlour, and her mother sitting at the little square table, fixing Helen with her lizard eye and saying, 'There are some things in life, Helen, we just have to accept with dignity.'

Helen battling to suppress a boiling rage and muttering, 'It's not healthy for her to grow up without brothers and sisters.'

'The child will have everything you and Nicholas can give her,' – conclusively, as Helen's mother adjusted her glasses and turned back to the *Daily Mail* – and she'll be all the better for that.'

She was trying to comfort me, thinks Helen. That much is obvious, now. But at the time, with Lisa wriggling and grizzling and Nick working late and Amelia Berwick Blake taking on that supercilious tone – at the time, Helen detested her mother for suggesting that she count her blessings.

Helen was born towards the end of the war, conceived during a snatched week of leave. She was a mistake that was not repeated. She reckons her parents had lost the strength for a family, among all that exhaustion and fear, hunger and death and horror. They never said so, of course; her parents only ever mentioned the war as something irritating and occasionally comic. The rest, they put aside with their wasted youth. But Helen knew she'd been one more trouble, just as she knew that her peacetime problems would always seem petty and selfish. It made her resent them all the more.

Lisa downs her wine and holds her glass out for Mark to fill. The colour has deepened in her cheeks and her eyes are sparkling. *Always spoiling for a fight*, thinks Helen. Does she know how much Helen wanted to give her sparring partners? Probably not. It occurs to Helen now, with new clarity, that Lisa thinks the way things turned out is the way they were always planned. *I must put her right some time*, she thinks. *I must talk to her, properly.* But not now.

After their meal they move from the table to the sofa and chairs, arranged around a contemporary gas fire that's built into the wall and looks to Helen like an illusion. She can't quite believe it gives out real heat. But this fire is their pride and joy, and it cost them a fortune; on her few visits she always makes sure to admire its elegance.

'Take your shoes off,' insists Lisa. 'Relax.'

Helen would rather not. Her blistered toes, squeezed into the arrowheads of her good shoes, are not for public view. She eases her heels free and balances her toes just inside the shoes, partially out of sight. Mark keeps pouring more wine; even Helen has had to succumb to a refill. The danger is that Helen will doze off and wake abruptly to find her mouth has sagged open or she's made a rude noise. She focuses on staying alert, and starts asking them about work. Lisa says, 'It was crazy last week. But it's easing up now. I think *you're* the busiest one at the moment, Mum!'

This kindly teasing reminds Helen of the way she used to speak to Lisa, when she was six and playing at offices with scrap paper and a toy typewriter.

'Yes,' adds Mark, 'it sounds like one mad social round, this history thing.'

'Hardly,' says Helen.

'You've even got your fancy man paying surprise visits…' says Lisa, slipping off the consonants. 'The man with a dog's name…'

'Actually,' Helen points out, 'to be fair, it's more that we had a dog with a man's name.'

'Quite right.' Lisa wags her finger. 'My mistake.'

As she grows tipsier Lisa takes on a sweet flirtatiousness, which Helen guesses was her manner when she first started seeing Mark. *Good*, thinks Helen. Better this than the usual tension. Far back in prehistory, Helen must have played the same games with Nick: the pouting and the dimpling and the widened eyes. She doesn't recall. She's reached the stage now when any reference to sex or attraction is a joke she's meant to share.

At midnight Helen crams her swollen feet back into their shoes and says, 'Well, it's time I got going.'

Lisa, slumped on Mark's shoulder, raises her head in amazement.

'You're not going *back*? Aren't you staying here?'

'No,' says Helen, 'thank you, but I didn't bring any…'

'Borrow mine,' squeals Lisa. 'Borrow whatever you need. I've made up the spare bed.'

Helen struggles to get up.

'Sorry – sorry. I didn't realise. But I really must go back…' She doesn't offer a reason.

'Well,' huffs Lisa, 'you'll have to get a taxi. I'm not fit to drive.'

'That's OK,' slurs Mark. 'I'm OK. I'll take you.'

Helen sways slightly on her imprisoned feet.

'No, no, you stay there. I'll phone for a taxi…'

She's such a fool. She didn't think about this – the alcohol, and who would drive her home. They're right to treat her like a child – that's what she is. A taxi, a stranger driving her into the dark – again she sees a flash of steel and feels the blow against her hip. Maybe she should stay. But Mark's up and fetching his jacket, saying, 'Nonsense, I'm absolutely fine and it's not far. It won't take two minutes.'

Helen hovers over Lisa, who's cross and avoiding her eye.

'It was a lovely evening,' she says. 'Thank you.'

Lisa says, coolly, 'It was lovely to have you here, for a change.' Then her voice slides into a whine as she adds, 'I just wish you'd *stay*.'

19

Guess what, Nick. Since you were unplugged I've been to London on the bus. I've been to Kew with one new friend and into the attic with another. I've been mugged. And I've discovered that my mother was a bastard and a workhouse kid.

'Americano and a croissant. Enjoy.'

The waitress beams. Helen breathes in the warm scent of coffee and pastry and enjoys a frisson of guilt. Extravagant, coming back here for her breakfast. *But this, Nick,* she adds in a footnote, *this is how far I've come. I'm now the kind of woman who treats herself to a continental breakfast before meeting her friends, because she fancies some time to herself.*

She takes the newspaper from her bag and puts on her glasses. She's seeing Barnaby in a couple of hours to pick up the workhouse trail. *But first,* she says to herself and to Nick, *I want some Me Time.* And she smiles, but doesn't giggle.

She's reading a review of a show she's never heard of when the table stutters and someone sits down opposite. Helen knows immediately who it is. She couldn't say, for sure, whether she came here partly on the off-chance that this would happen. She regards Foxy Woman over her glasses, keeping her newspaper open as a defence. Now that confrontation is imminent, Helen finds herself squaring up for it. Foxy's still in her coat. She leans forward, so that she and Helen are eye-to-eye over the page, and hisses: 'Where is he?'

'Who?' mouths Helen, producing no sound.

'Where's your friend?'

The waitress is watching from the counter. She thinks this woman is insane. Helen's beginning to suspect it too.

Without waiting for a reply, Foxy goes on, beating time to her words on the table with her index finger.

'Tell your friend it's no good setting his spies on me.'

Helen nods doubtfully and shoots a look at the waitress.

'Tell him,' Foxy continues, 'it makes no odds. I'll see him in court.'

The cavalry arrives.

'Can I help you, Madam?' the waitress asks Foxy haughtily. She gestures towards the café's empty tables. 'There are plenty of places to sit.'

Foxy looks around her in confusion.

'No,' she says. 'I'm going. I just came to say my piece.'

And suddenly Helen is furiously indignant. She's had enough of being reprimanded and ordered around and then left to try to gather up her dignity. She drops her inhibition with the newspaper.

'Just a minute.' Her mother's stern voice rings from her own throat. 'Let's get something straight.'

She nods reassurance to the waitress, who retreats a few steps, but stays on guard.

'I haven't the remotest idea,' Helen says, 'who your friend is, or why you'll see him in court. I'm simply going about my own business, researching my family tree, and I'll thank you to let me do so in peace.'

Foxy is shaken. Her eyes narrow and waver.

'You followed me,' she says, and Helen blushes, but she can sense that Foxy's lost her momentum now, and says, 'I certainly did not. Not intentionally, at any rate. I walked to the hospital, where my husband was a patient' – she delivers a calculated payoff – 'before he passed away.'

'Oh,' says Foxy, in defeat. She might be about to cry. High on adrenalin, Helen straightens her spine and folds away her paper.

'Right, then. Perhaps you'd better tell me what this is all about.'

They stare at each other. A muscle is twitching in Helen's cheek; to quell it she speaks again: 'I'm Helen. And you?' She seems to be in a play, reciting words supplied by someone else.

'Alana,' mumbles Foxy. That's a surprise. To Helen, it sounds like a made-up name, a label attached by the proud father: Property of Alan. She'd like to check the theory and ask, but this isn't the time. She just nods, and says: 'Carry on'.

As Alana speaks, her eyes glide from side to side, and she makes tiny, sharp gestures with her hand – gestures that would make sense if she had a cigarette. Helen guesses that she used to come here for a smoke, before the ban. Alana's fingers bunch. She swipes the air, touches her mouth; she rests her elbow on the table and holds her hand palm-upward, letting imaginary smoke drift away. Instead of puffs at a fag, she sucks in short breaths and spits them back out in streams of contempt.

'Marcus Edwards,' she hacks. 'Psycho. Arsehole. He should go under a truck. He should rot in hell.'

Helen swallows and checks the whereabouts of the waitress. This is obviously going to be about an affair gone sour, or a neighbourly feud, and such things can lead to trouble. She regrets her little exercise in assertiveness. Put your head over the parapet, and you catch the flak.

'What gives him the right,' – Alana shows long, parchment-coloured teeth – 'to fuck around with my life?'

Helen senses the waitress moving closer.

'I really don't know,' says Helen. 'I've only ever spoken to Mr Edwards once. All I know is that he's a historian of some…'

'Historian!' The invisible cigarette shoots to Alana's lips and away again. 'History! Family fucking history!'

The waitress clears her throat loudly.

'It's a madness. A fucking sickness,' continues Alana. Helen grips the table edge and summons her mother again: 'There's no need for that sort of language.'

(Guess what, Nick. This morning I turned into Dame Edith Evans.)

Astonishingly, Alana lowers her eyes and mutters, 'Sorry.'

'You and Mr Edwards, you're related, are you?' asks Helen.

'Related? To *him*?' Alana twists in her seat, then angles herself across the table, bringing the waitress a couple of steps nearer.

'Not related, not connected, don't know, don't care, just want him *out of my life*. Never asked him into it. Who the f... who does he think he is?'

She sits back and glares out beyond the café. After a moment Helen says, 'I saw you talking to him in here a couple of times.'

She doesn't know what else to say.

'Yeah, well, I thought I could warn him off. More fool me.'

'He's pestering you?'

Alana flexes her eyebrows to convey her scorn.

'Pestering! You could call it that!' She narrows her eyes, still scowling towards the street. 'No, you couldn't. Pestering – that's what a kid does, wanting sweets. *Pestering*.'

'Then... what's he done?'

'That's what they all say. That's what the law says. What's he done?' She shrugs. 'They don't give a toss. Police, lawyers, social workers, whatever. *Oh, keep a diary, keep records, take photographs...* Like I've got to hand over even more of my life...' She nods at something outside. 'Can you see him?' she asks, abruptly.

'Can I – who?' Helen searches the length of street framed by the café window. Two teenage girls stagger past, neighing with laughter and leaning in to each other. Then an overweight man, swagged with a cyclist's luminous yellow bands and straps. As Helen appraises the passers-by and traffic, Alana turns and smiles, and her face relaxes into a kindness Helen hasn't seen before. She says, 'Sorry I had a go at you. Keep watching.'

And she's left. The waitress is immediately at Helen's side, asking her something, but all Helen's attention is on the view through the window. Seconds after Alana's departure, a figure with dark ponytailed hair slips out of a newsagency on the opposite side of the road and sets off in the same direction.

20

'The address,' says Barnaby 'is deliberately misleading.'

'White Hill House,' muses Helen. 'It sounds rather grand. As if she were the lady of the manor.' *My mother would have liked that*, she thinks.

'It was a practice developed from the late nineteenth century,' says Barnaby, 'to avoid stigma.'

They're waiting in the reception area for Gangly Man. Helen wants to tell Barnaby about her encounter with Alana, but they're about to be admitted to the inner sanctum, and she feels it would be sacrilegious to start babbling gossip at him now. With an effort, she steers her mind back on track.

'How could you tell it wasn't a stately home? Or a rather pompous house?'

Barnaby rocks on his heels, hands in pockets.

'Ah,' he says. 'There you have a tale without end. Perhaps we should defer it to our post-match analysis in the Canteen.'

Gangly Man appears, bearing the depository keys like a sacrament, and leads them through the reading room to the reinforced door. The key turns; the door swings open. They're in a windowless vault, lined from ceiling to floor, wall to wall, with the slim files Helen glimpsed from the reading room. They march after Gangly, through another door and into a larger room, bordered with bound journals, all in regimental rows and embossed with dates and numbers. At a broad wooden table in the centre, a bald man in white gloves bows over an enormous ledger filigreed with writing. As he bends over the faded knots and flourishes, a circle of lamplight shimmers on his head.

Gangly Man takes them through a third door and down a flight of steps. The place seems to go on forever. They emerge in a maze of shelves and Gangly strides with confidence along a mysterious trail, Helen and Barnaby trotting along behind him. Without warning, Gangly swerves between two banks of shelving. His lips move as he checks reference numbers. Halfway down, he stops, reaches up and pulls out a deep box file. This part of the Archive has a more haphazard look – boxes, cardboard folders, sheaves and books jostle with each other, overreaching the shelves and lounging into triangles.

'You know the routine, Mr Keane,' says Gangly, handing Barnaby the file. Helen realises that she hasn't known Barnaby's surname until now. As they leave, Gangly waves towards the stacks and says, 'This lot will all be digitised if we get the funding. Then you'll have nice, clean computers to play with. No more fiddly stuff.'

Barnaby hugs the box file to his chest. 'I prefer the fiddly stuff.'

Gangly shrugs. 'That's what all our regulars say.'

Helen and Barnaby return to the wooden table to sift through the White Hill House records for 1923. Barnaby has a hunch, and after a forty-five-minute search it's proved right. Poring through the papers at Helen's side, he suddenly places the flat of his hand on the table in muted triumph, and directs her attention to one laconic, handwritten line: *Admitted 22nd October 1923. May Jones, 16 years, previously in service at The Willows. Condition: With child. Father unknown.*

Peering through her reading glasses at the officious purple ink, Helen feels a lurch of her grandmother's shame.

'She must have been desperate,' she says, and the bald man levels a silencing look at her from the other end of the table. Barnaby nods, slowly. He's getting a small notebook from his pocket, and one of the stubby pencils provided at reception. Helen thinks: *Oh, dear. I should have thought of that.* Barnaby is writing: *The Willows, up to 22/10/23.*

Later they decamp to the Canteen for tea.

'You're rather lucky,' remarks Barnaby, 'having a family who stayed roughly in one place. Very considerate.'

'Really?'

Barnaby gives his approximation of a smile. 'Suffice to say, my own search took me to twenty-three workhouse archives, with no result.'

'No result?' Helen takes a tissue from her handbag and mops up a crescent of spilt milk from the table. 'But I thought you'd traced your family back hundreds of years.'

'My adopted family. Of my biological family, I have found no trace at all.'

He was dug out of the earth. Buried and retrieved, like an archaeological find. He'd known only eight weeks of light and air, when the city exploded and the sky fell. The few houses cramped into that narrow alley took a direct hit. Nobody was left to tell his name, or to identify his mother's shattered face. He would have vanished too, stifled among the bricks and furniture and slices of glass, his mother's dead arm flung across his broken ribs. But a warden clambering over the rubble-dunes heard his screams, separated them out from the cacophony of aftermath, tracked them to a spot beneath his boots, and started clawing.

'It was a poor area,' Barnaby tells Helen, without emotion. 'It was, in point of fact, a slum. I'm given to understand, mainly from anecdotal evidence, that the ruins from which I was pulled had been a house of ill repute. A brothel.'

Helen blinks. A crash of china and cutlery from the Canteen kitchen merges in her head with shouts, screams, a crumpling of walls, the crack of flame, one man's hoarse cry: *There's a child down there!*

After a moment she asks, 'No trace at all?'

'None. It appears that I was born into a world without names.'

He tells Helen about his adoptive parents, who had lost a child of their own.

'A child of eighteen,' he explains. 'Killed on his first day of active service, three weeks before I was fished from the rubble.'

Barnaby opens his anorak. Helen sees now that it's a rather upmarket anorak, with panels of mesh and secret pockets. He unzips one and produces a wallet, which fans into a number of sleeves. Each one contains a photograph. Helen wouldn't have thought of Barnaby as the kind of man who carries photographs. Barnaby fingers his way to the back and shows Helen an old snapshot with crackling borders. A boy in shorts and vest, half-crouching, apparently about to launch himself into a headlong race along the beach. The boy notices the camera and is caught in a cry of surprise. His hair is blown across his forehead. Helen takes the wallet from Barnaby to scrutinise the image more closely. Two square inches of shades of grey; a throwaway instant over seventy years gone. Helen can hear the gulls, the calls of children, the waves. She feels the heat and the scratch of sand.

'It was my parents' favourite picture of him,' says Barnaby.

She thinks of Latisha's post-mortem portraits, solid and permanent. This picture is so fragile, so vivid; any minute, that boy might spring forward and go pounding again along a mile of firm sand. She returns the wallet and says, 'He looks a lively lad.'

'Yes,' says Barnaby, 'I believe he was.'

Helen imagines Barnaby as a child: taciturn, studious, shy. Her heart closes with pity.

'He was about eleven years old there,' Barnaby goes on. 'Weymouth, 1934. They went there every summer, first with him and then with me.' Then, as an afterthought: 'His name was Barnaby too.'

'Oh, how…!' Helen stops herself. The word 'cruel' resounds, imprisoned, through her mind. Barnaby and his namesake regard each other.

'I think it was meant as a… gift. Misguided, perhaps, but well-intentioned. They were very loving parents. I arrived in the fullest bloom of their grief.'

The fullest bloom. He makes grief sound sublime.

'I suppose,' concedes Helen, pulling out the handy phrase, 'grief makes us do strange things.' She considers telling Barnaby about following Alana, and their subsequent bizarre encounter. But instead, she says: 'When Nick died I kept getting the giggles.'

Barnaby's little eyes widen into perfect circles. 'How disconcerting,' he says. They both laugh. He says, 'When my wife died and the nurses were occupied in tidying her up, I sneaked into the hospital bathroom and dozed off. Slept rather soundly, in fact, for twenty minutes.' A quick spasm of the mouth, like a guilty schoolboy.

'Well,' says Helen, 'it's a tiring business.'

'Yes,' says Barnaby, 'it certainly is.'

21

It's the deepest part of night, as still and silent as outer space. Helen has to grope her way around the room. Her hand finds the wooden rail at the end of the bed and she shuffles along it. She can sense a mass of objects – wardrobe, chest of drawers – adding to the darkness.

'I can hardly breathe,' she says. 'Where's the switch?'

There's a thread of light ahead – so fine that it might simply be a quirk of eyesight.

'Put your bedside lamp on,' she says. 'Why won't you put your lamp on?'

She's angry. She clenches her back teeth until her skull hurts.

'Put it on!' she demands.

'No need,' says Nick.

Helen screws her eyes up and peers at the bed, but she can't see him.

'Nobody out there,' says Nick. 'Don't be an idiot.'

Helen is desperate with rage. She flings herself at the sliver of light and opens the door wide.

'Stop fussing,' says Nick. 'There's nobody out there.'

Helen turns to glower at his body, fully visible now, inert in the bed, sprouting wires and tubes. His eyelids are shut, stretched to near-transparency. Saliva glistens from mouth to earlobe.

Something occurs to Helen. A scoop of horror hollows her chest. She says, 'Who put the landing light on?'

Someone answers: 'I did.'

He stands like doom at the top of the stairs. His hair is loose, hanging down to his hips. His face is bony and bloodless. A conflagration sears Helen's veins. She's an X-ray, exposed, insubstantial.

The man says, 'What have I done?'

And then he hurls himself backwards, floating over the stairs in appallingly slow motion. Finally he hits the last step with a crash that yanks Helen into consciousness.

She waits. She's tensed against her elbow, straining to listen above the boom of her pulse. Something made that noise. Something real fell from the woken world, and smashed through her dream. The blade flashes. The fading bruise on her hip throbs. Her breathing is rapid and shallow as a cat's. Helen can tell from the mottled light and the faint rustle of life beyond the house that it's very early morning. She listens. Behind her terror, a calmer part of her brain calculates strategies. If there's an intruder, she must summon help. There's no party wall between her house and Nancy's. If she leaps for the window and yells, will they hear? Will she produce nothing but a croak, as in her nightmares? The phone is in the spare room, Lisa's old room. If she opens her bedroom door, will the burglar be looming there? Despite the racket in her head she finds room for gratitude that Lisa didn't come and stay. The thought of an armed and drug-crazed lunatic opening a door to her sleeping daughter's room – the knowledge that Helen would fail to protect her – that would be too much to bear.

There! She hears the sound and recognises it at once. Relief seeps through her, relaxing her muscles. She gets out of bed and lifts the edge of the curtain just as the fox is strutting up the path from the side of the house, having completed its investigation of the bins. Even as Helen is watching there's a shift in the quality of light. A motorbike revs up a few streets away. *Better get going, fox*, she thinks; *it's all starting up again.*

It's coming up for five. Helen puts on her dressing gown and goes downstairs to make tea. As she's pouring the water and mashing the teabag, a flash of recollection delivers an almost erotic charge. She sits at the table and chases the memory, as it retreats from her mind's surface to the ocean bed. If she leaves it much longer it'll be lost under the silt of events. She just needs to clutch at one corner of her sinking dream and give it a name.

Marcus Edwards.

Yes. Yes.

The whole scene is suddenly resurrected. The suffocating darkness. Nick's disembodied voice. Helen winces at the anomaly that her dreamself took in her stride. The flood of light, and Marcus Edwards, gaunt and messianic... Helen is suffused again with an emotion she can't define. Awe? Passion? She replays his words – *What have I done?* – and his slow fall. Her dream takes on the force of an omen. Helen thinks of Alana's hunted face, and the nonchalant way Marcus Edwards slipped out of the newsagent's and onto her trail.

I have to tell someone she thinks. To reinforce the thought, she repeats it aloud to the garden and the fox's vanishing scent: 'I have to tell someone, before he goes too far.'

Nancy calls round before the school run. She's armed with a sheaf of leaflets and flyers, and has a rolled-up newspaper under her arm.

'Flying visit, Helen, I won't intrude...'

Behind her, the car rocks. A pink satchel is flung against the back window along with muffled thumps and yells.

'I just wanted to give you these,' continues Nancy. 'Thought they might be interesting. I picked them up at the library when I took Florrie to the storytelling session...'

She deals out her collection: museums, courses, lectures, archives, all jabbering their opening hours and admission fees and website addresses. A small hand appears in the car's passenger window, brandishing a shoe, then disappears again. Nancy unrolls the newspaper and her voice descends to a contralto: 'Now, I don't know whether you've seen this...'

It's a local paper that Helen never buys. One headline takes up most of the front page:

Pensioner Mugged at Knifepoint

The doleful victim gazes from her photograph in confirmation.

'On the high street,' says Nancy. 'Broad daylight. Two lads with a knife.' She pauses for effect, then tucks the paper under Helen's elbow. 'Anyway, Helen, I don't like to labour the point, you know me. But I do think you should at least think about reporting your nasty experience, even now. I'd lay odds this is the same pair of thugs. I'm more than happy to come along for moral support. Any time. If it helps clear the streets of these vicious little... BE QUIET YOU TWO OR THERE'LL BE TROUBLE! I'll have to go, Helen, while the car's still intact – but whenever you need me... you know where I am...'

When Nancy's gone Helen puts the leaflets in the recycling bin and reads through the newspaper report. The muggers struck as the shops were shutting. An elderly woman was knocked to the ground and her bag was taken. Two Have-a-Go Heroes gave chase. The attackers got away but dropped the bag. '*One of them had a flick-knife. It nearly frightened the life out of me,*' said Mrs Peters, 71, who was treated for bruises and shock. Helen wonders whether her own mugging was a trial run. Evidently, they still hadn't quite got the hang of it.

The giggling starts. She'd thought that was over. Her breath comes in sharp hiccoughs. *This is no time for hysterics*, she rebukes herself. But the giggling accelerates out of her control. Guilt at her own weakness joins a maelstrom of other recriminations. Should have reported the mugging. Should have told someone about Alana's stalker. Should be nicer to Nancy. Should be a better mother. Should have been a better wife. The whirlpool spins faster. Her breathing is so violent that it lifts her from her chair. Her jaw drops open, her head hangs back and a bestial wail fills the house, rushing like water into every available space. It goes on and on, doubling her up, until finally it diminishes into a recognisably human sound: the sound of rhythmic, gut-wracking sobs.

22

At three o' clock that afternoon Helen is sitting in the lobby of the central police station, waiting for her turn. The officer at the desk is a young Sikh man with the world-weary air of desk sergeants everywhere. He promised Helen she'd be seen before too long.

'Quiet today,' he added, jutting his chin at the few others seated along the walls. 'We'll try and sneak you in before rush hour, Madam.'

Three seats along, a child in a pushchair grizzles on one low, relentless note. Its mother, who looks implausibly young to Helen, jiggles the chair with her foot and chews her fingernails, occasionally stopping to examine her work before resuming her task like a dog at a bone. Another few places away, a man is sleeping in his seat, arms folded on his chest, legs outstretched. His hair and clothes are a blur of grime, and a stench of unwashed flesh and alcohol pools around him. Helen remembers Nick's warning about the smell of dogs and tramps, and silently takes issue. *Not the same at all. Barnie never made me want to retch. He smelled of shrubbery, not despair.*

A girl at the far end of the lobby is performing a pantomime of revulsion about the sleeping man, holding her nose and rolling her eyes. Helen doesn't want to catch her attention and trigger any verbal protests, but she's fascinated by the girl's appearance. Her boots are maliciously pointed at the toe, and rear up at the heels into four-inch spikes. Her trousers are slashed to show stripes of bare flesh all the way up to the thigh. A complication of buckles, straps and studs criss-crosses her waist and stomach, and her jacket is busy with buttons, badges, pocket-flaps and strips of redundant material. Her hair is an extraordinary black plume, tipped with reds and blues. What a shame, thinks Helen, that the poor girl's face is so disappointing: pale and spotty and punctuated with metal hoops and circles. Helen makes an effort not to stare. She wonders how it would be to walk down the street in that garb. Like being an actor, maybe. Or a pirate. A swagger would be required. Helen rather envies the girl.

'All right, Mrs Pascoe, if you'd like to come through...'

As Helen is leaving the lobby she hears the girl calling to the desk sergeant: 'Oi, mate, I'm gagging here! Can't you spray him with something?'

Helen gives her account of the mugging to a policewoman, who takes perfunctory notes.

'And you didn't think,' says the officer 'to report this at the time?'

Helen squirms under the schoolmarm tone.

'I'm really very sorry about that. I just wanted to forget the whole thing.'

The policewoman looks unimpressed. Helen says: 'My husband died recently, and I haven't been thinking very clearly...'

'All the same, Madam, it would have been best to call us straight away.'

The interview ends. The officer stands and starts saying something about CCTV, but Helen has something else on her mind.

'One other thing...' she says '...I really think I should tell you...'

The policewoman sits again with resignation.

'Someone I know,' says Helen, 'is being stalked.'

'Someone you know?'

'A friend. Well, no, not really a friend... an acquaintance. I think she's being harrassed. He follows her around. I've seen him.'

In her anxiety to convey all the appropriate information, Helen hears herself start to burble. The officer thinks she's a bit dotty. Helen struggles for a more deliberate pace.

'I know it sounds silly, but she's quite distressed about it.'

'Has your friend reported this?'

'I think so. But she says nobody will help unless he does something…' The sentence wilts towards the inevitable reply.

'If your friend's been to see us, I'm sure we're doing everything we can.'

The officer gets to her feet and propels Helen to the door by force of will.

'She knows who the stalker is,' says Helen. 'His name's Marcus Edwards. He's quite brazen about it – I've seen him. I'm worried that he'll…'

'Marcus Edwards,' repeats the officer. 'Right you are, Mrs Pascoe, thanks for letting us know that. Keep a note of anything unusual or troubling and advise your friend to do the same.'

Helen catches the bus home. As it falters through the town traffic, she watches people hurrying along the pavements, following their tapestry of routes. Was that an idiotic thing to do, reporting Marcus Edwards to the police? After all, what *has* he done? Helen leans her forehead against the window and her head vibrates with the engine. If she and Alana are both watching Marcus Edwards, noting his every move and tagging each one with a time and a date, doesn't that make *them* the stalkers? It's true, what she told that police officer: she's not thinking clearly these days. On an impulse, Helen rummages in her bag and brings out the mobile phone. She wants a third party to vouch for her sanity. She's got three stored numbers. Lisa and Nancy will both be at work now. The third number is the hospital. For something to do, Helen puts on her glasses and deletes the hospital number from the memory.

That evening, Helen calls Nancy to tell her she's taken her advice.

'I'm so glad, Helen. I hope you don't feel I pushed you into anything, I'd hate you to think that…'

'No, no, you were absolutely right. I should have done it before.'

'Well, you've done the right thing. I'm only sorry you went through it on your own – I would have been more than happy to come with you – you only had to say the word…'

Then Helen rings Lisa.

'What? Which police station? What did they say?'

'They said I should have reported it at the time.'

'Well, maybe *they* should get off their backsides and start picking up some *real* criminals instead of spending all their time and manpower putting up speed cameras and fining people for exceeding the limit by two miles an hour…'

'Have you been fined for speeding?'

'*No*, Mum, I'm just saying – oh, for God's sake, you're so…'

'It was quite interesting, actually,' interrupts Helen, hastily. 'The police station.'

She pretends not to hear Lisa's impatient sigh. 'There was a girl there with the most remarkable hair…'

She describes the pirate girl to a tetchy silence, then concludes: 'She put me in mind of some kind of tropical bird.'

After a pause Lisa says, 'Sounds revolting. So what are the police actually *doing?*'

Lisa offers to come round. She sounds tired, and doesn't argue when Helen declines. Maybe, thinks Helen, maybe Lisa's been keening and wailing, too, up there in her immaculate flat. Neither of them would ever admit it to the other. In a way Helen's thankful for that. As long as Lisa's got Mark there to hold her, Helen finds it easier not to know.

That night, Helen opens a bottle of wine. When Nick was in hospital she got into the habit of buying a bottle at Tesco's every week and having a glass when she got home from her vigils. She craves it now in the same way. It helps – just the idea of it. That swelling warmth in her throat and chest, the pressure of the glass in her hand. She watches a programme on the telly – something clever and futuristic involving people who plug themselves into a parallel world. Then she pours another glass and watches an old film full of stoics in hats, with lockjaw accents. During one poignant scene she's surprised to find herself crying. But these are luxurious, calm tears, and bear no relation to this morning's paroxysms. *I'm all right now*, thinks Helen. Another mouthful of wine sunbursts through her skull. It's not over; it'll never be over. But she's all right for now.

23

Helen spends the next fortnight at the Archive searching for clues. Barnaby has gone to Suffolk on a quest of his own, but he's left her a list of instructions. She arrives early every day, consults Barnaby's pristine writing, and sets to work. Apart from a lunch break at the Canteen – with Latisha if she's around, or alone with a newspaper – Helen spends the whole day at the table in the inner sanctum, leaving in time to catch the bus home before dark.

She's trying to track down her grandmother's place of work – the place she left with scandal growing in her womb, and nowhere to go but the workhouse. Having found no trace of The Willows in the available census returns, she moves on to maps, starting with a 1930s edition and working her way backwards in time. She sees the town diminish with every decade. Streets of tiny, close-packed oblongs vanish, and fields open out and acquire names: Jacob's Meadow, Back Pasture, Middle Crop. Woods spread in neat circles over the surrounding hills. Every structure takes a title instead of a number: church, school, smithy. Helen uses a magnifier provided by Gangly Man, and picks out the name of every manor and farmhouse. Three Oaks. The Towers. Blythe Hall. West View. She tries maps of neighbouring towns and villages. Occasionally she forgets what she's looking for. The hours flow past, and at the end of every day when Helen ticks off another item on Barnaby's list, she knows there'll be an infinity of other sources waiting to be searched. Parish registers, indentures and probates… she half hopes The Willows will never be found.

'Got to hand it to you, Helen,' says Latisha one lunchtime. 'You've really knuckled down to this business. I knew it would get to you in the end.'

'It keeps me occupied,' says Helen. That was once such a patronising phrase. But she's come to believe that being occupied is the answer to everything.

'Any luck?' asks Latisha. Helen shakes her head.

'I've no idea *what* The Willows was, let alone *where* it was. It could be anywhere in the country.' She basks in the comfort of a future consumed by fruitless searching and list-ticking.

'Tell you what you *could* try,' muses Latisha, 'and that's Wallace.'

'Wallace? Is that a search engine?'

Helen's grown used to bandying these terms about. Latisha wheezes with delight.

'Come to think of it, that's *exactly* what Wallace is. A walking, talking search engine!'

She puts down her sandwich to enjoy the notion, then gives Helen's arm a friendly slap.

'That's what we'll do, lady! We'll have another outing. I'll take you to see Wallace, and I can pop in on my sister at the same time.'

*   *   *

Latisha's sister lives in Milton Keynes. Helen's never been there. As they cruise the gridwork of roads she gazes at a low dazzle of buildings. There's not a curve or a cranny in sight.

'Cartographer's dream, this place,' comments Latisha. 'Ruler, graph paper, and you're away. My sister loves it. Wouldn't live anywhere else.' She turns at a junction and the corporate gleam gives way to housing and gardens. 'Mind you,' she adds, 'my sister used to put her shoes away with the laces done up.'

The door is opened by a tall youth who moves with a dancer's easy grace. He accepts Latisha's avalanche hug, looping one long arm round her waist and extending the other to shake Helen's hand.

'My luscious boy!' Latisha is screaming into his chest. 'My gorgeous Grant! Look, Helen, isn't he a big hunk of gorgeousness?'

Yes, thinks Helen, as her hand is engulfed by Grant's, *he is indeed*. Grant winks at her over Latisha's head.

'Awrigh?'

Latisha disengages herself to reach up and grab his face with both hands.

'I can't *believe* how handsome he is!' She speaks through gritted teeth and waggles his head from side to side as if she's trying to prise it off. 'He's more handsome every time I see him!'

'Are you ever coming indoors,' calls a voice from further in the house, 'or are we having coffee on the doorstep?'

They parade into the narrow hall, Latisha bundling her nephew ahead of her.

'Look at his hair!' she cries.

'*What* hair?' says her invisible sister. Grant stoops to let Latisha rub his close-cropped head. Latisha turns to Helen.

'Used to have a great big mop of it, didn't you, Grant?'

'Got to get used to it,' says Grant, adding for Helen's benefit, 'Joining the army, see.'

The atmosphere sags.

'Not for certain,' insists his mother, finally coming into view from the kitchen behind him. 'Don't know if they'll take you yet.' She ushers them through a door into the other downstairs room.

'*Course* they'll take him,' Latisha is saying, glumly. 'Who wouldn't?'

The room is a lake of light. It splashes in from the front windows and the glass patio doors, and bounces off pale furniture and polished surfaces and the gold-framed mirrors on two of the walls. Helen blinks.

'Bit tidier than my place, eh, Helen?' says Latisha.

'Landfill is tidier than your place,' says her sister, then gives Helen a businesslike nod. 'Nice to meet you, Helen. I'm Jasmine and this is Grant – since my sister's too busy mauling my son to make the introductions.'

She talks with mock strictness. This is how Helen always used to imagine a sister would be.

'Oh, Helen's used to me now, aren't you, Helen?' teases Latisha, still kneading her nephew's arm.

'You must have the patience of a saint, Helen,' says Jasmine. 'Coffee and biscuits on the way.'

Grant allows himself to be pulled to the sofa next to his aunt and quizzed about his younger siblings.

'All gone off to the schools league match,' says Jasmine, returning with a laden tray. 'Their dad's taken them. About time *he* got lumbered, for a change.'

Grant unfolds from the sofa.

'I'm off, then.'

Latisha looks bereft. 'Not staying to chat with your favourite auntie?'

He bends quickly and kisses her on the cheek. The close haircut shows every contour and flick of muscle as he moves. Helen watches from the armchair and thinks: *gorgeous*.

'Meeting Sal,' says Grant, raising a casual hand to the room. 'See ya.'

Before the front door has shut, Latisha and Jasmine are exchanging cryptic grimaces. As soon as they hear the latch and Grant's receding footsteps on the gravel outside, Jasmine delivers her verdict: 'She's a good girl, is Sal. Not the brightest button in the box, maybe, but steady, you know. *Good* for him. Keeps his feet on the ground.' She passes Helen her coffee, with her eyes on the mug, and adds, 'Just as well. Don't want him turning out like his dad.'

'Oh, come on, Jaz,' says Latisha. 'It was only the one time…'

'One time is all it takes.' The answer snaps Latisha's sentence in half. Jasmine offers Helen a plate of biscuits and says, 'Sorry, Helen. Just that my dearly beloved has decided to do the midlife crisis in a big way and go off with some underage tart from Wolverhampton.'

'Not underage,' mutters Latisha.

'No – my mistake; she's a full two years older than Grant.'

Jasmine gives Helen an emphatic look.

'Oh, dear,' says Helen.

'I thought it was all finished, anyway?' ventures Latisha.

'That's what *he* says.' Jasmine drops onto the sofa beside her. 'It's all, oh, I'll be a good boy from now on if you'll only let me come back, I miss the kids so much… Misses the *kids*, you notice. Not the *wife*.'

Latisha's knee nudges her sister's leg.

'Of *course* he misses you.'

'Anyway.' Jasmine straightens and switches on a social face. 'Enough of my problems! Helen, Tish tells me you're a bit of a bloodhound, like her!'

'Family historian, I think she means,' says Latisha. 'Me and Helen are going to see Wallace.'

Jasmine crosses her eyes. 'Wallace! God, Helen, if you thought our Tish was a nutter…'

'Don't be horrible. He's a genius, is Wallace. Encyclopaedia on legs.'

'En-psycho-paedia, you mean. He's like that geek you used to go out with in the fifth form…'

'Oh, lay off, you were only jealous…'

And so they go on, bickering mildly, performing and reminiscing for Helen's benefit, and Helen is quite content to sit and watch a real family at work.

When Jasmine is seeing them out she suddenly asks Latisha, 'How is he, then?'

Although Helen has gone ahead and is outside the house, she registers the question and its disapproval. The tone reminds her of Lisa.

'Same as ever,' Latisha answers.

'Yeah, well. I won't say anything. You know my views on the subject.'

The sisters collide in a swift, tight embrace and raise their voices to say goodbye.

24

Latisha parks in the centre and leads Helen into a vast shopping mall.

'Welcome to CMK,' announces Latisha, as the doors slide open to admit them. 'Prepare for consumer overload.'

They pad along broad avenues and walkways, all lined with shops and laid out in chequerboard imitation of the roads outside. There are plenty of people around – their footsteps and voices echo under the roof, and occasionally a child's yowl explodes like a rocket overhead. But despite the families and toddlers and teens, the whole place has an unnerving sense of quiet. There are gift shops, fashion shops, nail salons, hair salons, beauty salons, cafés with tables set outside the door as if they're under a sky. Everywhere customers fiddle with bags and wallets, muse over TVs and consoles, pivot by mirrors on shop-stiff heels. And yet there seems to be no energy here. Just walking through the building makes Helen feel drained. Latisha beckons her to an exit. These are doors that have to be pushed open, and they lead to a different planet. The two women pass into the open air, and find themselves in an incidental space, buttressed by the massive concrete supports of an elevated car-park slipway. It would be a dead area, if it hadn't been colonised by stalls and tables and hawkers, crowding into every unused corner to sell their wares. The air crackles with laughter and gossip and smokers' coughs, and the peculiar serenades of the marketeers: 'Twelve for five, now, twelve for five, feel the quality, missus, lovely!'

'Fresh firm bananas, sweet, tender pears, come and getcha fresh fruit here!'

They squeeze between the shoppers until they reach a double trestle table. One half is a confusion of bric-a-brac: teapots, tarnished jewellery, a truncheon, a phone with an ear piece, Turkish slippers, pocket watches, a porcelain shepherdess, a top hat... The other half has a number of trays stacked with collectables – vinyl records, Victorian prints of romantic ruins; Latisha makes a beeline for the tray of old photographs and postcards. Helen's heart sinks. Passers-by are brushing and jostling her back, and she doesn't fancy hanging around for an hour while Latisha hunts for dead babies. But Latisha is signalling to the stallholder, who's been sitting on a stool in the shadow of a pillar. This must be Wallace. He moves into the sunlight and greets Latisha.

'Couple of new ones for you today, Tish,' he says, 'but they're nothing special. Calling cards, 1890s.'

He's a small man with a face squashed into horizontal folds under a flat cap. He looks like a mushroom, decides Helen. Latisha says, 'Got anything for us on The Willows, then, Wallace?'

'Got a couple of possibles,' says Wallace. 'There's a Willow Bank, River Road, but that's in the wrong county. I've got one in the same parish as your workhouse. That's your best bet, unless the lady in question went into service somewhere else, and found her way back when she got into trouble. So, I reckon your place is The Willows. Laurel Lane. Shottering.'

'I knew it!' Latisha tries to throw her arms up and knocks a customer on the head. Helen is baffled.

'I'm not quite sure I... er...'

Wallace turns towards her. She can't see his eyes under the peak of his cap.

'Seen it on a postcard,' he says. 'Dr and Mrs...' – he seems to scrutinise something – 'Calvin. That's it. Calvin, or Calvert, maybe – can't read the writing. Dr and Mrs Calvin or Calvert, The Willows, Laurel Lane, Shottering.'

'Wallace's thing is remembering addresses,' Latisha explains proudly. 'He's got a photographic memory. Reads all his stock,' she gestures to the tray of postcards, 'and a load of other stuff. Census, directories, visitors' books – you read 'em all, don't you, Wallace?'

'Used to do an act,' says Wallace, 'in variety. The Amazing Memory Man. But you don't get the gigs any more. It's all Celine Dion soundalikes now.'

Helen shows polite interest. She thinks Wallace might be making it all up.

'I do remember Shottering from the census,' she says, 'but I'm sure I didn't see that address.'

Wallace nods and his cap settles even lower.

'Could have been built after 1901. Or it could be one of them names only the locals use. Might have had a number, officially, like.'

'Wallace,' urges Latisha, 'do Helen's postcode. Go on, Helen – tell him your address.'

Helen is alarmed. For all she knows this man is a charlatan. He might employ heavies to raid the homes of gullible old ladies. Come to that, for all she knows, Latisha might be in on it too. A passing browser bumps against Helen's back. She can't move in any direction. The first tremors of panic putter in her chest.

'Don't need the number,' says Wallace. 'Only the street.'

Helen glances at Latisha, who's thumbing through the cards in the tray. She can't see any way of refusing.

'Woodland Street,' she admits. 'East Perriford, Forbridge.'

'FB23…' says Wallace immediately. 'Are you 1 to 30 or 31 to 60?'

'One to 30,' says Helen, still wary.

Wallace gives his punchline: '8EW!'

'Absolutely right!' For a moment Helen's astonishment overcomes her suspicion. Then it occurs to her that Latisha could have found out her postcode beforehand. Latisha, chortling beside her, reads the thought.

'He can do it for anyone. Pick someone out, Helen, go on – anyone from this crowd. Wallace's a walking Wikipedia.'

'Never really took off, to be honest,' says Wallace. 'When I started, a lot of people didn't know their own postcodes. I'd say, MK7 4EY, am

I right?' and they'd go "No idea, mate". It's different nowadays. Everyone's got it off by heart now.'

'You should give it another go, then, Wallace,' says Latisha. 'I can just see you treading the boards.'

I can't, thinks Helen. A man who delivers postcodes in a flat cap and a deadpan voice doesn't strike her as a top-of-the-bill attraction.

'Nah, I'm all right. Market suits me fine,' Wallace is saying. 'You'll want to write that down, then. That's your best bet – Dr and Mrs Calvin or Calvert, The Willows, Laurel Lane, Shottering. Can't tell you who sent it, or what they wrote; never read that bit. Came from the Lakes, though. Nice view of Windermere. Sold it to a feller collecting tinted landscapes, as I recall.'

Latisha is busy picking out some items from the tray. Helen and her bag are squashed against the trestle table, and Wallace doesn't seem to deal in pedestrian pen-and-paper methods. She'll have to write the address down later. *Dr and Mrs Calvin or Calvert, The Willows, Laurel Lane...*

Wallace takes Latisha's money and fishes for change in his leather money-belt. 'Prefer addresses to postcodes,' he says. 'But if you do it that way round, people think you're up to no good.' Helen shakes her head sympathetically. 'So I likes to do a bit of tracking down for the family tree lot,' he adds. 'Takes a bit longer, sometimes, digging a place out. But if it's there, it's there. And five is ten, Tish, thank you very much.'

Latisha and Helen move off with difficulty. The crowd is packed into a narrow passage between stalls and pillars, and Helen is beginning to find it claustrophobic. They seem to have stepped from CMK into a medieval time-bubble, with its fluttering stalls and hawkers' cries and sages who conjure answers from the air. She must make a note of that address before she forgets it. She daren't open her bag in this crush. So as they shuffle forward Helen recites the information over and over to herself. Dr and Mrs Calvin or Calvert, The Willows, Laurel Lane, Shottering. She lifts her face to try and escape the press of backs and shoulders, and gasps like a fish on the bank. The address spins round and round on its increasingly distorted loop. Dr and Mrs Willis, The Calvows, Laureling Lane, Shotter. Dr and Mrs Callous, The Laurels, Hardy Lane, Shocking… her knees soften. Nausea rises from her gut. Helen claws at Latisha's coat to save herself from falling.

'Woah, lady!' Latisha gathers her up and starts to bulldoze a path through the bottleneck. 'Let's get you free of this mob.'

They break into a clearing drenched with the smell of cooking fat. A hamburger van is parked to one side, with white plastic seats and tables set in front of it. Latisha deposits Helen in one of the chairs.

'Wait here. I'll soon get you fixed.'

A polystyrene box skitters against Helen's ankle. Pigeons squabble over some leftover chips under the table. Latisha returns with a wrapped bundle and thrusts it into Helen's hands. It's hot and moist and heavy.

'Eat that. You won't believe me, but I'm telling you, it will make you feel better.'

Helen's mouth waters to the hamburger's sizzling scent. Despite herself, she chomps into it. The meat has a thick, metallic taste. She's aware that grease is dripping down her chin. Her bag is looped round her wrist and it takes both her hands to grapple with the hamburger. Latisha's gone to fetch her own food; nobody else is looking. Helen dips her head and wipes her chin with the sleeve of her coat.

Latisha brings her own hamburger and two cardboard mugs of tea. 'Better?'

Helen considers, then nods.

'If you're about to peg out,' comments Latisha, 'a good dose of naughty food will always put you right. Never fails.'

After finishing her hamburger Helen finds a tissue to blot her lips. Then she retrieves a pen and rummages in her bag for paper.

'Dr and Mrs Calvin,' she says.

'Or Calvert,' says Latisha. 'Here – give us that…'

She snatches the biro, captures Helen's fingers and writes the name and address on the back of her hand.

'Don't worry,' she says, negotiating Helen's raised veins. 'It'll wash off soon enough.'

Helen examines the inky string of letters. 'Nobody's written on my hand since I was a schoolgirl,' she says.

'Suits you, honey!' says Latisha. 'You should get a tattoo.'

Helen's stomach has settled. She's glad to be outside, clearheaded, and free of the crowd. She tells Latisha about the pirate girl in the police station.

'I thought,' she concludes, 'she looked rather wonderful, in a way.'

Latisha smiles. 'You're a bit of a punk on the quiet, aren't you Helen?' she says. 'And why were you at the cop shop, Madam, if I might ask?'

So Helen tells her about the mugging, and Latisha's face reacts with a series of vowel shapes. 'No!' she says, and 'You're kidding me!' And Helen is so intoxicated with the novelty of a conscious audience that she carries on to tell her about Alana, and the sighting of Marcus Edwards on her trail.

'Not just a punk,' remarks Latisha, 'but a punk detective! Helen, my girl, you are full of surprises.'

'But I felt such a fool,' confides Helen, 'saying all that to the police, accusing him of being a stalker, with no real basis at all.'

'You saw him following her.'

Helen shrugs. 'He could have seen me doing the same thing.'

Latisha blows her lips dismissively. 'You were walking behind her. That's different. And anyway,' she adds, folding her arms, 'I'd believe anything of that Edwards guy. Gives me the shivers. Always has done.'

A spider-memory of her dream scuttles across Helen's scalp. She says, 'Even so, I wouldn't like to accuse him of something he hasn't done, on the word of a woman I don't know.'

Latisha ducks her head, conceding the point.

'Trouble with you, Helen,' she says, 'is you're too nice. People are drawn to you, because you're such a good listener.' She double-takes at Helen's incredulous expression. 'What? *What?* You *are!* Stop giggling, lady! It's true!'

When the crowd has started to disperse they head back towards the mall. Both rows of stalls are visible now, and Helen indicates a leather jacket hanging on its gibbet above a clothes rack.

'That's the kind of thing the girl in the police station was wearing,' she says. They stop to marvel at its bunting of tags and fringes.

'Can I help you lovely ladies?' sings the stallholder.

'No thanks, darling,' bellows Latisha. 'All a bit too crazy for the likes of us!'

'Cobblers,' says the stallholder affably. 'Everyone deserves to be crazy now and again, don't they, my love?' He appeals to Helen. 'No law against it, is there?'

Helen smiles and looks away, but not before he's caught her eyeing another jacket, displayed against the canvas behind him. He unhooks it and presents it over his arm with a flourish.

'Go on,' he coaxes. 'Try it on. Unique, this is. Handmade. Won't find another one like it.'

The jacket is denim, but dyed a rusty gold and flattered with tiny sparkles of glass, picking out the edges of collar and cuffs and the rims of pockets. In one deft movement the salesman switches it round to show a bluebird spreading painted wings across the back.

'Slip it on,' he urges. 'What's the harm?'

Helen takes a step away. She doesn't even like the thing, particularly. It's the sheer frivolity of it that captivates her; the pointless, whooping theatricality of it.

'This,' she says, 'is for someone young and pretty.'

'Well, you *are* young and pretty!' counters the stallholder, with brazen innocence. Helen laughs.

'I could never wear something like that,' she says. 'Never in a million years.'

At home that evening, Helen inspects the greasy blemish on her coat-sleeve. Maybe stain-remover would do it. Dry-cleaning is too expensive. She can still smell the market on her clothes and skin – food and cigarettes and exhaust fumes. She loads the washing machine and runs a bath. While the water's running, Helen stands in front of the long mirror in her wardrobe door, and inspects her naked body. It's a very long time since she's done this. For more years than she cares to count, she's only undressed to wash or put on other clothes. She'd rather not dwell on the stretch marks and pitted flesh and moles. But now that she looks at herself, turning to check different angles, she decides matters could be worse. She lost weight during Nick's time in hospital, and though she's heavier than she was in her youth, she has a figure. Helen draws her shoulders back and hoists up the sagging throat and breasts. A womanly figure, you might say. She puts her hands on her hips, and notices the lacework of ink on her hand. She must make a note of that address before getting into the bath. Helen thinks again of the pirate girl, and experiments with a defiant glare. Maybe she should have a tattoo. Somewhere private and hidden – the base of her spine, perhaps, or around her crumpled belly button. Why not? Who would ever know or care?

Guess what, Nick. I'm a 64-year-old punk detective. Well, there's no law against it, is there?

25

Helen wakes from another vivid dream. They've grown more frequent lately, delivering her from sleep around dawn. A calm breadth of sunlight lies across her. She breathes deeply, eyes closed, floating in the dream's last resonance. She can't pin it down. Already, the definitions of character and plot have dissolved. She knows there were young men – Marcus Edwards, probably, and maybe Grant. Her dreams tend to cast her as a teenager, and play out scenes with all the anticipation and wonder of first love. This morning, Helen emerges with serenity from a tranquil coda. She realises that her dream concluded with a vision of Nick, opening his eyes. Seeing her. Rising from his bed and shedding all the misery of his last years. Nick of the demi-smile and the dark eyes. Not a young man, but as he should always have been – gentle and funny and patient, relishing his life and his family. Nick taking Helen's hands in his own and saying, 'It's never too late.'

Helen is reluctant to acknowledge she's awake. When she does, this mood will slip away and she'll have to clear Nick's face from her mind to avoid weeping. Her blanket of sunlight grows a fraction heavier, as dawn shifts into day. Its maternal warmth allows her to open her eyes, and she focuses on her arm, resting across her ribcage, and the ghost of blue ink on the back of her hand. The Willows, Laurel Hill, Shottering. Helen imagines May Jones waking from her own dreams – dreams of home, maybe – and keeping her eyes shut to calamity as long as she can. If she was in service, she would probably be up by now, laying the fires, heating the water. But she might still have had moments such as this. She might have shared with her granddaughter the transient consolation of early sunlight on her arms.

Not all the family photographs are in the loft. There's a row of albums ranged on a bookshelf in Lisa's old room. Helen was never one to revisit pictures: once they'd been developed, shown around and stuck in an album, that was that. When Lisa was about fourteen she had a phase of poring over them, asking who was who, but that soon passed. Today Helen takes out the albums. Their faux-leather covers creak as they open and she has to prise apart the plastic-covered pages. She starts with the latest additions. She's accustomed, now, to reversing into the past. Lisa, posing in her graduation gown and mortar board, clutching her rolled certificate with a tense smile. Helen took one of these to show her mother, who was seeing out her final weeks in a hospital bed at the time. She remembers handing over the photograph in its cardboard frame and watching it shiver in her mother's unsteady grasp. Amelia Catherine Berwick Blake held her granddaughter's image inches from her face. Helen could see the misshapen fingers fluttering at its edges. For a long time her mother studied the picture, working her jaw to ease her sore and toothless gums. Then she returned it, with a peremptory gesture towards the bedside table. Helen fiddled with the back of the frame and propped up the photograph as directed. Her mother spoke through a wall of catarrh: 'Lisa's done well.'

Helen recalls the jealousy that mingled with her pride. She had gone to secretarial school. To her mother, that wasn't doing quite well enough.

The plastic slurps as she turns a page. School photos of Lisa, neat in her uniform, same tight little smile. Holiday snaps: Lisa in her stripey bathers on the beach. Lisa feeding the pigeons in Trafalgar Square, holding her hands up to a flurry of wings. Helen standing by, on guard, half out of shot. Another page turns and a loose print falls out: a shot of Barnie, sitting up for the camera, tongue lolling, eyes laughing. This must have been taken by Lisa. Helen and Nick had stopped bothering with photographs by then. The old boy's daft face makes Helen smile. Then she thinks of Barnaby, and has a brief fit of giggles.

Back she goes. Lisa's first day at school. Lisa standing in her cot. Lisa's scrunched, hour-old face in the crook of Helen's arm. She moves on to the next album. Her wedding day. She and Nick stand on the chapel steps, flanked by parents. Helen's mother in that awful hat. Nick's father, red cheeks evident even in monochrome, wondering when he'll get a drink. Helen's hair curled up like apostrophes at the ends. Her mother disapproved of the dress – too short – but Helen admires it again, deciding that her legs look rather good. The next one is of the happy couple, turning to face each other, apparently sharing a joke. She stares at this for several minutes, before turning back another few years. Nick and his first car. Nick and two of his student friends. A picture of Helen, looking over a stile into a cornfield. They'd gone for a country walk on one of their early dates, and Helen remembers fretting about her inappropriate shoes. They'd walked miles. She was tired and hungry and had mud on her stockings. But look at her, in profile, contemplating the view, hair tucked behind her ears, hands resting lightly on the wooden stile. Here is Helen, seen through Nick's eyes, and she's lovely.

26

'I can't believe,' says the voice on the receiver, 'you haven't got email. Helen, love, it would change your life.'

Until now Helen has had no real memory of the voice at all. She recognised the name, offered like a fanfare when she answered the phone – but only vaguely. If her surprise caller hadn't announced herself as 'a blast from the past', Helen might have assumed she was selling insurance.

But one phrase, and its condescending cadence, immediately gives that name a face. Patricia Fife. Of course. She always did address her as 'Helen, love,' and always in a way that implied her forebearance of Helen's stupidity.

'Never mind,' she goes on, and now Helen can visualise the horsey face, and the red lipstick outlining her words. 'Lucky for us you're still in the same old place, so it didn't take us long to track you down, and Harry reckons he can still find the way there…'

Harry and Pat. They appear in Helen's mind as she last saw them, a couple in their thirties, bearing down on her at some terrible dinner party given by a colleague of Nick's. There they are, each wielding a glass; Harry assessing her in silence, Pat releasing a geyser of chatter from that blood-red, elastic mouth.

'So, when can we come over, Helen, love? We're only in the country for a couple of months and I said to Harry, we've got to see poor Helen before we go back. I couldn't believe it when I heard about Nick. So terrible, so hard to believe, I always knew him as such a cheerful guy…'

The memory sharpens. Pat never made any secret of her attraction to Nick; whenever they met she would clamp herself to his side, horse-face tilted up as her lips went to work, making their red shapes and circles. Helen remembers what Nick used to say: *Pat Fife doesn't make small talk. She makes monstrous talk.*

Helen plays for time.

'It would be lovely to see you,' she says, 'but as you can imagine I'm not very organised at the moment…'

Pat hacks through the excuse.

'Don't you worry, Helen, love. No need to stand on ceremony with us. We take as we find. Look, why don't we drop by now? No time like the present, and we can't let another thirty years slip by, can we?'

Can't we? thinks Helen. She'd quite happily see out the rest of her days without getting round to a reunion with Pat Fife. But the decision is made and sealed with a 'Be right there!' and Helen is stranded in the hall with a buzzing receiver. She sees the house with a visitor's eye. Reasonably tidy: she hasn't lived in it enough, over the past two years, to cause disorder. But that's the trouble – it's choking on neglect. Helen moves the phone on its table and reveals a dark oblong in the dust. The carpet is freckled with specks of fluff and human sheddings, and the air is stuffy with past meals and lethargy. She must hoover. Hoover and dust – quickly – then attend to herself: comb hair, change clothes… she wants to present to her callers an elegant widow in a modest but stylish home. But her limbs are leaden. A cliff-face of effort looms sheer before her, a physical impossibility. Helen swaps her slippers for shoes, passes a brush over her hair and opens a window. And she reminds herself that Pat Fife takes as she finds.

By the time the doorbell rings, half an hour later, Helen has seriously considered running away, or summoning Lisa from her office, or at any rate dashing to the corner shop for supplies. She's done nothing. She sees their fizzy silhouettes through the glass and knows they can see her too. No escape.

'Here we are! Just as I said – found our way without a hitch. Even took a short cut!'

Pat's bluster carries them through the first shock of encounter. Helen's thirty-year-old image sags into reality, and she sees the same wince of adjustment pass across their eyes. Actually, Harry and Pat haven't changed a great deal. Pat is still as thin as a stick, moving like a girl in her bright sweater and tight jeans. Her hair is straightened and dyed, her nails painted; only her drooping cheeks and stringy throat give her away. Harry is stockier and has lost all his curly hair, but he has the same discomfiting stare. As Helen leads them into the sitting room, she wonders what they must make of her, and raises her hand instinctively in a futile attempt to quell her hair.

'Just look at this!' Pat is saying, scanning the walls and furniture. 'It's like stepping into a time capsule, isn't it, Harry?' She goes to the patio doors and looks out. 'Even your garden's exactly the same! I do admire you, Helen – you're so … *constant*. Not a flibberty-gibbert, like me. Always needing to chop and change, that's my trouble. Which is why we left the country in the end. I said to Harry, when they kicked out Lady T, I said, there's nothing for us here any more. Didn't I, Harry? And off we went.'

Harry's eyes nail Helen to the spot.

'How are you bearing up?' he asks.

Pat rushes to join in with commiserations and disbelief. 'Nick,' she says, with bafflement, 'was never that desperate type.'

Helen remembers to offer tea, and Pat insists on making it.

'Point me in the general direction of a kettle,' she orders. 'We'll take care of ourselves. Friends don't need formalities, do they, Helen, love? You stay put and have a chat with Harry.'

Helen sits, cowed by Harry's glare, and he sits opposite her and asks, flatly, 'Was it depression?'

Helen catches her breath. Most people have skirted around that topic. She says,

'I don't really… well, yes, I suppose it must have been.'

Of course it was depression. She knew that. She even used the word, or variants of it: *Your father's a bit depressed*. That was what she'd tell Lisa, on his worst days. *He's a bit down*. As if they were one and the same condition, a harmless inconvenience that would soon pass. Harry's question hits her like a train. He follows it up with another: 'Was he on medication?'

Helen shakes her head and searches frantically for a valid reason why not.

'He wasn't really…' she starts, then forces herself to meet Harry's eyes. 'I don't think we really understood what was going on,' she admits. Harry absorbs the reply and gives one short nod of absolution.

Pat returns with the tea. She's unearthed the best china – a set Helen inherited from her mother and has hardly ever used. She's not sure it's as clean as it could be.

'Terrible, terrible thing, depression,' Pat says, catching the end of their exchange. 'And of course that surgery of his was such a burden to shoulder on his own – such a responsibility, I always think, to be the sole earner.'

Helen clenches her fists in her lap.

'Nick had retired,' she says, and her voice is high and strained. Across the fuss of Pat's catering, she feels Harry's eyes steadying her resolve.

'Oh, yes, love, I realise that,' says Pat, arranging cups and saucers, 'and I'm not casting judgements, Helen, please don't think that. I only wonder whether the stress of running a business – you know. And Nick wasn't a business man, was he, when all's said and done? He was a vet. He wanted to cure animals. Not balance the accounts.'

Even as she aims a roar of *how would you know?* at Pat's dancing mouth, Helen recognises the truth. This gibbering woman with a backdated infatuation has made a better job of diagnosing Nick than Helen managed in four decades of marriage.

Pat serves tea and asks about Lisa – 'such a wilful little girl, I always thought' – and about a few mutual acquaintances who are only half-familiar names to Helen.

'I'm sorry,' Helen says finally, 'I'm absolutely hopeless at staying in touch.'

'Well, you never really got in touch in the first place, though, did you, love,' says Pat, without rancour. 'Always a bit of a loner, you were. Took us all by surprise when you and Nick took up with each other. He was such a laugh, you know? Such a sociable guy. And you were this sweet little bashful thing. Attraction of opposites, I guess.'

'Nick was quite shy,' Helen protests. Her voice is climbing again. 'He wasn't the same, out of company.'

'Yes, well, we've all got different sides to us.' The mouth stretches and snaps around its verdict. 'I guess you brought out Nick's quiet side.' She drinks more tea. Every mouthful dissolves a little more lipstick, and there's now a distinct boundary between the clotted colour on her lips' outer edges and the inner circle of raw meat. Helen has an urgent need to shove Pat off the subject of Nick. She delves into her conversational depository.

'Which part of Australia did you say you're in?'

Pat veers on to the new topic without a pause. She tells Helen about their marvellous house with its spectacular views, the long hikes they take, the fabulous friends they make, and Pat's hectic schedule of leisure pursuits.

'If you've never tried Salsa,' she assures Helen, 'you haven't lived. Harry won't come, of course. All too sensuous for his liking, isn't it, Harry? And then on Thursdays I do my silk-painting class. And believe it or not, Helen, I'm learning the clarinet...'

The first drops of a shower rap against the patio doors, and Helen wonders whether putting the light on would brighten the room or show up the dirt.

'We're all getting older,' Pat is saying, 'but that's no excuse for being idle, is it? Time is short, so make the most of it, I always say. That's what *you* need, Helen – you won't mind me saying this. Get out and about. Shake off the cobwebs. It's hard, I know, love, but let's face it, life goes on.'

'I've started doing my family tree,' offers Helen.

'Very nice,' says Pat. 'Good for you. But that won't really get the blood flowing, now, will it?'

When they leave Pat grabs Helen's neck in a violent hug and smacks a faint red mouth onto her cheek.

'We'll have to get you out to Oz,' she threatens. Just before the door shuts, Harry reaches back and squeezes Helen's hand.

There's a mirror over the hall table. Before going out Lisa used to go through a ritual of last-minute checks. Tweak the hair, smooth the eye shadow, inspect the teeth and finish with two sidelong views of her profile: left, right. Without Lisa there, the mirror was reduced to a shudder of movement as Helen or Nick passed it by. It's only since Nick's death that Helen has reintroduced herself to her reflection. She stands in front of the glass and conducts a ruthless inventory of her features. This is a much harder task than posturing, full length, in the nude. Only the passage of time is marked on her body; its impact is all in her face. But she perseveres. It serves as a kind of penance. Pat's imprint throbs on her slack cheek. Maybe Nick would have been better off with Pat Fife at his side, instead of an Opposite and a Bore. Helen sees herself jump as the phone rings.

'Mrs Pascoe? This is PC Wellbeloved. We met at the station the other day. I'm ringing to give you some news.'

27

'Two brothers,' Helen tells Lisa, 'and the youngest is only thirteen.'

'God! Unbelievable! And where's the mother in all this?'

'Only thirteen,' says Helen again, 'and already running around the streets with a knife.'

'Appalling,' says Lisa.

Waves of indignation travel along the phone lines between them like comfort. Helen can hear the pattering of keyboards and office conversation in the background. She never usually rings Lisa at work, but felt this could be an exception.

'About bloody time!' was Lisa's initial reaction, but she sounds relieved and gives no sign of impatience to return to work.

'What happens now?' she asks.

'I'm not really sure,' admits Helen. 'They just said someone would be in touch.' A new dread grips her. 'I don't know whether I'd have to go to court…'

A picture forms of a raised dais, a judge in comedy wig and, in the dock, a hooded, faceless spectre. 'I don't know what good I'd be,' she goes on. 'I didn't see what they looked like.'

'Oh, I shouldn't worry, Mum. It'll take ages to get to that stage, anyway. I'd be more worried that the whole thing falls apart before they even get to court.'

How does Lisa know such things? Helen suspects she's simply acquired a mish-mash of terms and notions, as Helen has, from TV dramas. But she accepts it all mildly and says, 'I expect you're right.'

She hears the indistinct rise of a query in Lisa's world, and Lisa's muffled response: 'It's my mum. They've arrested the kids who mugged her.'

A crescendo of interest, then Lisa's voice again – 'Yeah, only thirteen, one of them. Can you credit it? Yeah, coffee, please – white, no sugar.'

Helen peoples her imagined version of Lisa's office, placing her daughter at a grand desk from a 1940s film. She's never seen the place. She hardly ever visited Nick's surgery, come to that. Helen didn't like to corrupt their professional domains with the whiff of domesticity.

'I'd better not keep you,' she says. 'I know you're probably up to your eyes.'

'No, it's fine,' insists Lisa, who sounds unusually laid-back. 'I'm having a bit of a lull. It's nice to have a chat.'

So Helen tells her about Harry and Pat and their impulsive visit.

'Bloody nerve!' cries Lisa. 'Turning up on the doorstep! I'd have told them where to go.'

Encouraged, Helen relays some of Pat's more galling remarks.

'She said I brought out his quiet side. She meant I was dull as ditchwater.'

She means to say it lightly, but her voice catches against the word 'dull'.

'Stupid bitch,' says Lisa. 'Mum, I hope you haven't let her get to you. It's all bollocks.'

'Well,' quavers Helen, 'I suppose in a way she was right. Your father *was* always quieter, with me.'

'You and Dad,' says Lisa, placing the words with precision, 'were always laughing. That's what *I* remember, before he got ill. You two, laughing, all the time. It was the illness stopped him laughing. *Not you.*'

Helen squeezes the phone until it threatens to crack. She takes a few seconds to master the wobble in her throat and find the voice of Amelia Catherine Berwick Blake. Then she says, 'Anyway. *Her* husband never gets a word in. So *she* can bloody talk!'

28

Barnaby's back. Helen is sitting at an Archive computer when she sees his approaching anorak in her screen. Relief laps over her like a hot bath. Conducting her research without his guidance must have been more nerve-wracking than she realised. Barnaby greets an air vent and asks it how the search is progressing.

'Quite well, I think,' says Helen. 'But it's taken rather a curious turn.'

She starts to tell him about Wallace. Before she's reached the second syllable of his name, a minimal tightening of Barnaby's jaw conveys his displeasure.

'Ah yes,' he says. 'Wallace Bird. The postcode man.'

Helen squirms in humiliation.

'He did come up with an address,' she pleads. 'And it does seem to be a genuine one.'

She indicates the screen, where *Laurel Lane, Shottering* is scattered through a page of search results, picked out in bold like a taunt.

'Yes, I've no doubt of it,' says Barnaby, apparently without opening his mouth. 'It's an impressive trick.'

They go to the Canteen for tea. Barnaby gives her a precis of his research trip. He seems to have harvested a vast amount of information, shunting his adoptive family's story back by another century.

'How far do you think you'll get?' asks Helen, with awe.

'Probably as far as the Norman Conquest,' replies Barnaby.

'Possibly further, if there are any records of the French line.'

Helen thinks of her trawl through the local maps. She hasn't even waded out of the twentieth century yet, and she's started to understand how Latisha can spend so long on one generation. While Barnaby strides purposefully upstream towards the source, Helen's family history keeps expanding like a flooded drain. May Jones makes her way to the workhouse, the catastrophe in her belly growing heavier by the day, and Helen doesn't know how she can leave her behind.

'It must be satisfying,' she suggests, 'to see everything falling into place.'

'For a family like mine,' says Barnaby, 'it's easy.'

Helen pictures him in his anorak, sifting through parchments in the library of a stately home, while his other, nameless ancestors sink another inch into the soil. She returns to the matter of Wallace and his magic tricks.

'Do you think he's a fraud?' she asks Barnaby.

'Oh, no. No, I wouldn't say that. More of a throwback, you might say. Once upon a time, after all, that was how all our history was stored and passed on. By rote, and by word of mouth.'

'But you have doubts?' persists Helen. Barnaby's eyes wrinkle.

'I'm a books-and-paper man,' he says. 'I'm suspicious of anything else. But...' he raises his cup in a toast – 'I'm sure the address he supplied is sound, and you're on the right track.'

Helen reports her findings on Laurel Lane. The electoral register has thrown up several ordinary addresses, plus a solicitor's office and a nursing home.

'Aha!' says Barnaby, glittering with interest at last. '*They* sound promising. These large Edwardian houses often end up as businesses or care homes, if they're not knocked down. That's how people fill 'em up, now that they're less likely to have a horde of children or an army of staff.'

'I'll give them a ring,' announces Helen. She's on the verge of asking Barnaby to accompany her to Laurel Lane. But she changes her mind. She's a grown woman. The hooded demons have been caught and cast out. She can find her own way there.

She rings the solicitor's office first. The secretary is effusive and helpful. Her uncle is looking up his family tree, she tells Helen, and she herself is addicted to those celebrity-ancestor programmes. And yes, the nursing home just up the hill is called The Willows, and the warden is a delightful woman who went to school with her mother, and she wishes Helen all the very best of luck in her search.

29

Helen has never learned to drive, and can't contemplate learning now. Besides, she has no car. She knows the garage is empty; she senses it there, a locked space lurking beside the house like a tomb. But she's not entirely sure when or how she was rid of the car. Lisa and Mark dealt with all that. Her only recollection is of a rushed exchange in the hospital corridor. Lisa told her the car had gone, and Helen said: 'Nick *needs* the car. He'll be furious, when he gets home.'

It's not an easy journey to Shottering, even though it's only seventeen miles away. Helen plots the trip with military care. She has to take a train to Merringdon and a bus from there. The price of the ticket almost puts her off the whole idea. But she's persuaded by the embarrassment of begging a lift, and an increasing compulsion to follow in her grandmother's footsteps. She'll make up the cost somehow – perhaps by walking the three miles to the Archive, in future. That'll get the blood flowing, now, won't it?

She takes the early train. It's delayed by twenty minutes, and judging by the fixed expressions on the other passengers' faces, this isn't uncommon. Helen worries about the bus connection and unfolds her timetable again, without registering what it says. Above her the seconds clack away on the platform clock. She becomes mesmerised by the changing patterns of lozenge-shaped digits. The train might never come. She and the other passengers might be held in this vacuum of time forever, listening to the metronome beat of nothing at all. Like being by Nick's hospital bed.

A stirring around her, and a yellow nib appears on the horizon. Helen checks her watch, despite having noted every passing second since she arrived. She should be all right. If she misses one bus she'll catch the next. If she's running late for her appointment with the warden, she'll call ahead on her mobile to apologise. Why is she fretting?

The train journey is short. Helen wishes it were longer. She enjoys the progression past indefinable yards and buildings at the town's margins, and then the expanse of fields and hedgerows, streams and woods. Scenes whip by, keeping their stories to themselves. A man with a fishing rod balanced on his shoulder, clambering down to a riverbank. A young girl running after her dog in a cornfield, lifting her knees high. A farmer swinging down from his tractor cab as white birds wheel over the twisted earth. Helen wonders why she hasn't travelled by train more often. Her life has been contained within a circle of daily landmarks: Lisa's school, the shops, the dentist, the park where she took Barnie for walks. She was content with that. Unlike Pat Fife, Helen never wanted to chop and change. Today, though, the notion of boarding a train and breaking through the circle is exhilarating.

She catches the bus with seconds to spare. The last five miles of the trip take twice as long as the first dozen. This is a rural bus that grunts and whinnies round sharp bends and up narrow lanes, and the driver addresses everyone except Helen by name. Two women call at each other over the engine's growl, gossiping across a gulf of empty seats. Helen consults the directions provided by the warden. She's quite excited now, and glad that she came on her own. Arriving by car would be too easy. Too glib. May Jones is worthy of more effort.

Helen and most of the other passengers get off at Shottering. The bus drops them in Market Square. Today, cars are parked there instead of stalls. As the other passengers scatter and the bus rumbles off, Helen realises she should have planned her visit for a market day. That would have been a setting recognisable to May Jones, and Helen would have stood, as her grandmother stood, watching the flap and fluster of trade, trying to settle the nervous sickness in her stomach, mustering herself for the first uphill walk to Laurel Lane. A car reversing from its bay yaps its horn in warning and Helen crosses the road to read again her first direction: *leave the square along Drover Street, at corner by internet café and Pizza Hut*. She skips to the last: *Willows halfway up Laurel Lane on left*. She didn't think to ask whether this would be the original Willows. When she gets there and looks left, she may well see a clinical, concrete block, punctured with identical windows. This isn't May's world, she reminds herself. Nothing about the way Helen feels or the things she sees would be familiar to May. And yet, as she walks along Drover Street and starts her slog up the long, leafy curve of Laurel Lane, Helen can hear the hammering of May's young heart.

It's a bright day but Laurel Lane is drenched in shade. The houses are set well back, and most are hidden by shrubbery and walls, but Helen does catch sight of a couple as she passes their gates. Large cars, gravel drives; one house a johnny-come-lately with flat roof, doric pillars and lions on the gateposts. At the next gate there's a plaque: Bowman & Clarke, Solicitors. Helen pauses for breath and is tempted to wave at the chummy secretary. Not far now. As she approaches The Willows, a Land Rover pulls in to its drive just ahead of her. Helen hangs back, waiting to hear the car doors slam and the knot of voices unravel into the distance. Then she moves to the entrance to take her first look. When Lisa was small, Nick used to take them on day trips to castle ruins, and he'd always say, 'Try to imagine what it looked like when it was new'. But Helen never could. All she ever saw was the scene before her: heaped stone, chewed towers, sightseers with their audio guides, frowning at the same view as another voice exhorted them to see it through different eyes. Today, Helen makes an extra effort to blank out the anachronisms littering her vision: the sign at the entrance (*The Willows, Private Residential Care, Warden Mrs R. Lloyd*); the cars on a tarmac forecourt; the low brick extension. She focuses on the house itself – the house, she's now convinced, that May Jones saw some ninety years ago. A great muddle of a house, with a bristling of chimneys, pointed gables of varying sizes, bay windows bulging out in several directions and a 'front door' wedged awkwardly to one side, embellished with ramp and railings. Helen eventually heads for this door, and wonders whether it was originally the tradesmen's entrance. She rings the bell and scans the walls quickly for any clues, but every trace of that old segregation has been whitewashed away.

Helen is led through a broad hallway to Mrs Lloyd's office. Much of the interior has clearly been scooped out, but the wooden staircase, the solid doors and the high, coved ceilings seem to have survived. Helen glimpses a large sitting room, where a couple and their child are crowding round an armchair. 'Hello, Mum!' Helen hears. 'Aren't you looking…' the phrase fades as Helen hurries on after her escort. They pass double doors leading into the modern extension, where tables and chairs are set out, and a mist of cooking smells emerges.

'First shift at twelve,' explains the nurse. 'Only seems like ten minutes since breakfast!'

Mrs R. Lloyd has a smiling voice and a humourless face. She processes Helen's visit briskly. She presents her with a photocopied picture of the house in about 1932, and a brochure for the home, which includes a page on the building's history.

'A few of our residents remember this place as the local doctor's surgery,' she says. 'What I suggest is that you talk to Violet. She's Shottering born and bred. Ninety-one and sharp as a pin. Don't let her talk through lunchtime, though – she'll forget to eat.'

Helen and Violet sit in the day room's sunny bay and talk about the past. Violet is curling in age. The withering of flesh has turned her nose into a beak, and there are pink expanses of scalp between her puffs of white hair. But the life in her eyes and tongue have weathered the changes, like the period features of the house. Yes, she assures Helen, she can remember The Willows in the twenties.

'Never set foot in the place, in those days,' she adds, to Helen's disappointment. 'Not for our likes, the surgery. Couldn't meet the bills. My ma used to say,' her finger prods Helen's shoulder in strict time '"Keep well, and if you can't keep well, keep quiet!"' She gives way to the remnants of a laugh, then shakes a feathery fist. 'I'm in 'ere now, though, in't I?'

'And you like it here?' asks Helen.

Violet braces herself on the arms of the chair, easing the pressure of sitting.

'S'allright,' she says. 'Grandson's paying the bill, so what do I care. Bless his heart. He done well, he can afford it. And I shan't be around long.'

Helen asks whether Violet remembers any of the servants in the house. Violet bunches her lips.

'Don't think so … I was a little girl, in them days. Like I said, we didn't used to come up this end of town. 'Cept my brothers came climbing the fruit trees round the back. Scrumping – you know what I mean? And got a whipping for their trouble.'

Helen listens to Violet's reminiscences – about her brothers, her parents, the way they made ends meet, their squabbles with the neighbours, the day everyone crowded out to the square to see the doctor's new motor car. Helen pounces.

'You remember the doctor, then?'

'Remember the doctor?' Violet flattens her with nine decades' worth of scorn. 'Of course I remember him. I in't gaga yet!'

'Dr Calvin? Or Calvert?'

Violet shakes her head firmly. 'Nope. That were the last one. The old man, him what passed away. In *my* day it were Dr Adams.'

There's a slow tideswell of movement around them as the first shift is summoned to lunch. The nurse's wheedling falsetto reminds Helen of the way people talk to their pets.

'What was he like?' Helen persists. 'Doctor Adams – what did he look like?'

Violet's lips suck again at a memory.

'Looked like another old man, to me. Grey hair, big black eyebrows. But I was a little gel. He'd be a young lad to me, now!'

Violet pulls out a few more strands of detail. How the doctor's wife was short and stout, and thought herself a cut above. How Dr Adams never let his patients owe him a penny, not like some of the decent ones, who'd let you pay them when you had the cash. How there was some scandal about the cook – Helen's heart leaps – but that was a long time later, in the thirties, and everyone said it was Mrs Adams lost the ring, and only called the cook a thief to save her own face.

The young nurse is standing over them.

'Ready for your shepherd's pie, Violet?'

'Mrs Parks to you,' snaps Violet, but lets herself be helped to her feet.

Helen thanks her, shakes her boneless hand and watches her being chaperoned to her lunch. Time to go soon, anyway, to be certain of catching the bus. But Helen's lost all her anxiety about times and schedules. She's been sitting with someone who probably crossed paths with May Jones, who could easily have brushed past her in the market, or watched with baleful, six-year-old eyes as May trudged towards Laurel Lane. If only Helen could tap into the hours and days stored in Violet's sparrow skull. Only a leaf's-width of skin, a brittle dome of bone separates Helen from the world of her grandmother's youth. And as Violet pointed out, she won't be around much longer. Helen gathers up her things in a whirl of sudden urgency. There's someone she needs to see.

30

Every wave that slaps onto the pebble beach sends an afterthought of spray against the tearoom window. Helen rubs a circle in the condensation and strains for a view up the seafront road. She can't for the life of her see why Aunt Fay is so fond of this place. Even in midsummer it's pretty bleak; on a wet day the sky, the ocean and the dismal strip of shops and eateries on the front all seem to merge into one big blotch of grey.

Two train journeys in a week. Helen promises herself she'll cut down on the wine to make up for the cost. At least this was a direct trip, and the station's only a five-minute walk away. It was Fay who suggested meeting in the tearoom.

'I go there every day for my elevenses,' she explained. 'Next best thing to room service.' Aunt Fay should be a long-term resident at the Grand, tottering out for a turn along the prom before nipping back to her usual table for dinner. A bit part in an Agatha Christie book – and, knowing Aunt Fay, she probably dunnit. The reality is, though, that Fay lives in a small third-floor flat with a concrete balcony, which she may feel isn't fit to receive a guest.

Another crack of water against the window. Hard to tell whether it's spray or rain; they seem to amount to the same thing here. There are two shelters down the road. One faces the sea, the other faces the street. Helen can see a bundle of macks and plastic rain bonnets: three women sitting hip-to-hip, discussing this and that as the surf ricochets behind them. One of them raises a hand at someone across the street, then leans in to her companions to share a comment. Aunt Fay must be heading this way.

The tearoom door gasps and Fay sweeps in. High-heeled boots and a gold-coloured, hooded cape.

'Usual, Fay?' asks the owner. Fay gestures affirmation and regards the sickly display of pastries. 'And an almond croissant,' she adds, pronouncing the *croissant* with more flamboyance than it deserves. She tosses a look at Helen's metal teapot.

'Aren't you eating, Helen? Nonsense. A *pain au chocolat* for my niece-in-law, please, Audrey.'

She hands her cape over imperiously with her order, and takes her place, brushing invisible crumbs from the table.

'Such a nuisance,' she remarks 'that one can't smoke in here any more.' She opens her handbag and produces a pencil-thin cigar. 'These don't count,' she assures Helen. 'Cigarillos are bound to have a loophole.'

Despite the No Smoking signs on all the tables, Audrey evidently makes an exception in Fay's case. After serving her usual – a hot chocolate topped with a bouffant of whipped cream – she places an ashtray on the table and withdraws.

Fay sits with her legs crossed and one arm resting along the back of her chair, letting the smoke dawdle towards the door. She savours the first lungful with half-closed eyes, then turns to Helen.

'Well,' she says, 'I was expecting to hear from you. I suppose there's all manner of rubbish to clear up in poor Nick's wake.'

Helen pinches a corner from her pastry and says, 'I've been looking into my family history.'

'Christ, have you really?' Fay taps her cigarillo over the ashtray and raises a painted eyebrow. 'I've never understood why people are in such a hurry to open every can of worms in the cupboard.'

'I just sort of fell into it,' says Helen.

'I'd scramble straight out again, if I were you. Families are a pain in the *derrière*, dead or alive.'

Her eyes sidle away after the cigarillo smoke, and Helen realises for the first time how awkward Fay finds this situation.

'Well,' Helen ploughs on, 'in a way, that's beside the point. Except that it got me thinking. About… I don't know…'

She searches for a diplomatic phrase. Fay cuts in: 'About quizzing the old bird before she kicks the bucket, you mean? Yes, well, I suppose that's inevitable, given that I'm the Last of the Mohicans. Ironic, really, when you consider my history of drink, drugs and depravity.'

Her eyes swivel mischievously back to Helen, who can't help chuckling. Fay studies the purple nails on her right hand.

'I always suspected,' she says, 'there was more to you than met the eye, darling.' She smiles broadly, revealing perfectly straight brown teeth. 'Our Nicholas was no fool.'

Helen has been trying to formulate questions for Aunt Fay since her return from The Willows. But this isn't a nostalgic interview about a far-off episode in period dress. However sympathetic Helen has started to feel towards her grandmother, May Jones is, to all intents and purposes, a fiction. When it comes to gathering clues about her own husband, she can find no way of untangling past from present, herself from him. Sitting in the Sea View Tearoom, breathing in the musky scent of Fay's cigarillo smoke and eau de cologne, Helen flounders. She doesn't know how to begin. Luckily, Fay has no such trouble.

'No doubt,' she comments, 'you and Lisa have been castigating yourselves since Nick pulled the plug, and wondering where you went wrong.'

Helen submits, and carries on nibbling her food.

'You really mustn't bother, you know,' continues Fay. 'Absolute waste of time and energy. Nick took after his mother. That's all it was.'

'His mother?'

A solitary figure in the kitchen, cleaning, smoking, glassy-eyed and cocooned in her own thoughts. Nick would always greet her the same way when they visited, squeezing her shoulders in a held-off, accordion hug: *How are you doing, Mum?* And her reply was always the same: *Same as ever, don't fuss.*

Helen blinks at Aunt Fay.

'How do you mean, took after his mother?'

'He had that same dark thread,' says Fay.

Helen considers this, then objects: 'I know his mother wasn't happy. But she did lose a son.'

Fay draws out the last of her cigarillo and thumbs the stub into the ashtray.

'Yes. Well, that's how I saw it too, darling. Lose a son, and part of you will always be in hell. Natural reaction. *Sane* reaction. That's the way *I* saw it.' She's already searching in her bag for the next smoke. 'But of course, that's exactly why Nick and I fell out.'

Nick and Aunt Fay had a falling out. Helen didn't know that. But she's getting used to hearing about her husband as a character in other people's plots. Nick the mate, who used to be great company till he married a mouse and was broken by his business. Nick the father, who was always laughing till he caught an unnameable disease. And here's Nick the nephew, who apparently had a knock-down, puce-gilled row with Fay about how to deal with his mother.

Fay was the younger sister.

'Younger by five years,' she points out, 'and more feckless by a score.'

Helen lets Fay yatter on about her wild youth, her adventures in the WAAF, her string of lovers in all ranks and uniforms – 'I'm an egalitarian, darling, in every possible respect.' To Fay, the war seems to have been a six-year party. Helen says, 'My parents would never talk about the war.'

Fay shrugs.

'War is frightful. *Frightful.* Drives everyone a little…' The index finger of her cigarillo hand taps against her temple, making the smoke dip and leap. 'But, you see, darling, a little madness can be rather delicious now and then.'

She starts talking about her sister, about the marriage to Patrick Senior.

'That clown,' she sneers. 'Great bullying, bellowing, big-booted clown. The kind of clown that frightens the kiddies.' She releases a long dragon-stream of smoke from her nostrils. 'Tried it on with me every time her back was turned.'

Helen thinks of Nick's father, pink-eyed on the sofa, paunch bulging over his ill-fitting trousers, and cringes.

'Yes, I know,' says Fay. 'Ghastly, isn't it? Even *I* couldn't countenance *that*. But he never let up. The day little Pat was born. Again when Nicky came along. There was Sissy, like a wet rag in her bed, baby at her booby, and Patrick outside on the landing trying to get his hand up my skirt.'

Helen sits up at the mention of Nick's birth. She sees him, crooning at his mother's breast, wrapped in white flannelling, safe from the tussles and rebukes beyond the bedroom door, safe from the gunfire and bombs beyond the house. Fay says, 'Sissy was pretty low after having Pat. And after Nicky, too. She was really struggling, when I look back on it now.'

Helen is startled.

'Struggling? Do you mean post-natal depression?'

Fay puts out another cigarillo and inclines her head.

'Do I? I've no idea. I know she had two small boys and a useless bastard clown of a husband, and everyone in the world was trying to kill everyone else. Whether she had anything extra on top, I couldn't say. And neither could she. You didn't start bellyaching about things like that, in those days. You *muddled through*, darling. Ha!'

Fay hurls a laugh into the tearoom as an elderly man enters, measuring his way with a stick, and doffs his hat to her. Fay gives him a queenly wave.

'Looking marvellous, darling!' she cries, and then, hardly lowering her voice, informs Helen: 'On his last legs, poor soul.'

Helen watches the man take a table in a smoke-free corner, parking his stick and hat with slow care. He's probably a good ten years younger than Fay.

The day has calmed. The tide's gone out and the waves have diminished to a faint bloodbeat: push and drag; push and drag. The sun's come out. The women have left their shelter to stroll to the Winter Gardens, and there's a fiesta of barks and yelps as the dog walkers make the most of the dry spell. Fay says, 'Let's stretch our legs, shall we?'

Helen suspects she wants to escape further interrogation. But as Fay leads the way towards the pier, trailing her cape-wings like an Elizabethan courtier, she resumes her account unprompted. She describes Nick and his brother in childhood: 'Chalk and cheese – Nick at his books, Pat up to all sorts, right from the off.' They cross the road and come to a breach in the sea wall, where a wooden walkway leads down to the beach. Below the bank of pebbles is a gritty width of sand, where the dogs and their walkers chase or battle the wind. Fay stands to watch them, and her cape flowers around her. She yanks in a painful breath and says, 'Oh, Christ. That dreadful day…'

Helen knows she's talking about Pat's death.

'That dreadful day…' she says again, and all at once her profile, her entire frame seem to lose definition and begin to liquefy. Helen waits. She has no wish to hear Fay's stalactite voice shatter and splay. She would rather not see this well-honed, tough-bird act fall apart in a mess of feathers and gore. So she waits, and lets her eyes be soothed by the horizontal sheen of sea and the rapturous sundance of the dogs. Eventually Fay is ready to speak again, this time with scientific detachment.

'I thought it would crush Sissy,' she says. 'But it didn't. It didn't destroy her, didn't destroy anyone. Or at least…' her head motions minimally towards Helen – 'that's what I thought.'

She recalls the phone call, the heartsick journey from her home in London; of finding Nick at home, ashen and silent, and his father still denying the news, fighting it off. 'He was like an explosion,' she says. 'But Sissy – she was the opposite. She was so *still*. Almost an absence. Maybe I mistook that for strength.'

Closing the vista to their left is the pier, a simple wooden affair with a round, low pavilion in the middle. This was meant to be their destination, but now Fay takes Helen's arm for support and says, 'Let's walk on the beach.'

Helen fears for Fay's ankles in those heels, but Fay's stepping over the pebbles with expertise, and it's Helen who's losing her balance. The stones click and grind; the two women lift their feet like show horses till they reach the firmer, tide-compressed ground. They walk on towards the sea, a world away now, just a mechanical rhythm, like the passage of air through comatose lungs. Aunt Fay says, 'Nick was the strong one in that family, you know. He was so young, and more wise than I realised.'

Helen is taken aback. She's not sure what she was expecting from Fay – a narrative, a few shocks and jokes, maybe a revelation or two. She hadn't bargained for emotion. And despite her stirling performance, Fay can't conceal her involvement in this story. This was part of her life too, this tragedy. It's Helen who stands outside it. Fay describes the way Nick kept the household going from day to day. Making his parents breakfast, insisting they eat, leaving school early to buy groceries, dealing with callers and opening the bills...

'Of course,' she adds, 'I did try and lend a hand. But I was in London, darling, I just wasn't on the spot. I didn't realise... not fully, you know. I didn't realise...'

She flings her arm out, throwing her guilt to the wind. A gust catches her cape and wrestles with it. She has to raise her voice to say: 'Poor Nicky. He was only thirteen.'

Only thirteen. A knifeblade slices across Helen's mind. She says, 'But it can't have gone on that way for very long. I mean – his parents *did* cope, in the end.'

Fay gives her a nudge, directing her along the beach towards the pier.

'They made a fist of it, you could say. But you remember how they were, don't you? Hardly on top of things, with hindsight. Nicky was right about that.'

Then she tells Helen about the rift that occurred years later, when Nick was about to leave home and start his college course. Just before Helen entered his world. He was worried about leaving his parents. His mother, in particular. He went to see Fay in her London flat.

'Eighteen,' she recalls, 'and handsome as a king. Mature beyond his years. My heart went out to him, darling. I thought he should be out there, having fun, being an idiot, making a few mistakes – not cosseting his elders at home. And I told him so.'

Helen lowers her head against the wind and thinks of Nick at eighteen, handsome as a king. Fay shouts: 'He wanted to get medical help. For Sissy. I thought he was fussing over nothing.'

They reach a wooden barrier running from tideline to sea.

'It's called a groyne,' Fay says, touching one slimy post. 'Only reason I moved here, darling – someone mentioned all the big sturdy groynes in town!' She cackles, as she hoists up her cape and skirt to step over the bar.

'Come on. We'll carry on as far as the pier.'

Nick had wanted his mother to seek treatment. He wanted to recruit Fay's help.

'She'd listen to you,' he told his aunt. 'Even if she pretends not to, she respects your opinions.'

Fay was dismissive.

'Since when have I had opinions, Nicky darling?'

She poured him a gin and tonic and quizzed him about girls. She refused to return to the subject.

'The truth is,' she tells Helen, 'I was scared. Don't know why, or what of. But the whole damn thing scared me witless. Loony-doctors, pills, electric shocks – Christ. And I'm not accustomed to being scared.'

So when Nick had left, Fay rang her sister and reported the whole conversation.

'Warned her. Grassed on Nick, you might say. And she gave him hell. Accused him of all sorts. Wanting to drug her up to the eyeballs. Have her locked up. Betraying her trust. All that. So then Nicky came to me and we screamed at each other for a while, and that was that.

End of a beautiful friendship, darling. Barely ever spoke to me again.'

They reach the dank shadow of the pier and the wind drops. Seaweed cushions the massive struts. At the foot of each one is a dune of plastic bottles, cigarette packets, condoms and other debris.

'Charming, isn't it,' comments Fay. 'Humanity is so quick to shit in its own nest.'

They labour back up the pebble bank to the road. As they reach level ground Fay is taking out her next cigarillo. Helen says, 'Nick never told me any of that.'

Fay fumbles with her lighter and answers with the cigarillo bobbing between her lips.

'Well, darling, you were his new life. Probably didn't want to sully it with too much of the old.'

Fay walks her to the end of the prom and they say their goodbyes.

'I'd like to keep in touch,' says Helen 'if you don't mind.'

'Pleasure, darling. Have you got email yet?'

As they part, Fay grips Helen's wrist.

'Listen, darling,' she says. 'Don't worry about Lisa, will you? These things don't necessarily run in families. Anyway, she's *your* daughter too, remember. And you've got a healthy seam of iron in your veins.'

*　　　　*　　　　*

Helen toils up her road from the bus stop. Dusk is thickening and lights are coming on in her neighbours' houses. She's still not entirely at ease, out here in the dark, alone, and she quickens her step. But she's tired out from the sea wind, and the images summoned up by Fay's account. She's only dimly aware of her passage from prom to train, train to bus; her head's been too full of the din of old arguments to take in her surroundings. Helen turns the bend towards her house. Her skin is tingling and sticky with salt spray. For all its dreariness, Fay's seaside home has an addictive quality – Helen can see that now. The crash and sigh of the sea, the restless pebbles, the whip of wind – constant reminders of life beyond the chatter and angst.

A movement at her front door halts her breath. A man, tall and broad-shouldered, steps back to look up at the windows. Obviously he's just rung the bell. He moves again and she recognises Harry Fife. *Oh God...* Helen is resolute this time: she cannot face Harry and Pat a second time. As she alters her step, ready to duck across the road and out of sight, Harry hears the scrape of her shoes and raises his hand. *Damn*, thinks Helen, *damn you*, and starts towards him with her friendliest smile. There's no sign of Pat. Harry explains, as Helen's opening the door, that Pat's gone to see an old schoolfriend. He sounds edgy and stilted. Helen finds the day's revelations seeping into the present, and it occurs to her that Harry has come to 'help' her – in the same way Nick had wanted to help his mother. She closes her fist around the front door key as Harry follows her into the hall, and presses its cold metal into her palm as a safeguard against the loony doctor, the electric shocks, the haze of sedatives.

'I hope you don't mind,' says Harry. 'We didn't get much chance to talk, last time.'

Helen keeps her head down and fiddles with her coat buttons. What does he mean? When did she and Harry Fife ever talk?

'We're going back to Oz before very long, as you know...' He peters out and Helen is obliged to meet his eye. There it is – that same old stare. But as soon as she collides with it he looks away. Helen is perturbed. She says, 'Harry, you don't have to worry about me, you know. I'm perfectly all right...'

Harry looks rattled.

'Helen,' he says and suddenly Helen realises her mistake. Harry grabs her fist with both his hands. She whimpers as the front door key sinks further into her flesh.

'Helen,' says Harry again, and takes a full, rallying breath before blurting out: 'I'll be halfway across the world in ten days' time and I might never see you again.'

Helen has the impression that she's missed a slice of her own life. She leans away from him, trying to release the pressure of the key, and fails to find a response. Several possibilities race through her mind:

that Harry is going senile; that he's playing a cruel prank; that she's dozed off on the train and is dreaming the whole thing. Harry tugs her fist to his chest and the key bites harder.

'Ow,' says Helen, and he finally eases his grip. The stare is rocksteady now.

'We're past the age,' he tells her, 'of beating about the bush.'

It sounds vaguely smutty. Helen senses the spin of a giggle, deep inside.

'You know how I always felt about you, Helen,' Harry goes on. Helen wants to insist that it's all news to her, but she daren't open her mouth.

'When I saw you again the other day, the years just vanished.'

He's practised this. Helen feels sorry for him, but the muscles in her neck and jaw are aching from the effort of holding off that giggle. He lets go of her fist abruptly and her fingers gradually unfold. Harry's arms shut round her waist and pull her close, making her coat collar ride up around her chin. He tightens his hold, hoisting her onto her toes, and the key finally unpeels from her hand and drops noisily to the floor. Helen laughs aloud, and she's still laughing when Harry manoeuvres past her collar and lands his kiss.

31

'You look well,' says Latisha. She casts her eye from Helen's forehead to her feet and back again. 'In fact you're positively glowing.'

Helen says, 'I've been to the seaside.'

'On the hoof, huh?'

'That's right. On the hoof.'

Helen talks about Aunt Fay as they're collecting their coffees from the Archive drinks machine. Latisha listens, and responds, but her eyes are examining, calculating, concluding. Helen knows why. She knows her posture is different; the way she holds her coffee cup, the pitch of her voice. She's wearing a little make-up. She hadn't known that she still had any, but she rooted around in the box on her dressing table and found some ancient sticks of lipstick and congealed mascara. So while Latisha chortles about Aunt Fay's cigarillos and heels, she's preparing a question which Helen mustn't answer. She lobs it into the first break of narrative.

'What gives, lady? This is more than bracing sea air – am I right? What did you do – meet a scrummy Punch and Judy man?'

'Latisha, I've only been widowed a matter of months.'

Helen's rebuke is coquettish and unconvincing. *But it's true*, she thinks. *Five minutes after losing Nick and I'm twittering like a teenager.*

She's been split into two people. Helen the frivolous free agent, with an endless future ahead; and Helen the widow, still keening down there in a mineshaft of grief.

'No offence, honey,' says Latisha, 'but today you're the merry widow. Tell.'

Latisha is navigating her over to an empty table. Helen has promised herself she'll be discreet. But she's had a whole life of discretion, keeping confidences from herself and from everyone else. She's never had the kind of friend who provokes and cajoles her away from her better judgement. She can't resist. Helen and Latisha bow their heads together and lower their voices, and share secrets.

Helen doesn't have that much to share. After Harry Fife had kissed her, Helen saw him to the door. They didn't even take off their coats. Harry apologised, and assured her that he'd always been in love with her. Helen told him, gently, not to be ridiculous.

'We haven't clapped eyes on each other for decades,' she pointed out. Harry took her hands.

'That's got nothing to do with it,' he said. She could tell he was irritated by her refusal to stick to the script. 'Call me', he said, 'before we go back.' He took a folded piece of paper from his pocket and slipped it into hers. Then he kissed her again, and this time Helen didn't laugh.

'I haven't been kissed like that,' she tells Latisha 'for more years than I'd care to count.'

Latisha's face widens in scandalised delight.

'So what's he like, this Harry?' she prompts. 'Bit of a hunk?'

Helen says, 'Not bad.'

The fact of his kiss, its force and intention, overshadow everything else: age, looks, common sense. Only one immoveable obstacle remains: he's not Nick.

'And all this time,' sighs Latisha, 'he's been on the far side of the globe, pining after you.'

'Stuff and nonsense. Of course he hasn't. I don't think he even particularly fancied me when he was here. It's just a bored old man's fantasy.'

'Well, from what you say about the wife,' says Latisha, 'who can blame him?'

Helen thinks of Pat Fife and her dynamic lips, and is engulfed in sadness.

'This is terrible,' she says. 'It's all very well for me to play the merry widow, but Harry's a married man.'

She's expecting Latisha to chivvy her, to assure her it's harmless enough, that she hasn't done anything to feel bad about. But the mood has dropped. Latisha nods slowly.

'Yeah,' she says. 'Yeah. Best to steer clear. Being the other woman is nothing to write home about.'

Helen creases her brow in a tacit query. Latisha replies with a resigned dimpling of her cheeks. Helen says, 'You're...?'

Latisha says, 'Fraid so.' She fingers the rim of her plastic cup. 'I suppose you'll hate me now.'

Helen tuts. 'After what I just told you?'

'Oh, Helen,' says Latisha, mournfully, 'that's not the same.'

She's been seeing the man for eleven years. They met through work. Latisha was an administrator of further education courses, and he was one of the lecturers.

'I don't know why,' she says, 'but we just clicked. He's nothing to look at. Lot older than me. Family man. Really, he is. Kids, grandkids, hordes of 'em. Loves 'em all. Loves his wife. Loves me. Oh, yes, my Arthur's a very loving man.'

Helen can't tell whether her tone is sarcastic or affectionate. Maybe a bit of both. There's a pause and Helen rushes to fill it: 'Is that why you left your job?'

'No... Well, sort of. They were waving redundancies around and I thought: time to get out of this tangle. This dead end. Yeah. Come to think of it, that was quite a lot to do with Arthur.'

As she uses the name again, Latisha shoots Helen a look.

'This is between you and me, OK, Helen?'

'Of course,' says Helen.

'Don't tell anyone. Not even Barnaby.' Latisha considers for a moment. 'Especially not Barnaby. He might have come across him.

And anyway...' she glances over her shoulder, checking the room behind her '...I wouldn't want him to think less of me. Or of Arthur, come to that.'

'Do they know each other?' asks Helen.

'Wouldn't be surprised. Arthur's a historian...'

A memory unfurls in Helen's mind, with a smattering of others attached like briars. The flash of a blade. A blow against her hip. The gritty beam of a streetlamp. The clean lines of a business card against her fingers. The question is out before Helen can restrain it: 'Is his name Arthur Ballantyne?'

Latisha recoils in her seat.

'Jeez...! You know him?'

Helen explains that she only met him once, on a bus, and that she only recalls his name because of its association with the mugging.

'I can't even remember what he looks like,' she admits. All she retains is an idea, of a large and rather pompous man with obscure letters after his name; but she keeps this to herself. Latisha is determined to see portent in the coincidence.

'How spooky is that?' she demands, more than once. 'It's like destiny. Or fate. Or something.'

Helen doesn't argue. There's no reasoning with a woman who fills her days with spirits: dead babies, dead forebears, other people's children, another woman's husband. Latisha, so vital and present, seems to have ended up living life at one remove. Helen thinks about Harry Fife and his rehashed song-lyric speech and invented passion. She thinks of Fay's faultless performance as the hardbitten woman of the world. Maybe we all construct these myths, one way or another, to give ourselves significance. Maybe that was Nick's trouble: no story to tell. Then Helen's mind wanders back, as it often does these days, to May Jones. Poor May, who had no redundancy package or girlish chats in the Archive. Did May Jones, alone on the road to the workhouse, weave any tales to herself about who she was or where she was going? Well, Helen realises, she must have: because within a generation, Amelia Catherine Berwick Blake was instructing her own child to be a lady, to speak well and carry her learning lightly, to avoid all talk of God or politics, and to cross her ankles as she took her place in the world.

Latisha's family search has branched sideways again, and she's here to scroll through casualty lists from the Crimean War.

'Cannon fodder,' she tells Helen. 'Turns up in every clan. You'll find that out sooner or later.'

'I'm making very slow progress,' confesses Helen. 'I'm spending rather a long time getting to know my grandmother.'

Latisha winks. 'Knew you'd be hooked. Canteen, 12.30?'

'It's a date,' says Helen the Flirt, trotting away with a carefree new gait.

Helen's eyes are burning. She's been searching and refining at the computer screen for hours, and has almost forgotten how to blink. She's tried every conceivable term, euphemism and specification that might be remotely connected with domestic service. She's heard thirty-second sound bite recollections from oral history projects. She's made copious notes on the history and hierarchies of service. She knows, now, that in middle-class houses the cook was also expected to clean the dining room, doorstep and brasses. That a house parlour maid would see to the bedrooms, empty the slops, sweep the stairs and lay and clear the tables. That bigger houses had all manner of rank and file: under maid, laundry maid, lady's maid, kitchen maid, scullery maid, tweeny. A frenzy of washing, dusting, brushing, cooking, serving, sewing, water-boiling and fire-lighting, behind every panelled door. But though Helen has hunted down every online alley, diverting to obscure websites, creeping up with an oblique reference – still, she can find no database of ordinary household servants. There are registers for teachers and nurses, midwives and clerks, bricklayers, carpenters, bookbinders, lighthouse keepers, circus performers and town-criers. But a twentieth-century teenage servant is apparently impossible to track down.

Over lunch at the Canteen, Helen tells Latisha about her change of plan.

'I've decided,' she announces. 'I'm going after the Doctor.'

Her hunch is that, in death as in life, Dr Adams will have been noticed and documented, while his servants scuttle unseen into hidden back rooms.

'It strikes me,' she says, 'that I might be able to sneak into my grandmother's life by way of the Doctor's.'

'That's my girl,' cries Latisha. 'You're really thinking like one of us now!'

Helen spends the afternoon finding out about medical registers. She then searches the births and deaths register for a May Jones, born locally in around 1906, and, despite the cost, orders four possible matches. By now she's bleached by the screen, and needs to get out of its sapping light. She swings her chair round and comes face to face with Marcus Edwards. He's taken a seat at the computer next to hers, and seems as thrown as she is. Helen's colour rises. She moves her mouth in a feeble greeting and he responds with the hint of a nod. Helen scurries under the desk for her handbag, but before she can retrieve it Marcus Edward speaks.

'Tracing your line?'

The rising inflexion traps Helen in her seat.

'Yes. Yes, I… drifted into it.'

Perhaps he doesn't know about her visit to the police. With a bit of luck Lisa was right, and the police never follow these things up. Then she can get away with a few niceties and go, and maybe never set eyes on him again. After an eternal instant, Helen starts to rise from her chair. It squeaks on its spring and triggers him into more speech.

'I gather you're acquainted with Alana Kern.'

He knows. Helen tries to take in every fleck and blur within her peripheral vision, hoping one of them is Latisha. She says, 'Not really.'

The old dread is mounting: the dread of a situation that breaks all the rules. Helen has had this same disorientated sensation with cold-callers, door-steppers who'll seize a polite phrase and use it as a crowbar. She's had to learn to slam the door on them, and now she forces herself to issue a challenge to Marcus Edwards.

'What,' she asks, 'gave you that idea?'

A hairsbreadth of a pause, and then: 'I saw you together.'

His gaze is as direct as Harry Fife's, but it's not going to culminate in a kiss. Having prodded him into this admission, Helen is afraid to say anything more. For all she knows he's dangerous. One wrong word might pull the pin. Absently, Marcus Edwards draws his fingers through his ponytail. He says, 'I thought you and Alana might be friends.'

Helen replies as neutrally as she can: 'Alana thought I knew you.'

A change passes across his eyes as the pupils retract. He leans towards Helen, who sits back abruptly and sets her chair into a gentle bounce.

'I've got nothing against Alana,' he says, with quick intensity. 'I just want to find out the truth.'

He treads the ground, wheeling himself closer, and drops his voice: 'She's been to the police about me. Told them I was stalking her. That's all wrong.'

Relief cools Helen's cheeks: obviously he's unaware of her own report.

'Please,' he goes on, 'can you ask Alana to talk to me? All I want is the truth.' He nearly tips himself off-balance. His hands fly out and grasp the arms of Helen's chair.

'OI!'

A trumpet blast behind her.

'Back off, matey, and keep your hands to yourself!'

Both Marcus and Helen leap to their feet like guilty lovers. Latisha glowers over folded arms, and Helen turns to fling urgent reassurances at her, afraid of what she might say next. When Helen looks back, Marcus has gone, leaving the glass reception door to complete its lazy, closing arc.

32

Helen takes her seat on the bus home in a daze. Her mind darts around like Barnie let loose in a park, bamboozled by a muddle of trails. Two women are sitting in front of her; shopping bags perched like children on their laps. They natter away, adding to the cacophony in her head.

'I don't know how she puts up with it,' one is saying. 'I wouldn't stand for it myself.'

Helen's nerves prickle as Marcus Edwards' white face hovers before her again. *All I want is the truth...*

Latisha's warning chimes in the background: 'Don't get dragged in to anything,' she said, when they parted at the bus stop. 'Don't you get involved, lady. You've got your own life to lead.'

And now a current of excitement reminds Helen of Harry Fife's kiss and Latisha's revelations, and she smiles a small, private smile.

'Bloody squirrels,' the woman in front is saying. 'They're a pest. What I do, I tempt them out with hazelnuts, quick grab, bag over the head, drown 'em in the stream at the bottom of the garden.'

She gives an uncertain laugh. Helen can't tell how her friend is reacting. She hopes it's with horror.

Thank God, she tells herself, *Nick isn't here*. It would break his heart. Helen starts to comfort her dead husband: *She's probably lying. Showing off. She couldn't catch a squirrel. It wouldn't be that daft.*

Frantically, she searches for a happy ending, the way she used to for Lisa, if ever she was upset by a news item or an overheard snippet of the grim, grown-up world.

'Costs me a small fortune in hazelnuts,' the woman cackles away. 'But it works a treat. Amazing how trusting they can be.'

Helen has to grip her handbag hard and press her mouth shut. She wants to throttle this woman, to put her hands around the baggy neck and wring it like a flannel. She seems possessed by Nick's disgust and sorrow. Or maybe it's her own. Tears loosen her eyes, and she gives a loud sniff. The woman in front stops talking. She and her companion get off at the next stop, and Helen tries to fell her with a glower through the window. The bus waits, trembling, at the kerb, while more passengers embark. *I could get off now*, thinks Helen. *I could follow her home, the way I followed Alana. Easy. I could knock at her door, make up some tale about belonging to the same family tree, get her inside and – wham. Bag over the head. Drag her down to the stream, leave her lying next to the damp heap of rotting creatures on the bank. Squirrels avenged.*

The gears exhale and the bus moves off again. Helen waits for her distress to subside. She doesn't have to care this much any more. Nick's gone.

At four the next morning, Helen wakes crying. She's been dreaming about Harry Fife, but she surfaces thinking about Nick. Thinking something new and specific and suddenly very obvious: Nick loved somebody else. Of course he did. She's broken the code and everything immediately makes sense. The silence, the distance, the deepening melancholy… he couldn't have the other woman, whoever she was; maybe she had commitments of her own. Maybe she didn't love him back. So he left. Left them all. That must be it.

Four hours later, when the sun is up and the washing machine is chuntering to the radio, and the kettle's boiling and Nancy's car is revving up outside, nothing seems quite as clear. Helen sifts through names, women's names that might have been mentioned or avoided too often. But a man who says nothing gives nothing away. She reviews Nick's daily routine, when he still went through the motions of following one. Other than taking Barnie for walks, when could he have found the opportunity? Perhaps the other woman was a dog walker. Out of nowhere comes a flashback of the funeral. Caddie from the surgery, so scared and eager to please, stuttering over her eulogy, and that clumsy wording, so touching at the time: 'He loved his animals so much – and, of course, his family.'

How old is Caddie – thirty, thirty-five? Probably no older than Lisa. Well, it wouldn't be the first time a man had fallen for someone half his age. And Nick was an attractive man, until the very end, when the last of his humour and hope had seeped away. Helen sits at the kitchen table and cages her face in her hands. She can hear Nancy's car rumbling off down the road. All right then – why not Nancy? Just next door. Handy. So devastated when it happened...

For God's sake. Helen offers her mute apologies to Caddie and Nancy, and automatically adds her defence: it must be the grief. Then she whispers into the palms of her hands:

'Oh, Nick. I'm so sorry.'

*   *   *

'Mum, I've been thinking about your birthday.'

The word drops like a brick.

'That's not for ages yet.'

'But I want to make sure it's all sorted. If I don't do something, you just won't bother.'

Lisa's voice strains into a higher key. Helen keeps her own voice light.

'Let's not bother, then,' she says.

'You say that now, but how would you feel if...?'

Lisa trills onward and upward. Wearily, Helen interjects, as she does every year: 'The thing is, Lisa, when you get to my age...'

...and Lisa slaps back her annual response: 'It doesn't stop mattering just because you get older, Mum.'

As usual, Helen doesn't explain that, no, it doesn't stop mattering:

it matters far too much, this headlong rush through a reduction of years. Instead, she tries one last-ditch strategy: 'This year,' she says, 'of all years, I prefer not to make a big deal of it.'

Half a second's pause, and then Lisa's ragged voice returns: 'I'm not talking about a big deal, Mum. That's the whole point. I'm asking what you want. That's exactly why I want to sort it out now. It's not as if I can just drop everything at a moment's notice; I've got to plan ahead. I know it's a pain, but that's the way it is I'm afraid...'

She spirals away again, and Helen's mind wanders here and there. The kiss. Strange Marcus. The squirrels' payback. Nick's assignations with Nancy.

'...so all I ask is, give it some thought, so that I don't get it hopelessly wrong.'

33

Hopelessly wrong. That's what this is. Helen's americano is too hot. She scalds her tongue and her stomach complains. She sits upright, in her coat, doing her best to look like a woman on her way somewhere else. Not a woman with an appointment. Not a woman who's waiting in a café for a married man.

She re-runs her reasons for agreeing to meet Harry. Better to clear the air, before he and Pat go home. Best to meet in a public place, neutral territory, where he can't get up to any of his nonsense. And who knows, maybe Alana and Marcus will turn up for one of their dramatic confrontations, and provide a useful distraction.

She'd just said her goodbyes to Lisa and put the phone down when it rang again. She knew it was going to be Harry. For a long time, Helen couldn't hear the ring of a phone without foreboding. She'd forgotten what a different charge that noise used to deliver, in her youth. The split second before hearing the caller's voice. The frisson of vanity and pride at the sound of her own name, and everything it conveyed: his decision to call, the battle with nerves leading up to it, the strength of feeling that finally prompted him to pick up the receiver and dial the number... Helen hasn't known this thrill of conceit since she was eighteen and infatuated with Nick. But she's not infatuated with Harry. And she doesn't date married men. So why is she here, blowing on her coffee, feet writhing in the shoes she wore for her own husband's funeral?

Oh, yes. Because she's going to clear the air. In a safe, public place. She's going to put a stop to this idiocy once and for all.

He's here. He touches her shoulder swiftly, with the tips of his fingers. She's aware of the heavy texture of his woollen coat. He smells of aftershave – a formal, masculine smell. He takes a seat. His eyes are dark with worry and anticipation, like a child's. Helen has an unfamiliar sensation of power.

'Where's Pat today?' she asks, with only a hint of spite.

'Ladies' lunch,' says Harry, then hurries on: 'I know you don't believe me, but this isn't... I'm not... this is real.'

'Oh, for heaven's sake, no it's not,' says Helen.

His mouth curls as if he's about to throw a tantrum.

'Harry,' she says, 'we're in our sixties. We're...'

'So what?' he barks, unexpectedly. Before Helen can resume, the waitress is there, asking for his order. Helen notes the glint in her eye, and when she's gone, whispers, 'That girl is laughing at us. She thinks we're two old codgers playing at *Brief Encounter*.'

Harry is annoyed. He throws an indifferent look in the girl's direction and says, 'Let her. What does a kid like that know about anything?'

Without thinking, Helen starts to unbutton her coat.

'She knows we're too old to be acting like kids ourselves.'

She waits for his protest, but Harry has regained his composure. He sits back, and the stare is restored.

'Now is the time of life,' he says, 'to act like kids. There's nothing left to lose.'

Helen's hand stops unbuttoning at her waist.

'You,' she says, 'have a marriage to lose.'

They sit in silence until the waitress has brought Harry's coffee. He busies himself adding sugar from the plastic sachets. Helen watches the deft way he peels the corners down and lets the sugar hiss onto the surface. One, two, three sachets. Then he stirs, and his eyes go back to hers.

'You've got a sweet tooth,' says Helen, for something to say. But now it sounds disturbingly suggestive. She blushes. Harry says, 'Pat and I have always had a… a tricky relationship.'

Helen rolls her eyes. Everything he says sounds so contrived.

'You always struck me as fairly devoted,' she says, irritably.

Harry is still stirring his coffee.

'There've been… episodes.'

'You mean you've had affairs.'

Now we get to it, she thinks: the tawdry truth. She's torn between relief and disappointment. Harry shakes his head.

'No, I haven't. Not *me*.'

Helen's fingers go to work again, undoing the rest of the coat buttons. So that's what she is: Harry's revenge. Except, of course, that she's not. It's unthinkable, at every level. She and Harry are not going to sneak away for an afternoon's illicit sex. They're simply going to sit in a café, conducting a pretence of suppressed desire. It's a way of deferring the past and the future, the grief and the questions, the birthdays and the catechism of family rows. Just for an hour.

34

May Jones was a popular name in the early twentieth century. Helen discovered that in her hunt for her grandmother's birth certificate. Even after narrowing her criteria to Forbridge and environs, 1906, she has to choose between the four certificates that arrive within the week. And Barnaby has taught her to doubt everything. What if May was born in another part of the country? What if she lied about her age? All Helen can do (another tip from Barnaby) is make a decision based on her best guesses and all the available clues, and follow it up.

When Helen first paid to order certificates she worried that it was a pointless extravagance. Pieces of paper: dull, bureaucratic lists. She promised herself she'd save the cost elsewhere. But today, when four documents slide from their reinforced envelope, Helen's breathing is quick and shallow. Four new lives slither onto the kitchen table: four complete strangers, perhaps, whose faces are suddenly, randomly illuminated through the smog of the past. Helen spreads out the certificates.

May Jones. Born February 1906. Little Vale, Nr Forbridge. Father's Occupation: Baker.

May Ellen Jones. Born June 1906. South Street, Forbridge. Father's Occupation: Railwayman.

May Jones. Born October 1906. Five Acre Farm, Nr Forbridge...

Before the third May Jones is done, three words on the fourth certificate have made Helen's heart stumble. She picks it up and reads aloud to an empty house: 'May Jones. Born November 1906. White Hill House, Forbridge. Father's Occupation: Labourer (Unemployed).'

She holds the certificate in front of her and looks at it for a long time. A beam of sunlight falls across the paper, laced with the shadows of Nancy's apple tree.

White Hill House.

It could be a different May Jones, Helen reminds herself. But she's caught fast by those three words. There's no question in her mind that she's opened another window onto her grandmother's life. May Jones didn't just end up at the workhouse; she was born there. And when everything went wrong in her life, she made her way back home.

'Remarkable,' murmurs Barnaby. 'Remarkable.'

Helen shines with pride. She dashed to the Archive in the hope of finding either Latisha or Barnaby and sharing her discovery. But the fact that it's Barnaby who's here, and who's impressed, is particularly gratifying. He takes his time over all four certificates, kneading his lower lip with forefinger and thumb. He gives the inevitable caveat: 'We shouldn't jump to easy conclusions. It may be another May Jones altogether. You should really establish at least three points of evidence, to be quite sure.'

But Helen's not crestfallen. She can see that Barnaby's as besotted as she is by this finding. He lays the documents on the reading table and taps them, one by one.

'But it gives us something to go on,' he concedes. 'Most useful, indeed. Back to the workhouse records, I think.'

Three points of evidence. It sounds so clear and straightforward. But gathering evidence about the past is, Helen now knows, like trying to file water. Every clue, every fact, every solid name and date and statement thaws out and trickles away under Barnaby's interrogation. They've got the inner sanctum to themselves that afternoon, so he's free to fire questions at Helen as they sift through the registers of relief, minutes of the Board of Guardians, and workhouse master's diaries.

How can we be sure this is your grandmother?

How do we know she didn't lie about her age when she married?

Can we assume that she was born hereabouts, just because she ended up here?

How do we know...?

'Oh, how do we know *anything?*' Helen explodes. 'We have to gamble on it, don't we? Or we'll never get anywhere at all!'

Barnaby's eyes crease.

'Ah!' he says. 'You *are* a historian!'

The best way to be sure this is the right May Jones, he advises her, is to trace her grandfather as well, and see whether the two stories dovetail.

'I suppose so,' agrees Helen. Then she admits, sheepishly: 'I went off on a bit of a tangent. I started looking up May's employer. Dr Adams. Silly, really...'

She carries on searching through the papers. After a moment, Barnaby asks, 'Do I take it you regard the good doctor as your main suspect?'

Helen smiles at a column of admissions.

'I think he might have done the deed, yes. New young housemaid, harridan of a wife, easy access to the servants' sleeping quarters... And then, when poor May fell pregnant, the doctor or the harridan turned her onto the streets. That's my theory.'

Barnaby tuts gently.

'Careful, Helen. Use the facts to build your case, not to bolster your prejudice.'

Helen loses her place in the column of admissions and has to start the page again. It's the first time Barnaby's ever called her by name.

ADMISSIONS REGISTER, FORBRIDGE UNION WORKHOUSE.

10 February 1905. Admitted: Mrs Flora Jones age 28 with son Robert about 3 yrs. Husband a labourer, out of work due to injury these seven months past.

2 July 1905. Discharged: Mrs Flora Jones and son Robert, due to improved circumstances of Joseph Jones, husband.

MASTER'S NOTES, FORBRIDGE UNION WORKHOUSE, 1906.

15 June 1906: Mrs Flora Jones was readmitted at 5 o' clock. Previously resident with young son, who has since succumbed to scarlet fever. Brought to house by Joe Jones. Mr Jones in work intermittently but afflicted by back injury received in a fall. Mrs Jones is with child. Both arrived the worse for drink and possibly infested. Mrs Perkins arranged to have Mrs Jones' garments stoved.

'Fumigated,' Barnaby translates. He watches Helen as she reads the record again and again. Softly, he points out: 'We're still not certain that Mrs Flora Jones is one of yours.'

Helen's mouth hardly moves as she replies: 'It doesn't matter. I'm not disowning her now.'

Later, when Helen is drinking hot tea in the Canteen, she repeats her vow.

'Even if we're not related,' she tells Barnaby, 'I need to know how Flora Jones came to that pass. I don't know why. I just do.'

Leaning against her chair is a carrier bag full of notes and photocopies. Barnaby has offered to give her some box files, and she's planning to clear one of her bookshelves to make space for them.

Barnaby says, 'If you stick to Flora Jones it may mean leaving your own trail altogether.'

Helen nods slowly. 'I know. I know. But it seems important. To stick with her. More important than playing some kind of genetic Snap. There's got to be more to all this than DNA. Hasn't there?'

Part Three

35

Helen is overdressed. She's having to steel herself against the weight of her own clothes and make-up. Why on earth did she wear this great big coat? And why the pleated skirt, that makes her look enormous, and the nannyish blouse and cardigan? She's never had to dress for an occasion like this before. She even went out and bought foundation, which she's wearing now in a thick layer, like a warrior's helm.

'Take a seat,' says the receptionist. 'Gemma won't be long.'

But Helen isn't sure she can bend her legs, so she says, 'I'm fine, thank you,' and has difficulty fitting her mouth around the words.

She should have stuck to her guns. When Gemma first approached her, Helen was adamant. She was sorry, but she couldn't help. This new scheme sounded interesting – admirable – but it wasn't for Helen. Gemma was sympathetic.

'That's perfectly OK,' she kept saying. 'Perfectly OK. Not everyone is comfortable with it. It's entirely your decision.'

As she spoke, Helen could feel the old terror rising inside her. The flash of a blade. The impact against her hip. The dark, demolishing hostility of one instant on the street.

'It's just that...' Her throat had forgotten how to swallow. 'I don't think I can cope with meeting them face to face.'

'Not *them*,' Gemma corrected her, hastily. 'Only Darren. Only the youngest.'

Darren. The thirteen year old. The shadow beneath the hood

began to form features. Helen thought of Alfie, grinning at the rozzers' camera in 1892. But Darren wouldn't be anything like that.

'Sorry,' she said, again.

'Don't worry,' said Gemma. 'No problem.'

'What'll happen now?' asked Helen. She was unaccountably afraid that Darren would be released, silver blade hidden in his fist, to find his way to the other side of her front door.

'Well, he'll go to court, like his older brother. Juvenile court. To be honest, his brother Jake's already an old hand at all this, though it's always been petty theft, shoplifting, that sort of thing. Weapons are a new turn, for these two. That's why we thought it was worth trying something different with Darren. Before he's too far into the system.'

The system. It sounded like one of Lisa's managerial phrases. The career system. The ladder. Helen took Gemma's number as a courtesy, before hanging up, and went back to her reading. She was looking through a chapter in one of Latisha's books: *Tracing the Untraceable*. It had a section about workhouses, and who might end up there, or pass in and out, as her great-grandmother apparently had. She resumed reading where she'd turned the page down.

Some other residents turned to the workhouse because they had simply run out of other options.

Helen couldn't concentrate. Her mind was sniping at Gemma and her social-worker glottal stops. At Darren and Jake, who surely had plenty of options, in this day and age. Plenty.

She thought of something Gemma had said: 'Their home life's a bit of a mess, frankly.'

A bit of a mess. What an infinity of damage that term might cover.

Ten minutes later Helen was back on the phone and Gemma was thanking her with earnest emphasis.

'I really think,' she said, 'we might have a good chance with Darren.'

So here's Helen in her sartorial armour, and here comes Gemma, hurrying from the stairs with a satchel of files over her shoulder and gathering Helen up into a cloud of cautions and assurances.

'Just a chat. No pressure, no obligation, just feel free to say what you want to say, or not say anything at all. It might be frustrating. He might not speak. We'll just see how it goes…'

And then they've arrived at a room on the first floor, and Gemma's knocking on it and mouthing 'OK?' to Helen, as though they're about to go onstage. Helen is suffocating. If she breathes she'll be engulfed by the darkness in that room. The door opens, and she's about to turn and run. Then she sees a small, skinny boy slouched in a chair, pointedly not looking, and she sees that his hair is cut painfully short, and that his hand, lying awkwardly at his side, is twitching convulsively.

A bearded man, who opened the door to them, says, 'Hi! I'm Andy. Come in and take a pew!'

Andy introduces himself as a mediator, who will 'help things along'. He offers tea, which, contrary to her training, Helen declines. Apparently, so does Darren, though with no sound or movement that's discernible to Helen. There's another adult in the room too: Darren's social worker, Rose, a woman who looks, to Helen, little older than the boy himself. Rose is parked uncomfortably on a wooden stool next to Darren's chair. She's obviously embarrassed about being at a higher level, which probably contravenes all sorts of social codes. She rounds her shoulders and dips her head like a horse at water. Helen fears for her back.

As directed, Helen sits opposite the boy. There's a low table between them. Gemma and Andy sit on hard chairs, facing each other, to complete the square. Darren doesn't even raise his eyes to acknowledge Helen's arrival. Her back teeth clench. As she sits, the chair lures Helen backwards. Her feet leave the ground, and she wriggles forward to sit upright on the edge of the plastic cushion.

'Darren,' bearded Andy is saying, 'this is Helen…'

'Mrs Pascoe,' adds Gemma.

Darren's hand swivels back and forth. Helen says, 'Hello, Darren. Pleased to meet you.'

A noise emerges from his chin, a kind of animal mumble, but he doesn't look up.

Bearded Andy starts talking about the purpose of this meeting, and all the things they don't have to do or say. Helen becomes aware of expectation, as if a question has been asked. Andy and Gemma are regarding her without pressure. She searches wildly for an appropriate comment. Weather, general health and well-being, refreshments – yes, that will do.

'Perhaps,' she starts, then pauses to repair the crack in her voice – 'perhaps I could have that cup of tea after all?'

There's a kettle on the shelf at the back of the room. Andy, Gemma and Rose go into a complex choreography, clambering and sidling around each other to pass mugs and tea bags and a tin of biscuits. It reminds Helen of a scene from a Marx Brothers film. She feels a nervous giggle tap-dancing into her chest, and clears her throat. Quick as a fish, Darren steals a look, then disappears back under his eyelids.

'Will you have some tea now, Darren?' asks Gemma, cheerily.

'Yuh,' grunts Darren.

Helen resists the urge to remonstrate: *Yes, please.* She has an unexpected flashback: Lisa, in her early teens, brooding over her meal and forcing the word 'please' through clamped teeth. At that age, she viewed all such pleasantries as surrender. But this boy, thinks Helen, just doesn't know the form.

The tea is watery and Helen's mug has a hairline crack. Surreptitiously, she turns it away from her mouth. Once they're all settled, Andy summarises the event that brought them all to this airless room. He sets out the facts without emotion or embellishment. It sounds such a slight business, stripped of the hyperbole of newspaper or nightmare. *And after all*, thinks Helen, *it was.* Two minutes of scuffling confusion and the quick glimmer of a blade… even that turns out to have been a penknife, rather than the dagger that's been filleting so many of Helen's dreams. But those dreams are not a slight business. They toll between Helen's days – an infernal, subterranean note that reverberates through her waking mind. The flashbacks that torment her are more like threats than memories. Helen watches Darren's impatient hand, and hatred almost makes her gag.

Andy is beginning to guide Helen into the conversation.

'So perhaps, Helen, you could just talk about that evening, and how you felt about it…'

Helen takes a deep breath. The boy's chin has wedged itself into his collarbone. She speaks to the adults instead, tells them about coming back from London on the bus, about the emptying street and the darkness, and standing in the lamplight's beam.

'At first,' she says, 'I didn't know what was happening. I couldn't see very well… I was on my own…'

She hears the whine in her voice, and checks it. She's damned if she'll sit here and wheedle a child into sympathy. Andy and Gemma are nodding. Rose is nearly doubled up on her stool. Darren's hand swivels from side to side – the only indication that he hasn't fallen asleep.

Sit up straight, thinks Helen. *Sit up straight. You're pathetic.* She launches the words from her mind like a rocket, wanting to pierce the thirteen-year-old head, wanting to hurt him. *Pull yourself together,* she thinks. *Get a grip on yourself.*

She carries on: 'I thought someone had just bumped into me, until I saw the, er…' The word knife lodges in her throat. All she wants in the world is for Darren to be ashamed, and to get out of this dismal little room. But Darren hasn't shown any human feeling at all, and time is expanding around them. An image opens in Helen's mind of her great-grandmother, Flora Jones, pregnant, reeking, plucking at her oversized, flearidden coat, slanting her face this way and that to avoid the workhouse officer's disapproval. Maybe getting drunk was her only way to cope with that ignominious journey back to White Hill House.

For the first time, Helen addresses the top of Darren's head.

'I don't want to be here, either,' she says. 'No more than you do.' An avalanche is building inside her, gathering force with every sullen second. It finally crashes through her barriers of reserve.

'My life is already in pieces,' she says. 'My husband died. All I've tried to do is carry on. And you and your cowardly brother come along and make me feel old and stupid and helpless and afraid…'

Nothing. She slithers back in her seat again, appalled by her loss of control.

'Thank you Helen,' says Andy, 'for your honesty.' He thinks this is progress. Helen wants to slap his face. After a pause, Rose says, 'We're very sorry to hear about your husband...' with a prompting look at Darren's scalp. Helen feels sorry for the girl. She says, 'He was in a coma for two years. He...' She hesitates before handing over her last scrap of dignity. 'He tried to kill himself.' When it's said, it's said with such ease; she hammers out the syllables in steel. There are sympathetic murmurings from the adults and, from under Darren's clenched eyebrows, an infinitesimal, insect-wing stirring of interest. Helen's fingers are wrestling with each other on her lap.

'I was so tired,' she recalls. 'So tired. I'd been visiting him every day for two years. Talking to him. Reading to him. Telling him jokes.'

The motor in Darren's hand stalls for an instant, and she sees, as swift and as vivid as the blade of a knife, a toothy, childlike smile, before it's abruptly switched off. This child has learned to block his reflexes. That unguarded half-second tells its own history of spontaneity smacked down hard. In a few years he'll know how to sustain those smiles as weapons. And then it'll be too late.

Helen lapses into silence. Darren has won. He's worn her down. She senses contained exasperation among the adults. Darren hasn't played his part. Well, what did they expect? He has no reason to care that Helen Pascoe feels old and stupid and afraid. In his eyes she couldn't be anything else.

The session grinds on. Before it ends, Darren is persuaded to assent to a few leading questions: yes, he feels bad about what happened. No, he hadn't realised the effect it would have. Then, suddenly, he says something of his own accord, though to Helen it's an abstraction of sounds.

'Speak up a bit,' urges Rose.

'He wunt've cut ya,' he repeats, and the hand twists and flaps at double speed.

His eyes wheel warily towards Helen and away again. Helen says, 'But I didn't know that.'

Afterwards, Gemma escorts Helen downstairs. In the foyer, she touches Helen's elbow and says, 'Thank you. You were brilliant.'

'Was I?' Helen grimaces doubtfully.

'I think you genuinely made a connection, Helen. I know Darren doesn't say much. But it's all going on.'

Helen is sweating under her layers of sensible clothing. She wonders whether her make-up has run.

'Good,' she says, and shuffles towards the door.

Gemma says, 'It would have been useful to have his mother there. But she couldn't quite get it together today.' She gives a world-weary slide of her eyes, implying that Darren's mother doesn't get it together as a general rule. Then, softly, she adds: 'But she does try'.

36

Lisa drops round after work to ask about the session.

'What kind of a mother,' she demands, 'can't get it together for something like that?'

Helen spreads her hands.

'I'm just glad it's over,' she says. Lisa pushes out her lips and arches her eyebrows. She'd taken a dim view of the whole thing from the start.

Helen adds, 'The social worker thought it went well. She seemed to think something had got through to this... Darren.'

'*Darren*,' scoffs Lisa, as though he didn't deserve a proper name. She's tetchy today. Someone didn't turn up for a meeting, left her in the lurch... Helen hasn't really grasped the detail, and Lisa hasn't been inclined to explain. She sits without taking off her mack.

'Tea?' offers Helen. Lisa regards the castellated stacks of books and papers on the kitchen table.

'If I can find a space to put it,' she grumbles. She picks up a sheet of paper and reads aloud: '"Edward Blake. Clerk. Possible employers..." God, Mum,' as she casts her eye over a list of Forbridge institutions and companies, 'what *is* all this?'

'I'm trying to find out where my grandfather worked.'

'Don't you *know*?'

'Well... no. I don't. I never really knew my grandparents.'

'But didn't Gran ever say?'

Helen hands Lisa her tea without replying. *Did* she ever say? Surely she must have. But then Helen is only hazily aware of what her own daughter does for a living. She sits at the table and pushes aside a heap of notes. Some are ringed with tea stains, where she's absently put down her mug while absorbed in research. She had hoped to get back down to work this evening, and wonders guiltily how long Lisa will stay.

'Drink it while it's hot,' she says, automatically, then bites her lip in anticipation of a sharp retort. But Lisa draws her hair from her face and drinks obediently, and Helen recognises that look: the pale forehead, the downturned mouth and unfocused eyes. It frightens her.

'I'm trying to make sure,' she gabbles, 'I've got the right people.'

'The right people?' echoes Lisa, without energy.

'Jones is such a common name. So I'm trying to establish links between the Joneses I'm following up and the Blakes. Edward Blake. My grandfather.'

Lisa says, 'Does it really matter? I mean, they're all dead, aren't they? It's not going to make any difference.'

'No,' agrees Helen, thinking fast. Keep her talking. Keep her in the immediate world, safe from that plunge into silence. 'But I suppose… it's, it's…' She ad libs furiously: 'it's about connecting. With the family. You know. Holding it all in place. So that it doesn't just break apart and fall away…'

'Like Darren,' says Lisa. And then, to Helen's relief, the cheeks fire up again with righteous indignation. 'When I think of what you've been through, Mum, and what those little bastards did, and there's this woman, this so-called mother, just leaving them to their own devices…'

'I know,' says Helen, gratefully. 'But I suppose we can't tell what kind of life she might have had.'

'Who cares?' shouts Lisa. Her hair falls forward again and shields her face. Helen thinks there might be tears in her eyes. 'Who cares what sort of life she's had? Look at Gran. Look at *her* mother, coming from the workhouse and all that. *She* dealt with it, didn't she? I mean, why is it always the losers who get to have families? It's so…'

Her voice splits, and Helen waits, but there's no deluge.

'Lisa,' she says, 'sweetheart. Are you…?'

Lisa sniffs sharply and says, 'Oh, I'm just hacked off today. It's just work. Shitty day at work. That's all.'

'Sure?' ventures Helen.

'Sure.'

Outside, there's an outburst of squabbling as the Littles are released into Nancy's garden.

'Anyway…' says Helen. The word drifts over the table between them and settles over its mass of interesting facts.

37

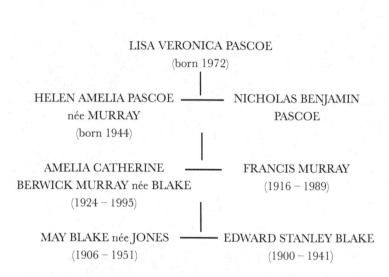

LISA VERONICA PASCOE
(born 1972)

HELEN AMELIA PASCOE ——— NICHOLAS BENJAMIN
née MURRAY PASCOE
(born 1944)

AMELIA CATHERINE ——— FRANCIS MURRAY
BERWICK MURRAY née BLAKE (1916 – 1989)
(1924 – 1995)

MAY BLAKE née JONES ——— EDWARD STANLEY BLAKE
(1906 – 1951) (1900 – 1941)

Edward Stanley Blake was a neat and methodical man. That much is
apparent in his trimmed whiskers, his immaculately parted hair, his
starched collar. It was apparent, too, in his daughter's proud accounts
of his domestic regime, segmented into tasks, duties, precise and
immutable schedules. All her life, Amelia Catherine Berwick Blake
continued his programme, rising at 5.30 and standing outside the back
door to do what she called her 'physical jerks' – a bizarre sequence of
movements that never varied in any way. Arms-up-arms-out-arms-
ahead-and-touch-the-toes ... from the day she could walk to the day
she could walk no more. And yet Edward Blake's physical jerks

couldn't save him from an early grave. Helen consults his death certificate again, and swills a mouthful of wine: *Cause of death: Coronary failure. Age: 41.*

So much for the wan and feverish deathbed. As it turns out, May Jones died young too. Somehow that fact had never really filtered through to Helen. *Cause of death: Pneumonia. Age: 45.* Nothing very romantic about that, either.

Helen shifts her weight and rearranges the blanket she's wrapped around herself. A plane passes overhead, making the glass putter in the dormer window frame. Otherwise, it's very quiet; it must be late. Helen's lost all track of time. She declined Lisa's invitation to try Mark's risotto – and she suspects Lisa was relieved about that. She couldn't be bothered to cook herself a meal, so she had cheese and crackers and brought some of her papers and a glass of wine into the loft to check what remains of her grandparents' effects, after the treasure hunt with Barnaby and Nancy. Everything they gleaned that day dated from after Edward and May's marriage. A deed transferring 14 Dover Way into Edward's name. A lease for the house they moved into after Amelia's birth. A receipt for delivery of coal. An advertisement for carpet sweepers, snipped from a magazine. All records of a slow climb to comfort; none to betray May's earlier penury. Still, they may have overlooked something. Helen retrieves a few scraps from the bottom of the box. A shopping list, scrawled on the back of an envelope. A couple of bus tickets. Nothing of any significance.

At least Edward Stanley Blake's life has fallen tidily into place. Born 12th January 1900, at 14 Dover Way, Forbridge. Twenty-three years later, still resident at the same address, married May Jones. Died in 1941, two years before Helen's birth. His heart gave out. Maybe the mess of war was too much for it. Helen tightens the blanket around her and tries to construct a story that could draw together the pregnant teenage workhouse girl and the tradesman's clerkly son. Maybe she's been on the wrong track altogether, falsely casting Dr Adams as a rapacious villain. Maybe May Jones met Edward Blake *before* returning to the workhouse door, and re-playing her mother's shame. When Edward married May, perhaps he was righting his own wrong, rather than another man's.

Helen's eyes are closing. She sets down her wine glass and leans against the crate of old velvet curtains. Edward Blake hovers over her solicitously and his moustache moves: 'Have you quite finished?' he asks, not unkindly, though he doesn't seem to have a mouth.

'Quite finished, thank you,' says Helen, and produces from the folds of her blanket a beautiful, sugar-scented baby. Edward Blake takes it gently and passes it to someone behind him, and for the first time Helen notices that a whole section of the loft is being used as a makeshift maternity ward. Babies are wriggling and squirming and dozing and gurgling on blankets laid out on the dusty floorboards; and squatting in the shadow at the lowest point of the roof, monitoring the scene, are two women. Helen can't make out their faces, but their thin legs and listless arms tell of exhaustion and despair. One of them has grazed and scabby knees, and her hand twists convulsively at her side.

'The state of them!' says Lisa, who's lying next to Helen, wrapped in a blanket of her own. Helen worries that her voice will carry, and stares at the darkness where the women's faces must be.

'Why are *they* in charge?' demands Lisa. Helen turns to her and sees the knuckles bulging on Lisa's hand as she wrings the edge of her blanket. Beneath it is a hollow, black void. Helen is overcome with distress and tries to reach for her daughter, but she's swaddled fast. The man is still moving around the loft, tending to the babies. Helen watches his back and wills him to turn, wills him to show her Nick's face. The urgency of it, the need to see Nick's features, clamps her like a stapler. She's mute with pain. In the far corner, one of the shadowed women smiles. The man finally turns, but it's the wrong face. She feels she should recognise it, but can make no sense of him. She just knows he isn't Nick.

Helen's head must have twisted off in her sleep. That's the only possible explanation for this agony. She opens her eyes with an effort.

The lids crackle with sleepdust. Cautiously, she alters her position, easing the pressure on her shoulder and neck, and noting the revival of that ache in her hip and some new pains in her knees and elbows. She groans, and takes in a measure of dust, setting off a coughing fit. There's a clunk and a drum roll as her empty wine glass topples and travels towards the wall. Gradually, Helen sits up, disentangles herself from the blanket and, in slow stages, gets to her feet and switches off the light. The loft is subdued into a silvery, early-morning pallor. Tiptoeing to peer through the dormer window, Helen can see the last depth of night sky retreating above the dawn. She must have been here for hours. She sees a bathroom light go on in the house across the road. Her mouth is sticky and foul with the taste of dead wine. *Guess what, Nick. I've turned into an alcoholic dosser.* Twenty minutes later Helen is outside the kitchen door, hoping Nancy is still in bed, and scaring the birds with arms-up-arms-out-arms-ahead-and-touch-the-toes.

38

Nancy's parents ran a picture-framing business. Helen never knew that.

'It never did very well,' says Nancy. 'But they were used to that. They had a go at lots of different things, and none of them took off. When I was a little girl they ran a mail-order business, selling lamps. The house was always full of lights. Standard lamps, desk lamps, tinkly things with bits hanging off them... you couldn't go in to the back bedroom, it was full to the gunnels...'

The wind lifts her hair in exclamation. She's got the afternoon off and has decided to tidy her garden. Helen just came out for the scent of grass and damp earth and a dose of weather to clear her hangover from the night in the loft. Nancy leans with her rake on the fence between them, and conducts her memories with a handful of gathered twigs and sweet wrappers.

'They were always borrowing, Mum and Dad. Always in debt. Kept it from me, of course, till I was old enough to help out.'

'Help out?' Helen clutches her collar against another flurry of wind.

'Oh, just the odd contribution here and there...' Nancy's eyes dart from side to side, searching for excuses. 'Not that they ever asked, you know – just... family; all hands to the deck, that sort of thing...'

Beyond Nancy, Helen can see other back gardens, reaching down the hill to the end of her road in precisely equal, sliced off portions. A eucalyptus tree four houses down curtseys elegantly to each new gust of wind. Brambles and bindweed explode from the student house further on and next to it clipped yew hedges border a flawless geometry of paths, pots and perfectly edged lawn. Helen thinks of all the lives contained in each of those homes, and all the ancestors, cousins, friends and acquaintances attached to each of those lives. In a few years' time some government official will come knocking on the doors in this street to compile another census, pinning down ages, occupations, relationships, like butterflies in a case. Or perhaps they don't knock on doors any more. Perhaps it's all done electronically now, and nobody actually sets eyes on the people who live on the street.

'My grandmother,' Nancy is saying '– my mother's mother, that is – she was a postmistress.'

The postmistress met her husband when he sent a packet of books to Inverness. He was a bookseller; new and second-hand. Nancy's paternal grandparents, now, they were both teachers, but the wife had to retire because school policy forbade members of staff to marry... names and anecdotes, birthplaces and dates are caught by the wind and hurled about their heads. The grandmother who taught had really wanted to be a dancer, but she broke a bone in her foot. *Her* father had been a very keen amateur singer, but could never make it pay... Nancy goes back through the generations, as if she's met them all, and Helen listens with envy. By comparison, her own family, past and present, seems to have grown within a silent shell.

'You put me to shame, Nancy,' she says. 'I don't even know what my own grandfather did to earn his crust.'

From another garden comes the rhythmic crack of a dog's bark. Nancy winces.

'That's Mr Lovell's terrier at number 42,' she says, surveying the descent of gardens like a captain on the bridge. 'He comes over all unnecessary when it's windy.'

Helen nods and struggles to put a face to Mr Lovell's name. Nancy knows everyone on the street, and all their doings and dealings, just as she knows all her forebears. Apart from her immediate neighbours, Helen has hardly ever spoken to any of them, except to pass the time of day.

The duned leaves in Nancy's garden shatter and whirl.

'Well,' says Nancy, grabbing her rake, 'I must get on, Helen, but remember, anything you need, any time – you know where I am…'

She returns to her raking, and Helen moves about her own garden, pulling a few weeds from the sodden borders. The light from her kitchen warms the afternoon. Helen's mind returns to Flora Jones. What would she have made of her great-granddaughter, in her lined coat and sturdy shoes, treading her square of suburban territory? Would she have been pleased, relieved to see the family recover itself? Might there have been a tinge of jealousy, as she cast her eyes into the future from the waste of her own life? Helen squats to tug at a clump of coarse grass, and watches the panic-flight of woodlice and spiders. *Thank God*, she thinks, not for the first time, *thank God the mortgage is paid off*. And then it strikes her that Nick may have been waiting to do what he did, until that debt was cleared and Helen was safe. Checking the statements, counting off the instalments, waiting for his exit cue… she flings the knot of soil and grass under a bush. No: she must not follow that thought. And besides, if he was planning it months, even years ahead – couldn't that be seen as an act of love?

You'll be all right, Lisa had assured her. *Dad made certain of that.*

So Helen has her roof and her four walls, and she has her garden. *And you think*, she challenges Nick, *that makes it all right?* She shivers in another whip of wind, and her anger subsides as quickly as it flared. If she gets too cold out here, if the rain begins again, she can go indoors, turn on the heat and the company provided on her TV screen. She won't think about the unravelling of it all, and how easily that could happen – first the payment defaults, then the plug pulled, no warmth, no light, no money coming in, and Lisa 'helping out' with the odd contribution, eventually installing Helen in another version of The Willows, where she'll sit in a bay window recollecting her girlhood till the nurse comes to badger her into eating her shepherd's pie…

Helen tells herself she would rather bed down with the tramps on the riverbank. But she knows that's not really true.

39

Another phone call from Harry. Helen is ruffled.

'I thought you'd gone back,' she complains.

'Three days' time. Three days,' he repeats. 'Seventy-two hours.'

Helen giggles quietly. There's a pause. She wonders whether he's calculating the minutes and starts to help him out: 'Four thousand, three hun...'

'Yes, yes, very funny, Helen. The point is, on Friday we go back. I'll probably never see you again...'

Helen waits for his maudlin speech to pass and studies the baggy skin of her finger-joints and wrist. When he stops for breath she says, 'Harry, really, it's not very long since I lost Nick. Do you think this is...?'

'You've still got a life to live,' insists Harry. Another well-rehearsed line. Helen doesn't even know what it means. What should she do, to 'live her life' any more than she already does? Whatever it is, she's pretty sure it wouldn't involve Harry with no clothes on.

Reluctantly he winds up the conversation. Helen has the impression he's in a public place – hotel reception, maybe – and has just seen Pat approaching. She wishes him a safe journey home, and Harry says, 'I wish you'd at least get bloody email.'

After putting the phone down, Helen tries to take her reflection by surprise in the hall mirror. She wants to see herself as others see her. As Harry sees her. Maybe other people don't focus immediately on the rucked flesh of her chin or the overflow of cheek into neck. She comes at herself from the right, with a passive expression. Then tries from the left, with an expectant look. By the third time she's laughing again, and Helen has never liked the way she looks when she laughs. The phone rings. *For God's sake*, she thinks, and snatches up the receiver ready with a rebuke. But it's not Harry.

*   *   *

Here she is again. Reading the local paper beside a hospital bed. Breathing in the mineral smells of treatment, hearing the padded activity of corridors and wards. So that was only an aberration after all, that interval of freedom and cafés and open air. And now she's back to the natural order. An infinity of hours. An oblivious companion. Click and suck. Click and suck. Click and suck.

But this is the sound of Aunt Fay's own breath, which rises and falls without the aid of electricity. And she'll wake, presently, or so they said, and will even be able to talk back. So it's not really the same, and it's not really forever. It only seems that way to Helen, as she reads about the new out-of-town Tesco for the third time.

The staff have been reassuring. A doctor on his rounds told Helen there were 'many positive aspects' to Fay's case. It wasn't a major stroke, and they'd been able to get help to her quickly. 'And Miss Pascoe is a fighter,' he added. Even when she was lying on the tearoom floor, near a splat of whipped cream and hot chocolate, Aunt Fay had manage to admire the paramedic's biceps. 'If anyone's going to suffer a stroke,' said the doctor, 'Miss Pascoe is going about it the right way.'

Helen is bored. And she's worried. Aunt Fay may be a fighter, but she can hardly stay on in that pokey third-floor flat, after all this. It was Helen they phoned in the crisis. Helen is the nearest relative, after all. So here she sits with her local gazette, summoned back to the district hospital from her nice, roomy house – a house that's a couple of sizes too big for a widow with time on her hands. She must look like an easy solution.

She doesn't want to think about that. On the other side of the curtain hemming off Fay's bed, a visitor is droning family news to the patient next-door. Helen shuffles her seat a little closer to Fay and in a low, self-conscious voice, begins to read: 'Campaigners against the development greeted the news with dismay and accused members of the council of "selling out".'

A sound emerges from Fay's pillow and Helen leans across to hear. It's a soup of consonants and vowels, but after two increasingly irritable repetitions Helen realises what Fay is saying: 'Bunch of bloody crooks'.

Helen stays a while longer, but Fay is soon tired. They manage an exchange of sorts. Fay's left eye and cheek are tugged downwards and she manoeuvres her mouth with an effort around liqueous phrases, as if it all belongs to somebody else. Occasionally she slides into a groan of 'Oh, bugger it'.

'This will get better,' Helen tells her firmly. 'They've told me. This is temporary, Fay. You'll get it all back.'

Fay regards her with lightless eyes. Those eyes are the worst of it. Worse than loss of speech or collapsed muscles: the absence in those eyes. Humour, mischief, eighty years' accumulated irreverence – all gone. Fay watches Helen's assurances with eyes that only endure.

Helen gets away as soon as she reasonably can. She promises to return the next day. As she takes her familiar escape route down stairs and through waiting areas, Helen feels the trap closing again. She can't ask Lisa to share the load this time. Lisa barely knows Aunt Fay and dislikes her on her father's behalf. If only Helen hadn't gone to see Fay, unearthing all those buried wires of history. Maybe then she wouldn't feel such obligation. The automatic doors hum open and Helen steps out into the hospital car park. She pictures herself manhandling Fay into a car ambulance, handing her out again at the journey's end like a footman at a coach. Placing Fay into an armchair. Offering tea. Will Fay be able to do such things? Drink tea? Eat her own food? An inventory of ordinary daily activity unrolls in Helen's mind. Eating, washing, going to the loo… she starts to walk faster. Not home, though. She won't go home. And she's too agitated for the café. Helen swerves off the main road and takes the turning into a housing estate – the route Alana took all that time ago, when Helen thought her captivity was over. She walks past the new houses, all built to a slimline, diminutive design and bonded together without fences or other lines of demarcation. A yellow toy tractor lies on its side on the strip of green outside one door. Otherwise there's no sign of life. Helen takes a footpath between two blocks, slaloming through a double metal barrier, and emerging into an identical street on the other side. She'll get lost, if she's not careful. *You never know where the hell you are.* She'll go back before long. She'll have to, sooner or later. Helen turns at the end of the street and abruptly the area changes character. This is the older estate – though Helen's mother always referred to it, with distaste, as 'the new houses'. These were built quickly to replace the old railway terrace, hit by a stray bomb in the war. As Amelia Berwick Blake bustled her daughter past the station she would invariably say, 'They're an absolute disgrace, those new houses. They just replaced one slum with another.'

Helen slows her steps, but someone is walking towards her and she's loath to go into such an obvious retreat. She'll wait until he's passed and is out of sight. The man approaching is small and shabbily dapper in an old yellow waistcoat and a green jacket. He reminds Helen of Wallace the Postcode Man. From two feet away she can smell the cigarette smoke that must be holding his clothes together. As they pass, he lowers his eyes but mumbles, 'F'noon'. A car revs through the street at absurd speed and brakes dramatically at the corner before whinnying off again. Helen hears the old man say, 'Idiots,' but isn't sure that he's said it to her. She walks on, promising herself she'll stop at the end of this road.

The houses here are patchworks of wood and concrete and corrugated iron. Helen's mother used to say they were never meant to last: only to fill a gap. Some have been painted and cleaned, and have pristine borders squeezed into the tiny front gardens. Some are rotting where they stand. The house at the end cringes beneath the pounding of music, which resolves itself, as Helen gets nearer, into an amplified litany of abuse. 'Muddafucka... bitch...' the chant lashes across the neighbourhood in a sinister monotone... 'muddafuckin whore...' and behind it a baby's cries battle with the boxed roars of a real argument. Helen sidesteps around a flowering of dog shit on the pavement and scans the bend in the road, which seems to lead back towards the station. A door opens somewhere behind Helen and she hurries on, turning into a wider road that runs parallel with the first. There's a row of shops here, all but one of them caged with a metal grille. Helen peers ahead as she walks, calculating the most direct way out of the estate. The tarmac road sucks in the daylight. Here and there, newer bandages of tar lie across its camber; the road's edges are crocheted with potholes. A youth appears, hood up, hands pocketed. Helen's legs begin to forget how to walk. This is probably where Darren and his brother come from. And the mother, who can't get it together. Drugs, Helen supposes. Violence. The sheer bloody effort of dragging through one dreary day and into the next. The youth is only yards away now. Without thinking, Helen crosses the road and heads into the open-doored shop on the opposite side.

It's a grocery, forested with tins and packets and boxes and bags. In a corner near the door a man is picking his nails behind the till. His recess is tiled with rows of cigarette packs. Their cellophane wrappings snag at the light and give off an ecclesiastical glow. Helen pretends to examine the shelves, and burrows towards the back of the shop, where there's a faint scent of spices. Someone enters the shop.

'Twenty Specials,' rasps the customer. Helen peers down the aisle and sees a girl much younger than her voice, with a pushchair parked and grizzling at her side. Her dark hair glowers under yellow stains of dye. When she stoops to tend to the child she exposes an inch of buttock-cleavage, a frilly V of underwear and a blotched tattoo. The shopkeeper passes a comment which Helen doesn't catch, and the girl replies: 'Fucking disgusting if you ask me. Shit all over the fucking place. Took 'im to the playground yesterday? An' it's all like beer cans and shit, and I'm sitting there, right, and there's a big chunk of

Kentucky Fucking Chicken Bargain Bucket. I mean, what if 'e got 'isself into that? Could be fucking maggots.'

Helen studies the dried soups and decides to buy a box of cream of chicken with croutons and a packet of cream crackers. As she takes her place behind the girl, the shopkeeper is saying, 'Kids round this way couldn't give a shit.'

The girl pays for her fags and starts to open the packet. The shopkeeper nods to Helen to pass over her goods; evidently the girl is settling in for a chat. While Helen fumbles for her purse, the girl is lighting her cigarette and talking about her stepdad, who's recently come back from Spain.

'Over there, right, they got *gold pavements*.'

The shopkeeper snorts in derision, and she raises her voice defensively.

'Not saying *gold* gold, you stupid tosser, they're gold *colour*, yeah? That's what they got over there.'

They laugh together at the notion of golden pavements, and cigarette smoke escapes from the girl's chapped lips in a series of blue-grey spurts.

'Wouldn't get that over here,' says the shopkeeper. 'I mean, who'd pay for it?'

'Yeah, and even if they did,' says the girl, 'it'd be knee-deep in bargain fucking buckets in a week!' She shakes her head towards Helen to include her in the discussion. 'Kids,' she says, as if youth is only a distant memory. 'What can you do? Can't tell 'em, can ya? So in-yer-face, you're too fucking scared to say nothing.'

Helen heads back towards the main road. She half expects to see Marcus Edwards lurking in an alleyway. But the only other pedestrians around are a very large woman, pitching and rolling her slow way towards the shop, and a small and stick-thin girl leaping at her side. When Helen reaches a lane out of the estate she's almost reluctant to go on. There are decisions out there, in the burr of through-traffic, and she doesn't want to confront them. Aunt Fay's stroke seems to have overshadowed all her other nightmares.

40

The following day, Helen goes to the Archive to search the database of local trades and professions. After a couple of hours she sees Barnaby emerging from the inner sanctum and reaches back from her computer chair to waylay him.

'I'm glad to see you.'

'Ditto,' says Barnaby, and Helen catches her blush in the computer screen.

'Could you spare me an hour in the Canteen? I'd like to pick your brains.'

Over coffee and biscuits, Barnaby considers a variety of possible connections between Edward Blake and the workhouse girl.

'He didn't work there,' reports Helen. 'Or, at any rate, I can't find any record of him in the staff lists. I was hoping he might be a clerk to the Board of Guardians, or something like that.'

She uses her fingers to tick off other likely employers. Suppliers of food, or beer, or fuel, all presumably delivered from somewhere to the workhouse and recorded by some literate functionary. Offices based in the same part of town as the workhouse, where Edward and May might somehow have crossed paths...

Barnaby chews his jammy dodger for a while, then swallows calmly and says, 'Perhaps his connection wasn't through his employment as such. He might have been a volunteer.'

A clearing opens in Helen's mind and all the convoluted lists and storylines fall away.

'Of course!' Her hands are frozen in the act of counting off alternatives. 'Of course! Why didn't I think of that?'

'I may be wrong,' cautions Barnaby.

'But I'll bet you're not!' Helen places Edward Stanley Blake at the workhouse door, cast in the perfect role: do-gooder.

'You might want to look up the League of Assistance archives,' suggests Barnaby. 'They had armies of volunteers, mainly visiting people at home to assess their needs and deserts. There are other possibilities too. I'll help, if you like.'

Helen checks her watch. She should leave before too long, if she's going to pay a call at the hospital. Every cell and sinew in her body rebels at the prospect. She won't go. She *can't* go. This is *her* afternoon, and she's going to spend it here, with Barnaby, ferreting through websites and logbooks. She thinks of Aunt Fay's demolished face and cadaver eyes, and she thinks of her promise to return. Maybe Fay won't remember. Maybe she's past caring. After all, Helen kept her promises for two years, sitting dutifully at Nick's bedside morning, noon and night, and he was none the wiser.

But Fay does know. Fay does remember. Her brain still whirrs and ticks behind her mask, and there's no one but Helen around to hear it.

'Everything all right?' asks Barnaby. Helen realises she's been staring at her watch for several minutes.

'There's somewhere I have to go,' she says. Then her whole body sags, and she has to put her hand to her forehead to keep her head erect.

'Problems?' asks Barnaby quietly.

So Helen tells him about Aunt Fay's stroke. And once she's started, she finds herself telling him about all the rest as well.

'I've got all this room,' she says. 'And all this time. And I'm really all she's got. But... I'm scared.'

Barnaby nods.

'And part of me thinks... I don't know... I think I'm being...'

'Punished?' he suggests.

Helen sighs, and shuts her eyes against a warmth of tears.

'Because... because, with Nick...' She slips a tissue from her sleeve and surreptitiously blows her nose. 'With Nick, I was afraid that if he ever woke up...'

'You'd have to take care of him.'

Helen knows Barnaby could finish the whole confession on her behalf. But putting it into words is part of her atonement.

'When he didn't wake up,' she croaks, 'I was... you could almost say... relieved. To have got away with it.'

Her voice hardens at the cruelty of the thought. Barnaby waits. A chair scrapes back from a table at the other end of the Canteen. Someone in the kitchen laughs at an unheard joke. Barnaby says, 'You wanted to be free of it all. There's no shame in that.'

Helen's eyes are still shut. Presently Barnaby speaks again: 'Would you mind very much if I came along to meet your Aunt Fay? She sounds rather an interesting character.'

Fay is sitting up and drinking tea through a straw.

''S'cold,' she complains, when she sees Helen.

'Maybe they're afraid you'll burn your tongue,' says Helen, and catches the humiliation in Fay's sideways glance. Barnaby hovers at a distance from the bed. Helen turns to introduce him.

'This is my friend Barnaby, who's been helping with all this family history business.'

Fay's weaker hand pulls at her nightie. Helen's heart sinks. Fay is embarrassed, exposed; this was a terrible idea. Barnaby steps forward and offers his hand. Fay lays hers limply over his palm, lending their handshake an unexpected courtliness.

'Tay'seat,' she says, and they pull up their chairs. Helen asks a few questions about Fay's health, but is quickly dismissed.

'Fie, I'm fie. Now, Baa-bay, te' me 'bout your fam-ee.'

Fay somehow manages to lean forward in her bed to fix her attention on her guest as he begins an account of his search through the archives. Helen smiles. No, this wasn't a terrible idea. It was the best idea possible. There's a spark of the old vitality in Fay's eyes. She interrupts Barnaby to order him, with a flick of the strong hand, to unzip his anorak.

For goodness' sake, thinks Helen. *She's flirting.*

After the visit Helen invites Barnaby back for supper.

'It'll only be bacon and eggs, I'm afraid,' she adds.

'Bacon and eggs,' says Barnaby, 'would precisely hit the spot.'

They take the bus. Helen asks Barnaby whether he drives.

'Not as a rule,' he says. 'Generally I prefer to cycle.' Then, in answer to Helen's quizzical look, 'I didn't cycle today, as it falls out. I walked.'

She doesn't believe him. She suspects he's left his bike locked up in the Archive car park, to save any awkwardness about escorting her to see Fay.

When they get back Barnaby sits at the kitchen table while Helen prepares the food.

'Your garden is in very good order,' he remarks.

Helen pays credit to Jim.

'He keeps it ticking over for me,' she says.

'Ah. Your gardener?'

Helen snuffles. 'That sounds rather grand. But I suppose that's what he is.'

Barnaby gazes at the trees where Lisa used to hide. After a while he says, 'My son is a gardener.'

'Your son?' Helen nearly drops the packet of bacon. 'I didn't know you had children.'

'Just one. Leighton. I don't see much of him these days. He lives in San Francisco. They're very keen on gardens over there.'

Helen continues with her task, heating oil in the pan, laying the sticky rashers in a row, watching them bridle and spit as they cook. She's intrigued by the appearance of a son in Barnaby's apparently solitary world, but she's not sure what to ask about him. Barnaby solves the problem by producing his wallet of photographs and holding it up for her to see. A young, tanned man with thick, black hair grins out from a sunnier place.

'Oh!' she says, then, feeling she ought to say more, 'Handsome!'

'Yes,' says Barnaby, adding, by way of explanation: 'Leighton was adopted, like me.' His wife's condition made childbirth risky, he tells her. 'She would gladly have taken that risk, but I was less… sanguine.' Leighton has recently started taking an interest in his biological roots. Helen shuffles the bacon around the rim of the pan.

'And how do you feel about that?' she asks.

'I understand.'

Barnaby swivels round to look at the garden again, and Helen nurses a cool curve of egg in her hand. She remembers what Nick would say when making Lisa's breakfast, before she turned fourteen and stopped eating it.

'Sunny side up,' she asks, 'or over-easy?'

'Sunny side up, please. Shall I butter some bread?'

Helen remembers with relief that she has both those ingredients, and accepts the offer. Barnaby stands at the table building a squat tower of bread and butter with neat strokes of the knife. Helen cracks one, two, three, four eggs on the side of the pan and eases their whites into neat circles.

'Do you ever visit your son?' she asks.

'Not since he moved there. We have a rather… *reserved* relationship. Should I make some tea?'

'There's a bottle of wine in the fridge,' says Helen. She notes with satisfaction that the egg yolks are rising into perfectly pert, orange domes.

Together, in a comfortable silence, they prepare, serve and sit. Helen doesn't ask any more about Leighton, but when they've settled opposite each other Barnaby continues where he left off.

'It all became rather difficult,' he says, 'after my wife's death.' He finishes a mouthful. 'Quite delicious. Thank you.'

He cuts his slice of bread and butter into small squares and adds an equal portion of bacon and of egg white to his fork. Then he pauses and addresses his glass of wine.

'This may be a delicate topic,' he says. 'I had considered…

accompanying my wife. When the time came.'

Helen's lungs expand sharply. She hears her own gasp. For an instant, Barnaby makes eye contact. 'It was never a very convincing plan,' he assures her. The giggling begins. But Helen's in control. She eats a little more, then says, 'What happened?'

He had made up his mind to get into bed beside his wife.

'Make sure we were both presentable,' he says, 'and then take the requisite number of sedatives.'

Helen pictures him diligently calculating the required dose. *At least,* she snipes at Nick, *he would have done it properly.*

'Susan,' says Barnaby, 'guessed what I was planning. She was vehemently against it. Read me the riot act, you might say.'

Susan. The name gives flesh to the notion of Barnaby's wife. 'She told me I mustn't think of leaving such a burden. A millstone, as it were, around Leighton's neck...' Barnaby hesitates. Helen tips her head: 'It's all right. Carry on.'

Susan had warned their son to keep an eye on Barnaby.

'And of course,' says Barnaby, 'when the time *did* come, it was hardly the tranquil scene I'd envisaged.'

A pandemonium of paramedics. The ambulance yowl, the businesslike dash of trolleys and equipment, the long limbo hours when hospital staff came and went and it wasn't clear whether she was alive or dead.

'When they finally broke the news I was too exhausted to do much at all.'

'So you had your surreptitious nap in the loo.'

'That's right.' Barnaby uses his last square of bread to mop up the egg yolk. 'And for a fraction of an instant, when I woke up, I'd forgotten that Susan was ever ill.'

After it was all over, his son was subdued and bewildered.

'We found each other's society rather... problematic.'

Helen doesn't dare answer. If she spoke now, she might release a jet stream of fury. How could he even have contemplated it? To abandon his son for the sake of indulging some operatic fantasy. To blot out all his own pain and sail into oblivion, leaving his boy to bear the full force of a hurricane. Helen starts to clear the dishes. The more she dwells on Barnaby's revelation, the less she wants him there. As she turns her back on him to put the plates in the sink, Barnaby says, 'I rather wish I'd kept my little plan to myself.'

Helen says: 'I'm sure. Because then you could have gone ahead and done it.'

There's a long pause while Barnaby notes her disgust. Then he says, 'On the contrary. Because I know I wouldn't have carried it through.'

Dishes and cutlery clash in the bowl. Helen turns the tap too hard and the water fizzes off at an angle and splashes her blouse. She curses under her breath and wipes it with a tea towel.

Don't tell me this, she thinks. *Bloody well tell your son.*

She rehearses a way of offering more refreshments that will encourage him to refuse.

The doorbell rings.

Lisa registers the wine glasses, the frying pan and Barnaby without a slip in her speech or inflexion.

'...and Mark came up with another idea,' she's saying as Barnaby gets to his feet, 'which is probably daft, but anyway see what you think...'

Helen introduces them.

'I'm about to take my leave,' says Barnaby, looking over Lisa's shoulder towards the front door. 'I've taken enough of Helen's time. She very kindly cooked me a meal after our sojourn to the hospital...'

'Hospital?' Lisa pinions her mother with a look.

'Yes... yes, I was going to phone you – it's about Aunt Fay...'

Helen stammers an explanation, under one of Lisa's affronted looks.

'Why didn't you tell me before?' demands Lisa. Helen is painfully aware of Barnaby's presence, and of her own hypocrisy. She ushers him back into his seat.

'I'll open more wine,' she suddenly announces.

'I'm driving,' says Lisa righteously, but she does take a seat at the table.

When Nancy calls ten minutes later, Helen is grilling toast for Lisa while insisting that Fay will recover her independence, and Lisa is pestering Barnaby for a second opinion.

' ...and don't try to sugar the pill, please,' she's saying; 'I know what Mum's like. She tries to pull the wool over my eyes.'

Nancy has brought some pictures of her grandparents to show Helen.

'I thought you might be interested,' she says, overtaking Helen in the hall, 'but if you've got company – you know me...'

Soon the kitchen is a bluster of activity, as photographs and plates of toast are passed from hand to hand, and voices and topics plait and collide.

'...she was still a teacher then...'

'...looks a bit stern...'

'...seemed exceptionally lively, given the...'

'...terrible thing, but you know where I am, Helen, if you ever...'

'...enough to deal with, she's not even directly related...'

'...most interesting, most interesting indeed...'

Helen leans against the sink unit and drinks her wine. She can't remember a time when the house was this animated. She envisages Aunt Fay propped in a chair, joining the mêlée, regaling them with tales of sexual deviancy and making Nancy squeal with shock. That seems possible. That seems like a life.

*   *   *

Helen gets up later than usual the next day. It's partly the deadweight of wine in her head. She was up during the night, wandering around, peering from windows in the hope of spotting the fox. It was so quiet, when they'd all gone home. And then, when she got to sleep, there was a stew of dreams and half-dreams, indefinable now but something to do with Barnaby marrying Nancy's grandmother, and always against the backdrop of Nick's waxen face.

She lies in bed for a while, waiting for a reason to move. If Aunt Fay were here she'd probably be on the rampage by now, stomping along the landing with her stick, calling for hot chocolate with a bonnet of cream. That would be stimulus of a sort. Helen fends off the decision for a few minutes more, then heaves and swings herself into a sitting position and lets her skull hang forward. All right. She'll tell Aunt Fay today. She can move in here, for as long as needs be.

The phone rings, finally hauling her to her feet.

'In all the excitement last night,' says Lisa, 'I never got round to telling you Mark's idea.'

'Oh yes,' says Helen hoarsely. 'Mark's idea…'

'For your *birthday*, Mum. Look – as I said, it might be a rubbish idea, but I thought it was brilliant.'

Helen attempts a sound of pleasant anticipation.

'How about,' says Lisa 'Mark setting you up with the internet?'

Helen's eyebrows lift her headache by an inch.

'Can he do that?'

'Of course he can. He can get hold of a pretty good second-hand computer at a knockdown price, and we'll fix you up with internet access and email.'

Helen's fuddled brain grapples with the concept of being fixed up with access. Does it mean laying wires, knocking down walls, rigging Heath Robinson gadgetry to send and receive alien signals? She says, 'Won't that be very expensive?'

'We wouldn't do it if we couldn't afford it.' Helen hears the plea in her daughter's voice and says, 'Sweetheart, it's the best present I could possibly have.'

41

The League of Assistance archive is housed in its head office in Castleton. Latisha gives Helen a lift en route to her sister's, and arranges to collect her on the way back. The head office turns out to be an upstairs room over the charity shop. As soon as Helen opens the shop door she's enveloped by the sour and yeasty smell of old clothes. She approaches two women behind the counter.

'I've got an appointment with Mr Ashley…'

'Kitty!' barks the older woman. 'Go and tell Ashley he's got a visitor!'

Kitty is a pale and nervy woman with long, white hair twisted into circles at her temples. Her face, too, is made up of circles, like a child's drawing: round eyes, round cheeks, a mouth set in a permanent 'O', ready for calamity.

'Oh, Mr – yes – I'll go and…'

Kitty flutters out through a back door and her companion growls to nobody in particular: 'Stark staring mad'. Then she commands: 'Have a look round while you wait. You never know, you might find something halfway usable.'

Helen browses the shelves and wonders whether she's obliged to make a purchase. Apart from a small display of third-world crafts, most of the stock is a jumble of second-hand goods. Helen examines an olive-green dinner set, a row of LPs in softened sleeves; she pulls down a book called *Hidden Gems of the Coast*, and turns the pages to play for time. *Crooked houses line the former harbour, now silted up two miles*

(3.2km) from the sea... There's a whirlwind at the street door and a large woman flaps in like a trapped bird. She keeps up a constant commentary, which propels her along the racks of clothing.

'Nothing too scratchy, don't like scratchy nothing black don't like black, what's the matter with black don't like it that's all not my colour black is not my colour...'

She snatches out a hanger with a voluminous summer dress and directs her prattle to the counter: 'This'll do dress in my colour this'll fit will it fit try it on...'

'Over there,' snaps the till-woman. The narrator lurches into a tiny changing booth and billows behind its curtain.

'Raving nutcase,' concludes the till-woman.

Kitty returns to announce that Mr Ashley will receive Helen in the office. As she's fretting past the changing booth, the customer's arm hurls the curtain momentarily aside, revealing a vast and braless sway of bosom. Kitty shies away, trilling: 'My word! You see all sorts in here!'

Helen is shown upstairs, where she's greeted by an unexpectedly young man, with a thin nose and a goatee beard. He apologises for the delay.

'The phone rang at just the wrong moment. But I hope our ladies looked after you well. Coffee?'

The archive turns out to be a collection of crumbling ledgers and a file. Mr Ashley – 'call me Ben' – means to organise them properly and publish a history of the league. It's one of many plans he has to raise the charity's profile.

'We need a brand,' he insists, showing Helen to a table overlooking the street. 'League of Assistance – it sounds grim, don't you think? So patronising. Colonial. I'm pushing for something snappier. Something that says – hey, guys! We're here if you need us! Something like... Here to Help?'

He raises his arms to place the name in lights, and Helen looks appreciatively into mid-air.

'Here to Help! Yes, that's really very... snappy!'

Satisfied, Ben provides her with a coffee and three ledgers.

'These should cover your period,' he says. 'I'll leave you to it. I'll be right over there, making a couple of phone calls. Go for it!'

Helen puts on her reading glasses, takes a pencil and notebook from her handbag, and goes for it. Each ledger is a confusion of case histories, accounts and lists of volunteers. Halfway through the second book, she finds her grandfather.

Forbridge Bible Visits. Fortnightly Sundays, for an hour following Evening Service. White Hill House Chapel. League Representatives:
Horace Kerr Esq
Mrs. E. Spencer
Edward S. Blake Esq...

Helen's hands bunch in satisfaction, but she says nothing. Ben is at his desk at the other end of the room, swinging his chair in time to a conversation about promo cards. It's another hour and a half before Helen is due to meet Latisha. She works her way slowly through the rest of the ledgers, and pictures her grandfather making his worthy way through the workhouse gate, across the yard and into the chapel, armed with his Bible and a mission to save the fallen. And there, waiting for salvation, is a dark-eyed 17 year old, with her drawn face and her big belly, offering up a prayer in the absence of other solutions.

*   *   *

'What's next, then?' asks Latisha, as they head for the motorway. 'Going to stick with grandad's line? Or go after great-grandma? Or both? That's the best thing about families – there's so many of 'em, they can keep you busy till the cows come home.'

She speeds up to join the traffic, leaning forward to assess the advance of cars into her wing mirror, and her laughter merges with the torrent of engines.

Helen says, 'I'd like to find out more about Flora Jones. But I don't really know where to start.'

'Barnaby's your man, then,' says Latisha. Helen smiles, but says nothing. Lately she's discreetly avoided Barnaby's company. She feels guilty about her reaction to his confidence. But the thought of his little escape plan – however fanciful it was – makes her feel physically sick. She can't help it.

Receiving no answer from Helen, Latisha provides one herself: 'Yes, Barnaby's the main man. He's amazing, really. Must be pushing seventy, d'you reckon? Sort of bloke who's always looked the same, so he never really gets old…'

The teatime traffic hurtles along like a hail of bullets. Ahead of them, the sky is congealing into a mass of grey cloud, singed with red. Helen thinks about Aunt Fay, about the visit she missed today, in order to go hunting the dead. Before long, going out on the hoof will be a rare treat, a major undertaking. Even her trips to the Archive might be impractical. She wishes they could drive on forever. Without meaning to, she heaves a deep sigh.

'Penny for 'em,' says Latisha.

Helen tells her about Aunt Fay, and Latisha responds with an aviary of whistles, whoops and collar-dove croons.

'Oh, Helen,' she says, accelerating to pass a truck, 'life can really stick its foot out and send us flying, can't it? And I was thinking you'd be on a flight to Australia soon with Mister Kissy-Kissy.'

'That,' says Helen flatly, 'was never going to happen.'

She reads the side of the lorry as they draw ahead. *Divinity Chocolates – The Taste of Heaven!* A woman's giant smile is spattered with motorway grime. Latisha reins her car back to the inside lane.

'And now here's my gorgeous boy Grant going off to join the forces. Snapped him up, of course, like I knew they would. And who knows where he'll end up? That's life for you, Helen – gives you a snog and then kicks you up the bum. When I think of that lad in some godawful hellhole, being shot at, booby-trapped…'

One hand flies away from the steering wheel to sketch the variety of horrors in wait. Helen says, 'He may not be sent anywhere terrible. They have to train him first, don't they?'

'Train him, yes! Train him to be fried to a crisp by a guided bloody missile…!'

The car swings briefly out of its lane and a foghorn blast from the lorry behind them makes Helen flinch. Latisha raises a conciliatory hand to her mirror: 'Yes, yes, piss off… sorry, Helen. I'm pretty cut up about it, as you can tell. Too many hours looking at casualty lists, see. All those young lives, all that potential, come to nothing. And that's how so many kids end up, isn't it? Just a heap of waste on the kerb.'

42

Gemma is touched. She hadn't expected to hear from Helen again. She meant to give her a call, but it's been so hectic… she tails away to convey the inexpressible calls on her time. She asks Helen whether she's had any thoughts about the session with Darren, and Helen makes non-committal noises.

'I think it was worth doing,' says Gemma. Helen may be imagining the note of doubt in her voice.

'I've never heard anything from the police,' says Helen, 'and I wasn't sure what would happen next…'

Gemma tells her the older brother has been released on police bail. Helen says, 'You mean he's free?'

She can't hide the tremor in her voice, and Gemma rushes to reassure her. There's nothing to worry about, they don't think he's a threat, he'll want to keep his nose clean before appearing at the magistrate's court…

'When will that be?' asks Helen quickly.

'Well… it can take ages I'm afraid. Best to put it out of your mind if you can.'

Helen agrees, and manages to sound quite convincing. And why wouldn't she? She's not a fool; she knows in her heart that Jason isn't going to track her down or lie in wait at every corner. This terror that bubbles under everything has nothing to do with any particular 17-year-old and his penknife. Still, she can see quite clearly how it will go: Helen and Fay, growing ever more frightened and decrepit together, bolting and chaining the doors as soon as the sun goes down, calling through the glass at every caller: 'Who is it? What do you want?'

Gemma has changed the subject, and is telling Helen about another new scheme. They want to provide Darren with a mentor – someone mature and reliable, she explains: 'a sort of surrogate grandparent, I suppose – someone who'll be there for him when he needs them, when things go belly-up at home...'

The back of Helen's neck is prickling. She can see the pulse in her wrist. She swallows air.

'Presumably,' she says, 'the victim of his crime wouldn't be eligible...?'

'Oh! Oh, no, Helen...' says Gemma hastily, '...don't worry, I didn't mean you! No, the fact that you were involved in this incident would be... an issue...'

'That's what I thought,' says Helen, and thinks: *Thank God*. Darren, she reminds herself, is not her problem. But when she's said her goodbyes and put the receiver down she stands for a long time, listening to the ticks and whimpers of the house, unable to shake off a profound and irrational disappointment.

*   *   *

Mid-morning and the café is full. People don't seem to go to offices any more. It's a menagerie of mobile ringtones and urgent discussions, and the smaller tables lining the walls are a sheen of laptops. Helen falters at the door. there are a few chairs occupied with bags and coats; she considers taking one, but her courage fails her. As she's leaving a voice says: 'Please!'

Marcus Edwards is tucked behind a table, masked by the open door. He indicates the spare seat with his slim and beautiful hand. Helen notices a movement at one of the pavement tables and says, 'Thank you, but it's such a lovely day I thought I'd sit outside.'

She would never usually do this – position herself at the shoulder of a departing customer, touching the back of the chair to stake her claim. She finds that kind of behaviour overbearing and discourteous. But in her eagerness to escape Marcus Edwards she slips into the seat almost before it's vacated. She sits back and closes her eyes. She could have gone somewhere else, of course – left the stalker to his domain. But this afternoon Helen is due at the hospital, where she's going to invite Aunt Fay to come and live with her. And before she goes, she's determined to spend an hour drinking strong coffee and watching the world go by.

It really is a lovely day – bright and chilly, soft with approaching spring. This is where Helen sat the first time she came here, after Nick had been spirited from his bed and signed away. Less than a year ago. Helen thought then that she'd never have to go back into that hospital again. She thought she was free.

The waitress clears her table with a juggler's dexterity, and Helen gives her order.

'A large americano please.' *As large as you can make it.*

So much has happened. So many new lives have braided with her own, past and present, since that afternoon when Helen sat at the salon, watching her reflected hair snipped and dried and sprayed, while Nick was busy stuffing insulation wadding up the exhaust. Helen paid the bill and tipped the stylist; Nick switched on the ignition. From that moment on, she would never be free again.

'Do you mind if I join you?'

Marcus Edwards looms over her, balancing his coffee cup with one hand and holding his bag to his chest with the other. He reminds her of Oliver Twist, asking for more. Helen catches her breath, but without real trepidation. She waves to the other chair. After all, it's partly due to the enigmatic Mr Edwards that she's constructed any manner of new and Nickless existence. Soon her universe will collapse into a two-room tedium of feeding, washing and biding time. She may as well enjoy his sinister sideshow a little longer. Marcus Edwards slips into the spare place and sets his coffee down with care. *So pale*, thinks Helen. Vulpine eyes and slanting cheekbones, that sinuous length of tied hair – he might be about to slink into the shrubbery and out of sight. The waitress serves her americano and Helen puts her lips to its biting heat.

'You really enjoy that, don't you?' says Marcus. 'I wish I could get such pleasure from a coffee. But I've got no sense of taste or smell.'

Helen sips the coffee and it's a mosaic of flavours on her tongue – treacle and peanuts and smoke and wood and honey… she tries to experience it as a blankness of liquid, but fails.

'I had an illness when I was a child,' he's saying, 'and that's how it left me….' He's unusually talkative today. Inadvertently Helen glances around her, looking for Alana. He continues in exactly the same tone of voice:

'She's not here. I don't know where she is. I know what she says about me but it isn't true. I'm not a stalker. I'm not obsessed – well, not with Alana. Not in the way she makes out.'

Helen blinks. She remembers what Latisha said: *Don't you get involved, lady. You've got your own life to lead.*

Only other people's lives, Helen thinks. That's all there is.

'I really don't know Alana at all,' she assures him. 'We've only ever had one short conversation.'

'But I can guarantee she used it to slander me.'

Helen can hardly deny it. So she tells him again that she doesn't know Alana, and is not in a position to pass on messages. She sees the muscles of his throat contract and his cheeks sink into even deeper hollows.

'Never mind,' he says. 'I want you to know. I want to tell my side of the story.'

So he does. He tells Helen about his Polish mother, born on a ship's deck as her own mother fled to safety. He talks of her four siblings – his uncles and aunts – who didn't get away, who were no more than names and photographs to him and to his mother; but who laughed and breathed in his grandmother's dreams to the end of her days, with their habits and hobbies and jokes and sulks and songs.

'All gone,' he says, with a terrible and graceful sweep of his hand. 'All gone in the camps, before they reached their teens. Their father too, and his two brothers. They thought the three of them, three big, grown men, would be able to keep the children safe. But they couldn't.'

They had a hiding place on a farm. The farmer had betrayed them.

'He wasn't a stranger,' says Marcus, crouching over his flavourless coffee. 'This farmer. He was a friend. They'd known each other for years, the two families. This man went to school with my grandfather and his brothers. They played together, chased girls together. But he gave them away.'

His bony face demands an answer. Helen says, 'I suppose... I suppose he was frightened.'

Marcus Edwards' lips draw into a bud of contempt. Then he says, 'That's what I want to know. *Why* he did it. Why some people protect, and some betray.'

Helen's mouth opens and shuts, as suddenly she understands.

'The farmer,' she says, 'was related to Alana?'

'Her great uncle. I had no idea, when I started this, that he had any living descendants at all. Let alone someone in Britain. She's the only one. She might even have met him. I don't know. She won't tell me.'

Helen recalls the two of them, with their oddly similar features, sitting opposite each other in the café: two heirs of atrocity, incapable of handling their legacies.

'She might be ashamed,' Helen suggests. He leans forward again, and the table edges towards her.

'I sold my house. I left my job. And my girlfriend. I came here, over a hundred miles from my home and my friends, and I started again, here. In *her* town. Where I knew I would finally...'

He breaks off to search his bag, and brings out a roll of paper, held with an elastic band. The band is rasped off and the paper falls open. At first Helen thinks it's a drawing – an exquisitely intricate drawing of a tree, branching in every direction, knotted with flowers and microscopically veined leaves. Then she recognises a name, a number, and sees that this is a different kind of tree, pushing its roots ever further into the past, driving its boughs and twigs horizontally through connections of blood and contract. She runs her eyes up and down, left to right. Births and deaths and marriages rustle from the page; names

appear and reappear through the undergrowth of generations –
Gregor, Magda, Mateusz… She shakes her head in awe.

'You've done so much work,' she says. 'You must know virtually
everything about your family.'

'That's not *my* family,' says Marcus Edwards. 'It's *hers*.'

A chill touches Helen's spine. The tree that had seemed so majestic
is transformed into a parasite, creeping down the scroll, eating into its
victim's heart. Marcus watches her reaction. Her words come out in a
whisper: 'Why have you done all this?'

His elegant fingers brush the paper's upper edge.

'It's all I can do,' he says.

43

Helen stands in the middle of the garage with Nick's keys hanging from her fingers. She found them straight away. Top right-hand drawer of the dressing table, among his bunched socks. He always kept them there, and that's where she replaced them, when she was given his belongings. She hadn't opened that drawer since. When she gouged the keys from their nest, she let her hand linger against the mossy resistance of wools and cottons. Nick's socks, still in the drawer; and behind the wardrobe door, a chorus line of Nick's shirts and jackets, preserving all that remains of him – his receding scent, the bend of his elbows, a few grey hairs on his collars. She hasn't opened that door yet. Her clothes are in another wardrobe, its twin, on the other side of the radiator. She's been able to put off the moment when she releases his spirit, sees a languid ripple of fresh air pass across the hangers. When she does, it'll be to start piling it all into bin bags. She'll have to clear space for Aunt Fay's belongings.

Helen isn't used to unlocking the garage door. It was always Nick who did that, while she waited outside. She had to fiddle with the lock for a minute, but eventually she felt it yield and turn, and then the door furled up with ease. There's a greasy window in the side wall, which admits a hesitant light even when Helen has rolled the door back down behind her. The concrete floor is swept clean. Maybe Lisa and Mark saw to that after disposing of the car. But then, Nick was always a neat man, so there probably wasn't much to do. There are shallow shelves opposite the window, stacked with tupperware boxes. Nails, she thinks, and drill bits and picture wire, and other odds and ends. Nick wasn't particularly interested in DIY, but he liked to keep things handy. Apart from the boxes, it's just an empty space. Helen sees the splash of her shadow, diffuse in the low light, and a laser-swing of reflection from one of the keys, strafing the wall and ceiling. There's nothing here. No sense of his presence, no clue to his final act of will. She'll glean no more from standing on a bare garage floor than Marcus Edwards will from compiling another family's history. Nick is not here, not in his clothes, not anywhere else. He's gone. She can add the date and close the brackets.

Helen wishes she could cry again, as she did that morning after one of her disturbing dreams. But she's done. She's desiccated, boulder-heavy, too tired to rest. An hour ago, she sat at Aunt Fay's bedside and asked her to come and live here. The two women faced each other with indifferent eyes. Fay said, 'Thank you, darling'.

And that was that.

Helen resolves to clear away the genealogy books. Her sympathy for Flora Jones, her hapless great-grandmother, has all but drained away. Seeing Marcus Edwards pillaging Alana's past has left her with a sick dread of it all. She doesn't want to end up a grave robber, turning corpses to check for items of interest. She'll get from task to task, keeping Fay alive as long as she can, looking no further forward or back than the passage of every day.

Through the wall she hears the phone ring, then stop. The key-light follows its trajectory across flaking plaster and high fringes of cobweb. To and fro. To and fro.

In her final hour, Amelia Catherine Berwick Blake roused herself twice from the mire of illness, and forced a rumbling of words to the surface. First she said, 'Helen, don't slouch'.

'Sorry, Mum,' said Helen, straightening in her chair.

Then, about forty minutes later, her mother said: 'It's all right.'

At least, that's what it sounded like. At the time, Helen thought it was her response to the apology, delayed by the fog of morphine. Now she wonders whether it was more than that. After so many decades of rules and exhortations about grammar and accent and posture and dress – maybe this was the message Amelia Blake chose to hand down to her daughter. *It's all right. I understand.* That's what most mothers want to tell their children, isn't it? That's what Helen wants to tell Lisa. That's what she wishes with all her heart she could have told Nick.

The phone rings again and Helen is spurred into action. She lifts the garage door and sees Barnaby standing in the drive. She hasn't the energy for his company; but she hasn't the energy to excuse herself, either. The phone stops ringing, and Barnaby is still there.

'It's such a lovely evening,' he says. 'Shall we take a stroll in the park?'

44

At the pond's edge, a father and his toddler are throwing crusts to the ducks. The water is ribbed with trails as the ducks steer in to the fray and make off again with their catch. Helen and Barnaby sit on the park bench to watch. After a while the father and son empty their bag and amble away, and the tangle of ducks loosens and expands, as they glide back to the last sunlit segment of pond. They drift there, in the warmth, or hop onto the bank to preen and comfort each other with small guttural sounds.

For the first time since they left the house, Barnaby speaks.

'The water must be rather chilly in the shade.'

A wide sweep of shadow has scythed the pond and the grass around it into two distinct areas. The darker part already has a forewarning of nightfall. The water there is steely and menacing, and the grass shivers low. All the colour and light of day is concentrated into one shrinking crescent, where the iridescence of drake feathers, the ripples, the blades of grass all sparkle and blaze as if the sun will never set. Barnaby says, mainly to himself, 'What is the colour of grass?'

Helen thinks it might be a quotation, but doesn't recognise it. So she answers, tartly, 'Green'.

Barnaby makes a whiffling noise, which seems to be laughter.

'Susan used to ask that,' he says. 'It's the sort of conundrum that gripped her imagination.'

He stares out into the parkland.

'It's quite different, depending on the fall of the light. Bottle green, lime green – entirely different colours. Susan used to puzzle over it: which is the real green?'

Helen hunches lower into her coat as the dusk touches their bench. 'I've never really thought about it.'

Some of the ducks are settling now, folding themselves into shallow domes on the bank. A cyclist speeds past behind the bench with a chainsaw buzz of wheels. Barnaby dips into one of the anorak's hidden pockets and gives Helen a folded printout.

'I do hope you won't think it presumptuous. I was checking the Medical Register for quite another item, but I thought, while I was there…'

Helen unfolds the paper with dismay. More ferreting around in other people's business. The printout isn't easy to read: blocks of faint type compressed into single-line spacing. But Barnaby has marked one paragraph with highlighter.

Dr Nathaniel Berwick Adams.
Date of Birth: 4 April 1887…

'I believe,' he says, 'this may be your grandmother's employer.'

Dr Nathaniel Berwick Adams. How many people would have known that middle name? Was this an intimacy shared by the doctor and his lover? A little pillow talk in the servants' garret? Or did May Jones do some detective work of her own, so that she could make her private point at the baptismal font? Helen feels sordid, as if she's read someone's diary. She recalls something Lisa said: *They're all dead now. It doesn't make any difference.*

A group of youths passes, and one of them breaks off to rush at the ducks, scattering them in panic before swaggering back with a bray. Helen's fingers tense, creasing the paper, as Barnaby turns in his seat to give an admonishing look.

'What you looking at?' shouts the youth, giving Barnaby the finger. Helen clutches his arm: 'Let it be,' she says, as if Barnaby had been about to wade into a fight.

The youths jostle away, and gradually the frightened quacking subsides. The birds return to their places, maintaining a nervous staccato for several minutes.

'It's a curious thing,' says Barnaby. 'We can't read their expressions or understand their language, so we take the poor creatures to be devoid of feeling.'

'That's exactly what Nick used to say.' Helen glares at the teenagers' backs. 'He said we treat animals as fodder, for the plate or for the lab.'

Barnaby nods slowly, still monitoring the ducks.

'Actually,' he says after a while, 'I was talking about those boys.'

The evening blots out all but a sliver of water. The ducks burrow further into their feathers. Helen folds the printout and slips it into her handbag. She can't sit on this bench all night. But she can think of no good reason to move.

Guess what, Nick. I think I might give up, too.

Her bag twitters wildly. Helen takes out the mobile and squints at the screen. *Lisa Calling.* As she presses 'Accept,' Lisa is already shouting over the din of another part of town. Helen holds the phone at a distance from her ear.

'Mum! Where the hell have you been? I've been trying to get hold of you for...'

Her voice is swallowed by a lorry's roar. Helen looks at the trees at the edge of the park, glowing in the last rays of sun. She waits while the phone spits and coughs. Then Lisa's voice returns, clearer than before.

'Mum! I'm going to have a baby!'

About the Author

Nia Williams is a freelance author and musician. She is the author of two other novels, *The Pier Glass* and *Persons Living or Dead*, which was longlisted for Wales Books of the Year, and her short stories have been published in magazines and anthologies and broadcast on BBC radio. For more information about her work see www.niawilliams.com